# HEART OF A REBEL

## A Cowboys of the Flint Hills Novel

TESSA LAYNE

**She is SO not his type...**

They might have shared a fiery kiss at his brother's wedding, but Brodie Sinclaire wants nothing to do with chef Jamey O'Neill and her sexy, all too sassy mouth. Except he desperately needs her to run the kitchen at his new hunting lodge.

**He's a pain in her....**

While Brodie may push her buttons in all the right places, Jamey doesn't need the deliciously handsome cowboy bossing her in the kitchen and meddling in her personal life. All she wants is him for dessert. They can't deny their chemistry is explosive, but can they handle the heat when things get messy in the kitchen?

*A standalone novel filled with racy shenanigans in and out of the kitchen, and a Happily Ever After that will have you reaching for the tissues!*

Sign up for my newsletter at
www.tessalayne.com/newsletter to receive updates, sneak-peeks, and freebies!

## Chapter One

*B*rodie Sinclaire stood pacing in front of the large stone fireplace that anchored the living room of the Big House. Even though he'd grown up here, he could count on his hands the number of times his family had gathered here. They'd always been more of a front porch family. Fine by him. The living room felt... confining. As confining as the starched shirt and fancy onyx and silver cufflinks he wore.

But hell, today was his oldest brother Blake's wedding. He'd do whatever was asked of him. Including wait patiently in front of the fireplace with his soon to be sister-in-law's wedding ring tucked safely away in his pocket. He could do this. Today of all days, he – Brodie Sinclaire, town clown and target for gossip, would get this right. He'd fucked up a lot of things in his twenty-eight years. His brother's wedding wouldn't be one of them.

"You have the ring?"

His older brother, Ben, strode into the room wearing the same get-up. Shined up boots, black denim, starched shirt, fancy cufflinks.

Brodie rolled his eyes. "Of course."

"Just checking," Ben chided. "You've been known to misplace things."

"Yeah, but not a wedding ring," he shot back. He might have misplaced a pair of diamond earrings meant for his mother, once upon a time. God only knew why his father, Jake, had entrusted a gift of that value to a twelve-year-old, but he had. With disastrous consequences. Brodie had tucked the earrings away for safekeeping, only it had taken until Easter to find them, stuffed on top of a stack of comics in his bedroom. In plain sight. Something his brothers still ribbed him about.

Brodie shook off the memory. It still bothered him. Especially when he looked at his half-brother, Simon, who was roughly the same age as he'd been during what had been fondly named as "the diamond incident." He'd never put that kind of pressure on a kid. Simon had begged to keep the ring while the men were suiting up, but Brodie had stepped in and offered to take it. Someone had to look out for Simon in the way no one had looked out for him.

Ben cuffed him on the shoulder. "Just kidding. No need to be touchy. Are you sure you have it?"

"Fuck you, asshole." Brodie couldn't stop his grin. If the comment had come from Blake, he'd have been more uptight. But this was Ben. Solid Ben. The brother who'd been there for him, no matter what.

Maybe it was their age difference. Blake was already in college when things had become unbearable at home. Maybe it was the fact that Blake kept their young half-brother Simon a secret from everyone until five weeks ago, but his relationship with his oldest brother had been… challenging. In spite of that, Brodie was determined to turn over a new leaf. Put together the kind of family for Simon they'd never had growing up. But there was still ground to cover. Brodie hoped that by agreeing to be Blake's best man, they were taking a step in the right direction. And making up for lost time.

Ben leaned against the stone hearth. "Come on. Show it to me."

"I buried it in the stable for safekeeping," Brodie deadpanned.

Ben threw his head back, laughing. "Fine. I'll quit harassing you."

"Who's harassing who?" Mason Carter, Blake's best friend from college, and an honorary Sinclaire, strolled in. "If you're going to harass Brodie about anything, harass him about Jamey O'Neill. What's up with the two of you?"

"Nothing," Brodie grunted. "Not my type."

Ben chortled. "Everyone's your type."

"Shut up."

He liked his women soft, curvy, and sweet. Compliant. Not bossy and prickly like Jameyson I Love Irish Whiskey O'Neill. Maddie's best friend. Brodie loved the sashay of swaying hips and lush curves. Not the strong, purposeful movements of a woman who might serve his balls on a platter.

She and her horde of loud, Boston brothers had descended two days ago to help with the wedding. They'd taken over the bunkhouses, the kitchen, couldn't ride horses, and had been the source of twice the usual ribbing.

But that hadn't deterred the ladies of Prairie. Oh no. They'd fallen all over themselves to meet the firefighters and cops from Boston. *"Oooh, your accent is so cute."* If Brodie heard that one more time at the Trading Post, he'd eat his socks.

Truth be told, Jamey fascinated him. She rubbed him the wrong way – like coarse sandpaper moving against the grain. But try as he might to ignore her and go about his business, he was drawn to her like a moth to flame. She made him want to poke at her like he would a marshmallow in a bed of coals, just so he could watch the sparks fly.

Hell, teasing her was more fun than teasing his little sister, Emma.

Where Emma just rolled her eyes at him, Jamey... shot off sparks. Big sparks. Roman candles. And it was glorious. Put a grin on his face every damned time.

His lips cracked into a half-smile. Jameyson O'Neill was as fierce as the whiskey she was named for. He was a scotch man himself, but Jamey's gangly movements and her sassy mouth intrigued him. She wasn't like the women around here, and not just because of her accent. Hell, he'd never seen anyone openly challenge Dottie Grace, Prairie's gossip queen and owner of the local diner. Not even her daughters. He'd witnessed more than one altercation between the two women over the last few days. The battles were mighty, and Jamey more than held her own.

Mason snapped his fingers. "Earth to Brodie."

Brodie waved his hand. "I'm here. Just practicing my toast."

Ben chuckled. "Keep telling yourself that."

Axel Hansen, one of Maddie's cousins, walked in, wearing the same clothes as the other men. "Time to get this show on the road. You ready to join our families?"

"Not if it means I have to smell you from the driveway, *Axe*," said Brodie.

"Shut up, bison breath." Axel clapped him on the shoulder.

Ben moved to the sideboard. "A toast?"

"High time someone offered us a beverage." Gunnar, Axel's older brother, walked in.

Brodie moved to help Ben pass out glasses.

Blake and Simon stepped through the threshold. "Were you going to toast without us?" Blake asked.

Brodie handed Blake a glass. "Here. And for you, kiddo," he ruffled Simon's head. "Ginger ale. Ben has a glass ready for you too."

"Can't I have a taste?"

Brodie shook his head. "No way. You're plenty man with ginger ale."

Ben handed Simon a small glass of ginger ale, then Brodie raised his glass, looking each man in the eye. "To burying the hatchet. To joining our families. To Blake and Maddie."

The group raised their glasses and drank. Blake clapped him in a hug, then pulled back, his eyes swirling with emotion. "I know it hasn't always been easy between us."

Brodie nodded.

"Thank you for being here." Blake's voice thickened. "For forgiving me."

Brodie's throat tightened. "Shut up. Your ring's burning a hole in my pocket. Let's get this show on the road."

They moved to the foyer, where Maddie's father, Warren Hansen, waited for them. Warren had nearly died few months back, and Blake had saved his life. He was a tough old cuss, but Brodie had learned Warren was responsible for saving the Sinclaire ranch years ago. And while Brodie didn't like owing a debt to a neighbor, it was better than being homeless.

The men took their places at the foot of the staircase. Hansens on one side, Sinclaires on the other. Brodie stood next to Blake in the best man's spot. Simon headed upstairs to escort the women down.

First came his sister, Emma. She caught his eye and

winked. Once she cleared the last step, Simon scampered up the steps for Jamey. She glided around the corner holding Simon's hand, and Brodie's breath stuck in his throat. Her brilliant red curls bounced lightly with each step, and her green dress hugged her narrow frame. Scrawny, really. She was sinew and bone. Yet he couldn't keep his eyes off her. Sound faded away as he zeroed in on her floating down the stairs.

Too soon, someone nudged him and whispered loudly. "The ring."

Shit. He'd totally forgotten his duties. He dug the ring out of his pocket and slipped it to Blake, who was staring goofy-eyed at Maddie. God help him if he was ever that whipped. Blake pulled Maddie's fingers to his lips, reverently kissing each one.

Words washed over Brodie, but he paid no attention. He kept staring at the curve of Jamey's neck. It had the same arch as his favorite horse in the barn. Was her skin as silky?

Blake was speaking again, all moony faced.

Brodie clapped his brother on the shoulder. "I know you want to start the honeymoon now, but the natives are getting restless. Time to kiss on the porch."

Laughter erupted from the men. Out of the corner of his eye he saw Jamey roll her eyes. "Is that all you men think about, kissing?"

"Nope. Much more," He muttered as he stepped around her. He wouldn't take her bait. Not this time.

"Oh you're one of *those* are you? All talk and no substance?"

On second thought, he couldn't resist. He reached out and pulled her close. "I've got plenty of substance whenever you're ready, honey." He winked broadly and waggled his eyebrows.

Her cheeks turned the most adorable shade of pink.

"Enough, Brodie." Blake spoke sharply. "She's our guest."

He was just joking. He'd never say something like that in earnest. She wasn't even his type. He opened his mouth to explain, but before he could speak, she jabbed him in the chest. "Back off you arse weed. You might think you're Mister Hotcakes, but if you can't make soup outta chicken shit, you better not piss off the cook."

Prickles of shame licked up his neck.

Shit.

He'd fucked up.

Again.

He always seemed to mess things up at the important times. He studied his boots for a moment, gathering himself. Surely if he turned on the charm she'd realize he was joking? Meeting her eyes, he winked and put on his best charmer smile. The one that always worked when people were mad at him. "Aww shit. I'm sorry, hon."

"Don't you honey me. I'll serve your balls for dinner if you cross me." She twirled on her heel and swept through the door.

His heart squeezed in disappointment as he stood staring at the empty doorway.

Blake shook with laughter, clapping him on the back. "Better watch out. I think you just met your match."

## Chapter Two

*J*amey stood busying herself at the buffet table.
Of all the nerve. Brodie Sinclaire wouldn't
leave well enough alone. He'd been a thorn in
her side from the moment she'd arrived. Following her
around, pushing and poking at her. Always with a twinkle
in his eye. He might be devilishly handsome with his dark
hair and sky blue eyes, but he was not for her. She was
finished with the male species. Too bad her stomach flip-
flopped every time she caught him staring.

And earlier, at the wedding, when he'd pulled her close.
Heat rushed to her pussy at the memory. He might drive
her nuts, but her body didn't seem to have a problem with
that. She just needed to avoid him a bit longer. Tomorrow
she'd head back to Chicago, and the current nightmare
that was her life. Brodie would be nothing more than a
distant, irritating memory.

Jamey recounted the biscuits. They needed replen-
ishing for the third time. She grudgingly had to admit that
Dottie was right about them. People couldn't get enough.
It killed her that she couldn't taste them. Stack them up

against her own. Pain knifed through her stomach, nearly doubling her. Out of habit, she'd stupidly tested the brioche batter for the bison slider buns. And now, hours later, she was in agony. There would be no biscuit tasting in her future. Not ever again. Bitterness rose up in the back of her throat. Of all the injustices. She bent over the table, trying to slow her breathing as another stab of pain shot through her.

She just had to make it through the next hour or two. See Maddie and Blake off to wherever they were going to spend the night. Then she could crawl into bed and curl up in a ball. But for now, she'd have to grin and bear it. She wouldn't let anything blemish Maddie and Blake's wedding.

Dottie stood at the far end of the table serving wedding cake. Her eyes narrowed suspiciously at Jamey.

"Don't worry, Dots," Jamey called out. "I haven't laced the biscuits with arsenic."

Dottie gave her a quick frown, but continued serving wedding cake. Jamey bit down on her lip to keep from crying out as another shot of pain wrenched through her insides.

Jarrod, one of her older brothers, approached, eyes full of concern. "You don't look so good."

"I'm fine," she bit out. "Go back to the celebration." She couldn't meet his eyes, so she focused on brushing crumbs off the tablecloth.

"You got glutened, didn't you?"

She nodded once, willing away the tears that suddenly pricked at her eyelids.

Jarrod was the only family member who knew about her celiac diagnosis. He'd flown out to be with her when she'd collapsed and ended up in the hospital. Her own boyfriend, now ex, and soon-to-be ex-business partner, couldn't be bothered. He'd come up with every excuse in the book to not visit her, namely that he needed to do double duty at the restaurant.

Jamey grit her teeth at the memory. She'd clearly been charmed by his... Frenchiness. All charm and no substance. He might be a stellar cook with an outstanding reputation for building a brand, but after a year of working with him intimately, in and out of the kitchen, she'd discovered his nasty side. His lazy side. He treated the bussers with disdain. Left her to do the heavy lifting in the kitchen while he schmoozed the important guests. Worst of all, he belittled her. It wasn't the partnership she'd imagined. Far from it.

During any other crisis, Jamey would have called Maddie immediately. After all, they'd been best friends for over a decade. But Maddie had rushed home to Prairie after her father, Warren Hansen, had suffered a massive heart attack, and was embroiled in her own crisis. She loved Maddie like a sister and refused to add to her stress. It hadn't made sense to tell Maddie when she returned to Chicago, brokenhearted, or during the flurry of wedding preparations over the last few weeks. So Jamey had soldiered on and tried to make the best of a shitty situation on her own.

"Why don't you come back to the pub?" Jarrod asked, his eyes serious.

They'd had this conversation three times in the last five weeks. She was over it. "I've already told you no. There's no creativity in pub food. And I can't be around gluten there any more than I can be around gluten in my own restaurant. You should see the rash around my midsection." Not to mention feel the knives slicing through her gut.

"But there's an escape clause in your contract. Why not use it?"

"About that…"

"Jamey," her brother's voice grew sharp. "For God's sake, Jamey. You used the contract I sent you?"

"Jean Luc had a fit when I showed it to him. Said if I didn't trust him, that we couldn't be partners."

Jarrod groaned. "And you fell for that shit?"

"I didn't want to upset him any more than I already had."

"I don't give two fucks about that asshat. That contract was for *your* protection. To keep *your* investment safe. What were you thinking?"

Shame heated her. God, she'd been so naïve. Star struck that Jean Luc had chosen to partner with her. He'd pursued her with the ferocity of a pit bull. No one pursued her. She was always the loudmouth. Bossypants. Most of the time she liked it that way. But in the beginning, Jean Luc had made her feel feminine. Desirable. Until he started pressuring her to change. Get a boob job, fix her hair. At first, she'd made excuses for his behavior. But after she disclosed her illness, he'd become cold, impatient. Dismissive. And the pieces fell into place.

He'd been using her this whole time. Using her talent in the kitchen for his gain. It had never been a partnership. And as soon as she was back in Chicago, she'd begin the difficult task of extracting herself from the partnership that wasn't.

"Obviously, I wasn't thinking," she snapped. "A mistake I won't make again."

"It's for your own good, sis."

"Are you ever going to stop bossing me?"

Jarrod draped his arm across her shoulders and grinned. "Nope. Never."

And that, in a nutshell, was why she'd gone to Paris to study at Le Cordon Bleu, and why she'd moved to Chicago to make her own way. She adored her family. Loved all her brothers to pieces. But they couldn't leave well enough alone. As the only girl, she was saddled with five well-meaning protectors. She'd never move back to Boston. Not if she wanted any kind of life for herself.

She leaned her head against Jarrod's shoulder. "Do me a favor?"

"Save you a dance?"

"You know I don't dance."

"I think there's a certain cowboy that would love you to save him a dance."

She twisted to study her brother. "Not dancing with anyone. Sexy cowboy or not."

"We see the way Brodie follows you around. Need us to take care of him?"

"I can handle him just fine, thank you." She gently cuffed Jarrod. "Now grab that pile of dirty plates and make yourself useful."

"Whatever you say, bossypants." Jarrod gave her shoulders a squeeze and moved to collect the plates.

She followed, collecting another stack full, holding them out from her body so she wouldn't get food on her dress. Of course her brothers had noticed the way Brodie looked at her. They weren't blind. Neither was she, for that matter.

A body moved in front of her, and the plates were lifted from her hands. "Let Me."

Brodie.

Did he have to look so delicious holding a stack of dirty plates? She rolled her eyes. "Do I look like some helpless little lady?"

He smiled slow and sexy. "No way to mistake you for one, darlin'."

She pursed her lips, shaking her head. "Don't call me that." She attempted to take back the plates, but he tightened his grip.

Fine. Let him help. She stepped around him and made her way to the back door.

"You prefer something more intimate? Like babe?" He kept pace with her and reached the back door in time to open it for her.

What was it with cowboy chivalry? She snorted as she bustled to the sink. "Go fack yerself, Brodie Sinclaire. Did you notice there's a party outside?"

"What? What I do to set off your Irish?" He followed her around the island and leaned on the counter.

She narrowed her eyes at him as she began rinsing dishes.

"Wait. Are you mad about earlier? I was just teasing."

He looked genuinely contrite. She didn't know why he'd set her off like that. Under normal circumstances she could dish out as good as she got. But these weren't normal circumstances, and Brodie kept her off-kilter. Tied her in knots.

"Forgive me? Kiss and make up?" He waggled his eyebrows. No shame. The man had no shame.

"I'm impervious to your charms. And I don't dance."

"I can teach you."

"I didn't say I don't know how."

"Now don't get your panties in a bunch... you're wearing them aren't you?" He winked at her.

She rolled her eyes fighting the urge to giggle. "Do you really want to lose your balls?"

"Quit sweet-talkin' me darlin'."

She'd learned growing up that when she felt vulnerable, her best defense was a strong offense. Jean Luc had only reinforced that conviction. Hanky panky with the brother of the groom at any other wedding might be a pleasant diversion. But Brodie got under her skin. Made her hot and agitated. That made him off-limits, no matter how many butterflies he launched in her stomach.

"I have five brothers and know how to wield a knife. Are you a betting man?"

Damn.

Had her voice just gone breathy?

"I've been known to make a few bets in my life."

She arched an eyebrow at him. "Cocky bastard aren't you?"

"Wouldn't you like to know?"

The back door opened. "Sis, he bothering you?"

Without turning around, she answered. "I already told you. It's nothing I can't handle, Jarrod. In fact," she slid Brodie a sideways glance. Time to have a little fun with him.

"Brodie here has just offered to take care of the dishes." She cocked an eyebrow at him and winked, handing him the scrubber. "Thanks, *sweetheart.*" She whispered so only he could hear, then sashayed away to join her brother at the door.

## Chapter Three

*B*rodie stood staring as the screen door slammed shut behind Jamey. Damn. She was good. And way too sexy for her skinny frame. The smirk she'd shot him indicating she knew she'd won this round had gone straight to his balls. He needed to have a talk with his balls. Jamey wasn't remotely his type. But the whole time they'd talked, he'd found himself focusing on the way her mouth moved.

He had no desire to kiss her. None whatsoever.

Except that suddenly he did.

Damn.

Where the hell had that thought come from?

She was too tall. Too skinny. Too mouthy. But there were surprising benefits to having a woman's face so close to his own. For starters, he could see every expression, every thought that passed over her features. Second, he was close enough to observe the crinkles around her eyes and the faint freckles splashed across her nose. Third, he wouldn't have to tilt his head to swoop in for a kiss. Her mouth was right there. Ready for him. All he'd have to do is step close.

Blowing out a breath, he tossed the scrubber in the sink. He wasn't going to consent to dish duty. Not when there was a party to help wrap up. Dusk would be falling soon, and he and Ben would have to saddle the bride and groom's getaway horses before they began the fireworks. He wanted the horses well on their way before it got noisy. He had half a mind to collect Simon and take him to the barn to show him how to turn the horses out to pasture. Then he could supervise Simon in the horse saddling. The kid was smart. Learned fast. But he didn't quite have the mechanics down well enough to saddle horses by himself.

Brodie stepped out on the back porch and surveyed the party before him. The late afternoon sun lit everything in gold, and sharpened the contrast between light and shadow. He scanned the dance floor but didn't see Jamey. Where was she?

Back over by the buffet table. Head bent toward Travis fucking Kincaid. Jealousy shot through him with the force of a charging bull.

Huh.

She wasn't his type. He couldn't possibly be jealous. Maybe he needed one of the celebratory Irish whiskey shots being passed around by her brothers. That would scratch the insane itch that had developed around her.

He spotted her brothers standing in a circle with Mason Carter, Blake's college roommate and a billionaire playboy. Stepping off the porch, he made a beeline for them, narrowly avoiding Millie Prescott, who ran the local organic market.

He should ask her to dance. She was more his type. Curvy, soft spoken, vivacious. He glanced back at Jamey, who was still speaking with Travis. She threw her head back in laughter just then, and jealousy surged again.

No way.

He wasn't jealous. He couldn't be. Shaking the feeling off as he reached the men, he extended his hand. "How about a toast, gents?"

Jarrod, the obvious ringleader, looked him up and down.

Brodie got the distinct feeling he was being measured and wasn't quite up to snuff. The desire to put these city boys in place surged through him. He stood his ground and looked each of them in the eye.

Jason, another of Jamey's brothers, clapped him on the back. "Seein' as we're almost family, you bet."

Mason handed him a glass.

"Sláinte," saluted another brother whose name Brodie hadn't caught.

Clearing his throat, he lifted his glass. "To the bride and groom." He tipped his head back and swallowed the fiery fluid, feeling every bit of its heat sliding down his throat.

The whiskey didn't do anything to cool the itch. If anything, it made it more persistent. Would Jamey taste like a shot of Irish whiskey?

Jarrod stepped close. "I noticed you following our sister."

"Just making sure the guests are happy."

Jarrod's eyes narrowed. "So long as that's all it is."

Defiance pressed against his chest, and he lifted his chin a notch. "You have a problem with me, city boy?" He'd be damned if he'd be subjected to this kind of scrutiny on his own property.

Jarrod stepped closer and took a sip of his whiskey. "We see the way you look at our sister."

"Oh?"

"Yeah." Jason crossed his arms, biceps bulging. Was he the firefighter? Brodie couldn't keep them straight. "Like she's a five course meal."

Huh.

He'd show them how wrong they were. He gave them his best smile. "You're barking up the wrong tree, gents. The one you gotta watch out for is Travis." Brodie cocked his head over his shoulder, sliding another glance Jamey's direction. She was laughing with Travis. Again.

The brothers moved as one.

"Thanks for the drink," he called after them. He kept his eyes trained on the brothers as they descended on Jamey and Travis. Jamey stepped away and caught his eye, giving him a scathing glare.

He waved his fingers at her, chuckling. Then mouthed the words "Payback" before he drifted away to search for Simon. Another round for him. She'd probably make him pay next time, but he didn't care.

Thirty minutes later, he still hadn't found Simon. Blake had signaled that he and Maddie were more than ready to escape the party, and it was past time to saddle up. Maybe Simon was waiting for him at the barn. So long as he didn't handle the horses.

Brodie began to make his way to the barn, stopping to accept congratulations every few yards. He was halfway to the barn when he realized Jamey was in front of him, wobbling her way across the bumps and ruts. What was she doing away from the party? And trying to navigate the barnyard in frilly shoes?

Suddenly, she stopped and bent double. Was she hurt? He quickened his pace. "Jamey?" he called after her. A shudder wracked her body and she lurched forward, obviously heading for the barn. What the everloving fuck was going on? "Jamey. Wait."

She heard him this time, if her dismissive wave was any evidence.

The barn door opened. Simon stood straining against the heavy door. Shit. *Shit. Shit. Shit.*

Blake's horse, Blaze, stood saddled. But Brodie could tell from the tilt of the saddle that the cinch was loose. Simon must have tried to saddle him alone. He broke into a jog, calling to the boy. "Simon. Stay there. I'll be right there."

A flash of movement by the corral caught his attention. The McPherson boys had found their stash of fireworks. *Goddammit.* Axel and Gunnar had assured him the fireworks were stashed out of sight. "Boys, get out of there," he bellowed. What in the hell were those boys doing down here anyway? Then he caught it. The whiff of cigarette smoke.

Of course.

Three things happened simultaneously. An object bounced off the barn door. Simon reached for the reins hanging from Blaze's bridle. And Jamey finally stopped to stare at him.

The air filled with the deafening sounds of firecrackers. Christ almighty. Did the boys have to choose the string of Black Cats? At the same time, Blaze reared, pulling Simon.

"Let go, Simon. Let go of the reins," Brodie yelled, breaking into a run. Blaze gave a little hop and bolted, saddle listing precariously, heading straight for Jamey. The horse was going to trample her.

"Jamey. *MOVE.*"

Out of the corner of his eye he could see the McPherson boys hopping the corral fence. He'd deal with them later. He had to reach Jamey. She stood frozen to the ground. He charged with a final burst of speed, and captured her waist, diving and twisting so that she landed on top of him.

"Oomph." The air left his lungs in a whoosh, and her startled eyes met his. He caressed the back of her head. "It's okay. You're safe." For a moment, he'd visualized the worst, and his heart had leapt to his throat. He'd never forgive himself if anything happened to her.

She shifted on top of him, and he became aware of her thighs pressed against his. Hard and muscular. His other hand rested dangerously close to her ass. The urge to squeeze and caress her radiated through him. All he'd have to do is raise his head, and her mouth would belong to him.

She arched her back, pulling away from him. "What in the devil's whiskers are you playin' at, Brodie Sinclaire?"

He gave her a wry smile. "Glad to see your Irish is intact."

"Jamey, Jamey. Are you okay?" A worried Simon appeared above him.

A curious light flashed in Jamey's eyes. "I'm fine, kiddo. Just had the wind knocked out of me by Cowboy Courageous, here. Help me up?"

Simon extended his hand. "I thought for sure Blaze was going to run you over."

"Nah. I'm too ornery." She pushed off him, and took Simon's hand, hauling herself up. She dusted herself off and glanced back at Brodie, her face all business.

He pushed himself to sitting, looping his hands over his knees. "Simon. What were you doing down here by yourself? You could have been trampled when the horse spooked."

Simon's eyes widened. "I guess I didn't think of that."

Brodie shook his head grimly. "I know you didn't. You

have to remember there are reasons for our rules. We don't want anyone to get hurt."

A look of panic crossed Simon's face. "Are you going to send me home? I didn't mean to, honest. I wanted to help."

Brodie pushed himself to his feet and crossed to Simon in two steps, wrapping an arm around the boy's shoulders. "No one's going to send you anywhere. You're a Sinclaire. This is your home. Even when you make mistakes. Hell, I've been making mistakes on this ranch my whole life, and I'm still here. Just do your best, and follow the rules."

Simon's arms wrapped around his waist. "You won't tell, will you?"

He ruffled the boy's hair. "Yep. I've got to. Part of being a man is taking your lumps when you mess up. Now go find Ben and let him know about the McPherson boys. Gloria's going to tan their hides."

"Sure thing." Simon gave him an extra squeeze, then took off for the Big House at a jog.

The horses could be properly saddled once he assured himself Jamey was really okay. Blaze had circled the barnyard, and stood about ten yards away, munching on a patch of spring grass.

Brodie gave a low whistle to the horse, gently strolling closer. Blaze gave him a side-eye, but remained where he was. "Come on, boy." He kept his voice low. "Come on back. No one's gonna hurt you."

He kept advancing on the horse, murmuring soft endearments until he came abreast of him. Reaching out, he gave Blaze a gentle stroke along his neck. "See? You're okay. Come on back." Brodie slowly reached down and clasped the reins. Blaze's ears flicked, but the horse didn't back up.

"You're good with him, you know," Jamey called out behind him.

Warmth blossomed and settled low in his gut. "I've been around horses my whole life."

"I meant Simon."

Pride surged through him. Jamey didn't seem like the kind who freely dished out compliments. "You sure you okay?" Better to steer the conversation to safer territory. For both of them. "Before the horse spooked–"

She raised her hand, mouth tightening. "I'm fine. *Really.*" She lifted her dress and picked her way over the bumpy ground to the corral fence.

He followed her with Blaze, looping the horse's reins over the fence post. "Why are you down here? Why'd you leave the party?"

Jamey stared across the corral, brows furrowed, refusing to meet his eyes. "What is this, twenty questions?"

Whatever had been bothering her must have passed. She was back to her usual piss and vinegar. "You're a pain in the ass, you know?" he growled.

"You're not the first person who's told me that." She held her body rigid.

"You're prickly as hell and you drive me crazy." He reached out and tucked a curl behind her ear. Soft and silky. Just like he'd imagined.

Her lips flattened grimly. "You know what your problem is?"

"Let me guess," he drawled. "I'm a cocky bastard." That, at least, earned him a half-smile.

"You're all hot air. Like a popover."

He scowled at her. "What do you mean?"

"You know, a popover. All air and no substance. A two-hundred-pound popover."

He pushed down a flash of annoyance. "And you know

what you are? Some kind of insane Irish crazy. First you threaten to serve my balls on a platter, then you say I'm great with Simon. Now I'm a popover? You need lessons in good natured flirting." He focused his attention on tightening the cinch, and double-checking Simon's work on the halter.

Indignation crackled off of her. "I know how to flirt just fine."

He gave Blaze a little pat and checked the cinch one last time. "Do you now? Not unless your prickles are all an act." He aimed a pointed glance at her. "Maybe you're the popover in this relationship."

She snorted. "This isn't a relationship. It's an... annoyance."

"You're right. Relationships involve willing parties. And kissing."

She glared at him. "Not interested."

He crossed his arms. "Neither am I."

"You're not my type."

"You're the farthest thing from mine."

"I don't date cocky bastards."

"I don't date bossy mouths."

She raised her eyebrows quizzically. "You think I'm bossy?"

"You think you're not?"

A blush crawled up her neck, mirroring his own rising agitation. "I didn't get to be one of the top chefs in Chicago by sitting quietly on my hands and waiting to be told what to do." Anger laced through her voice.

Setting his jaw, he tugged on her hand and started for the barn.

"Are you a sandwich short of a picnic you gobslice? Where are you takin' me?"

"I may be an arse weed, or a gobslice, or whatever else

23

Irish you want to throw at me, but I'm not enough of an ass to ruin my brother's wedding by having an argument in plain sight of the bride and groom," he ground out, leading her around the corner of the barn.

As soon as they were out of sight of the guests, he pulled up short, and spun around, pulling her close.

She clutched at his arms to avoid falling into him, and something slow and sensuous twisted in his gut. "Tell me again I'm not your type," he rasped.

Her eyes widened a bit, and she rolled her lips together, shaking her head. "Not even close."

"And you're not mine. Not remotely."

"Good." Her response came out more like a sigh than a statement.

He nodded, his gaze locking on her lips. "Good." He paused, the air suddenly crackling between them. "Then you won't mind if I confirm it." Without waiting for an answer, he tightened his embrace and covered her mouth with his.

There was nothing soft about her. Her thighs against his were hard. The muscles under his hands, rigid. But her mouth was another story. Her lips were softer than his favorite down pillow. He moved his own against them, willing her to open. And with a shudder and a sigh, she did. Hunger flooded his veins, urging him on. He swept his tongue across her lower lip, exploring.

Tasting.

Sweet as honey and soft as silk. He drank her in like she was the last drop of water in the well. A groan ripped from his throat as he spun her against the wall, his hand fisting in her dress.

She deepened the kiss, inviting him in further. Her own tongue sliding against his in a battle of wills. His cock stood rigid against his denim. And he ground against her, at the threshold of losing control.

Jesus.

If her mouth tasted this good, what about the rest of her? Her pussy must be a slice of Irish heaven. His balls tightened at the thought of dropping to his knees right now and lifting her skirt.

Just as quickly as it started, she gave him a push, and tore her lips from his, eyes glazed and gasping for breath. "Have you lost your marbles you nutter? You can't go kissing me."

"Why the hell not?"

"I-I-I have a business partner." She crossed her arms.

"What's that have to do with anything?"

"We- we're… getting married."

His eyes flew to her bare left hand, then back to her face. "Bullshit," he stated flatly, rubbing his hand over his face.

Her eyes widened.

"That's right. I call bullshit. If you haven't already married him, darlin', and from the looks of your left hand, it appears you haven't, he ain't interested."

She scowled at him, eyes sparking in challenge. "And you know this because?"

He braced an arm against the wall, leaning in close. So close her breath tickled his skin. "Because I don't care how scrawny and mouthy you are, I'd never let you out of my sight if you were mine."

Before she could protest, and before he could stop himself, he brushed his lips against hers one last time, savoring the sensation. Then he pushed away from the wall, and stalked around the corner back to the party. Only a two-by-four to the head and a bottle of scotch would purge Jamey Irish Whiskey O'Neill from his system.

## Chapter Four

hree Months Later

The summer sun beat ferociously down on the pavement as Jamey hurried past the neon sign of Frenchie's. She'd never enjoyed summers in Chicago. Especially this summer, when every time she passed her beloved restaurant sign, a knife twisted in her ribs. The O'Neill's part of the sign had been taken down weeks ago. Frenchie O'Neill's – now just Frenchie's, was *her* restaurant, dammit. *Her* concept, *her* baby, *her* money she'd stupidly sunk in without the contract her brother Jarrod warned her she should have. All for the love of a conceited, lying, cheating, man-whore of a Frenchman.

Not only had he screwed her out of her savings. He'd been schtooping the hostess, right under her nose. Because Barbie Bimbo's daddy wanted to franchise the *Frenchie's* concept – without her.

She might have been able to live with the sting if Jean Luc had been willing to part ways fairly. But no. When she'd threatened to go public with the scandal, Froglegs had threatened *her*. *"Good luck, Cherie. Where will you go when ze entire town knows you refuse to work with flour?"*

It wasn't that simple, and he knew it. Jean Luc had refused to budge on making the kitchen gluten-free. Even though she'd run numbers and showed him the bottom line was safe with a few modifications. Plus they would have a new and very loyal clientele once word got out their kitchen was gluten safe.

But her concept had been too much for his ego. The fatal flaw in her plan to turn the kitchen gluten-free was that it took the limelight from him. And what had he done to remind her this had been his gig from the get-go? He'd made good on his threat. Every chef in Chicago now knew she had celiac. Colleagues she'd had drinks with suddenly wouldn't take her calls. She wasn't worth the risk. Damaged goods. She'd gotten that message loud and clear.

Jamey grimaced, taking the stairs by two up to her apartment right across the street. Never again would she blindly trust someone else with the business side of a food venture. Never again would she enter into a business relationship without a contract. Never again would she mix business and love. The cost was too high. At this moment, her life could not possibly be more pathetic.

A turd floating down the sewer drain had it better than she did.

By a longshot.

She jammed the key into the door a little too vigorously, and once inside, shut the door a little too hard. She didn't care. It was the middle of the afternoon, and the old lady next door was deaf. She tore off her chef's coat and stomped to the kitchen.

Chicago hadn't been the same since Maddie had moved back to Prairie, Kansas, and married a handsome cowboy. A cowboy with a sinfully hot and very obnoxious brother.

She wrinkled her nose at the memory of Brodie Sinclaire. A few inches shorter than Blake, and broader. Beefier, thanks to all that hard ranch work. And hotter.

So hot she could fry an egg on his abs. His kiss had flat out incinerated her. His piercing blue eyes had a way of boring through her and making her all hot and itchy. But – and this was a big *but* as far as she was concerned – he was an ass. All hot air and no substance. Too much like Jean Luc.

And it irked her that in the span of thirty seconds he'd accurately summed up her non-relationship with Jean Luc. And told her she'd needed lessons in flirting. It double irked her that he'd called her scrawny. *If you were mine, I'd never let you out of my sight...* What the hell was that supposed to mean?

As. If.

Did all the cowboys in Prairie use some kind of cowboy testosterone spray?

"Never let you out of my sight, my ass," she muttered as she rifled through the sink for a glass that looked passably clean. "Who talks like that?"

She might run a spick-and-span kitchen, but her home life had always been a bit of a disaster. For too long, she'd counted on Maddie's sense of order to keep her functioning outside of a professional kitchen.

Jamey rinsed a little water through the glass, then poured out the last of her crisis bottle – 12 year Redbreast Irish Whiskey. In her opinion, the best of its kind. Who cared that it was three-thirty in the afternoon? This would be the last drop she'd enjoy for the foreseeable future. Swirling the whiskey in the glass, she leaned against the counter. Best to make the toasts count.

She would toast every blessed sip remaining, then swallow her pride and call her brother, Jarrod. What was a little more humiliation after the day she'd had?

Without a doubt, today had been the crowning turd on the shitpile of her life. Bad enough she'd had to take the most humiliating temp job for a chef of her standing – dishing up slop in the cafeteria at the local elementary school. Worse still, she'd gotten fired by a battle-axe in a hairnet for refusing to serve pink slime. As if that goo was fit for human consumption.

Raising the glass, she spoke into the silence. "Here's to never depending on fuckwits, numpties, or shitdonkeys ever again."

She sipped, letting the warmth settle in her belly.

"Here's to self-humiliation and listening to *I told you so's* from your family." She swallowed down a lump of despair right along with the whiskey.

Her throat hitched a little. "Here's to never having beer, or croissants, or-or bread... ever again."

The lump of despair she'd swallowed, ballooned, and threatened to close off her throat. She squeezed her eyes shut, willing the tears that were pricking behind her eyes not to flow. Five months into a celiac diagnosis and she was finally coming to terms with the reality that cheating had violently painful and lasting consequences. And while she'd tried valiantly, she also had to accept there was no way she could ever work in a standard kitchen again. Breathing flour dust wreaked nearly as much havoc on her body as taking a sip of beer.

Her final toast came out in a whisper. "Here's to being blackballed by your so-called fiancé, and never working in a five-star kitchen again."

Taking a deep shuddering breath, she tipped her head back and downed the last of her liquid sanity, licking the inside of the glass to catch every drop. She slammed the glass down on the counter, the echo of it momentarily ringing against the cupboards.

God she hated living alone.

But she sure as hell couldn't slink back to her family in Boston after the disaster she'd made of her life here. They'd begged her not to move to Chicago with Maddie in the first place.

But *noooo*.

She wanted to prove something to them. Prove she could manage on her own, creating art out of food. She'd gambled everything and come up short. In every aspect of her life.

Jamey tipped up the bottle a final time, hoping for one last tiny drop. No such luck. "Oh how the mighty fall, Jamey. How the mighty fall."

How on God's green earth was she going to make rent next week without calling Jarrod? When she finally disclosed what went down with Jean Luc, he'd strangle her through the phone. She'd managed to put him off the last three months by insisting she was fine. But now she had to face the music.

Her phone buzzed in her purse. Reaching for it, she smiled for the first time that day. "Mads! How's the little mummy?"

Maddie's delighted laugh crackled through the speaker. It warmed Jamey's heart to see her best friend so happy in life. She pushed aside the twinge of envy that sparked. Maddie's childhood had been difficult. She deserved every happiness.

"Jamey, I'm glad I reached you. I wasn't sure if this was a good time."

Jamey plastered on a fake smile, hoping it would come

through the phone. "Oh, it's always a good time to talk to you. You know that."

"Are things still rough with Jean Luc?"

Guilt wound through her. She should have at least told Maddie what was happening.

"Ah. About that… you could say we're pretty much through."

The sympathetic gasp on the other end of the line was all the confirmation Jamey needed that she'd been right in not saying anything.

"Jamey. Oh no! When? What are you doing about the restaurant?"

She pinched her nose. Craptastic. All her chickens seemed to be coming home to roost today.

"About that too… umm…" Best just to get it out quickly and have it out in the open. "He's a witless man-whore, Mads. Was boffing the hostess right underneath my nose the whole time. Then sold out my interest to an investment group to make a chain."

Maddie's gasp of horror made her cringe.

"Nooo! Jamey. He can't possibly do that. Can he? I'll ask Blake. He knows all about that stuff."

"No. No need. I ah… didn't insist on a contract."

Shame and humiliation rolled over her in waves. Saying it out loud made her sound like the world's biggest idiot. "Jarrod tried to tell me, but I was too stubborn, an-and in love, and too scared Jean Luc would bail if I demanded a contract. I should have known. I should have suspected he wasn't above board. But…" She took a shuddering breath. "I needed his name and his connections. Oh God, Mads." Tears pricked her eyes for an instant. "I was such an idiot."

There. At least now, some of the worst of the last few months was out in the open.

"Why didn't you tell me?" Maddie's voice was sharp with accusation. "I'd have come up to help you. My new job didn't start until last week."

Jamey let out a heavy sigh. "I didn't want to rain on your parade. You've had enough to deal with settling into a new life."

"I'm hurt, Jamey. You know I always have time for you. No matter what."

Great. The guilty knot in her chest stabbed at her. Now she'd offended her best friend. And she still hadn't fessed up about having celiac. What would happen when Maddie found out she'd been holding out on her for months?

"Are you okay Jamey? Do you need anything?"

Maddie's question about did her in. Tears threatened to spill again.

"Yeah… Yeah… You know me. I always manage."

"Stop it, Jamey. You know you don't have to go it alone."

There it was. That pitying tone of voice. The reason why she couldn't go home to Boston. Or ask anyone for help – her brother or Maddie. Why she had to figure out something. Anything. Even if it was, God help her, scooping ice-cream on Navy Pier.

"Do you have anything lined up?"

Jamey shrugged. "A few things. I'll be fine."

Maddie was like family, which meant Jamey couldn't disclose how precarious things were to her, either. Maddie would phone Jarrod in a heartbeat and send the cavalry in.

"How lined up?"

"What do you mean?"

"I mean, have you made a commitment to anyone?"

Jamey cocked her head. Maddie never beat around the bush this way. "What's going on Mads?"

"Oh God, Jamey. We're in a pickle down here with the

hunting lodge. It's only been up six weeks and already it's a disaster. Brodie's messed everything up and Blake's ready to kick him off the ranch."

That perked her up.

"So bad boy Brodie can't seem to keep his nose clean, huh?"

As hot as his kisses had been, she was still pissed he'd called her scrawny.

"Blake was hoping he might be able to retain you for six to eight weeks to get the kitchen running properly."

She cocked her eyebrow, reaching for the empty bottle of Redbreast and turning it upside down to see if anything dribbled out. "Tell me more."

"There's not much to tell. He needs a strong hand in the kitchen, and someone who can manage a simple budget."

"I've always worked alongside business managers, but if you promise it's simple, I could do it. Who else would be in the kitchen?"

"Just you, unless you wanted to hire help. You know how Blake loves your food. You'd really be helping us." Maddie took a deep breath. "In addition to salary, Blake will pay the condo lease through the end of the year, so you can come back to Chicago, if you choose, and have time to find something new. Although, maybe if you like running the lodge, you'd stay? I figured it was a long shot calling you, but I've missed you. I'd be thrilled to have you close again." Maddie's voice held a note of hope.

"So I'd have complete control in the kitchen?" Would Blake and Maddie care if it was a gluten-free kitchen?

"Absolutely, and no rent. You can stay down at the lodge."

Jamey bit her lip. Regret, shame, loss, and hope vied

for space in her chest. Blowing out a sigh, she weighed the proposal.

Six weeks.

*Tell her.*

But if she took six weeks to prove to herself and everyone else that a gluten-free kitchen was as good as any other kitchen... Why worry them unnecessarily over a detail like gluten when they already liked her food? She'd never consent to serving anything that wasn't delicious. Her conscience momentarily pricked at her. More for not confiding in Maddie *again* than the possibility of a gluten-free kitchen. Jamey knew she could deliver great gluten-free food. She just needed time to prove it. Might as well take the opportunity and run with it.

"Okay. Tell Blake I'll come."

Maddie squealed into the phone. "I'm thrilled Jamey. Your touch is just what the lodge needs to be successful."

"So when do you need me down there?"

"How about tomorrow?"

## Chapter Five

 *wo days later…*

Jamey's lips hovered over his cock, a wicked smile playing on her lips. "Ready, cowboy?" The heat in her emerald eyes scorched him.

His breath caught in his throat and he nodded, savoring the view. Her wild red hair tumbled every which way and he fought the urge to fist his hand through it. This was her gig.

Her tongue flicked out to circle the head already slicked with pre-come.

"Jesus, Jamey. You're killing me."

She laughed quietly. "Don't die yet, cowboy, I've just started."

He groaned, thrusting his hips in an attempt to relieve the agony building in his balls. She gave him a little squeeze and stroked up, her eyes never leaving his face. God, it was exquisite, this sensation. Killing him.

He was going to die in the throes of bliss.

He reached down and lightly caressed Jamey's neck.

Her breath caught in her throat, giving a little sound that made his balls vibrate. Good. She was enjoying this torture as much as he was.

And from the look in her eye, she was going to suck him like a Goddamned popsicle. Holy hell, he was going to blow his rocks off just looking at her, but he couldn't look anywhere else. His cock twitched in anticipation.

"I'm ready for dessert," she said breathlessly, giving him a wicked smile. She licked her lips slowly, dipping her head to take him fully in her mouth…

Ice-cold needles assaulted him, and her head twisted strangely.

"Wait, Jamey…"

A second wave of ice-cold hit him.

"JAMEY??"

Wait. What?

Pain stabbed behind his eyes as he opened them to the form of his brother, Ben, who stood beside the bed with a bucket. A dull throbbing started drumming in his temple and realization dawned that his bed was soaking wet. A dream. Pinching his temples, he tried to sit up. "What the fuck, Ben?"

"Jamey, huh?" Laughter laced Ben's voice. "Maddie know you're having wet dreams about her bestie?"

Brodie groaned and flopped back onto the soaked bed. "What time is it?"

"Time to drag your ass out of bed and down the hall before Blake comes in and loses it."

Brodie could barely hear Ben over the roaring in his head. His mouth tasted like a shit pile. He screwed his eyebrows together trying to piece together the events of the previous evening.

"I'm not fucking around. Blake's hot under the collar. I'll hold him off, but you gotta get up, man." Ben threw him a robe and left the room, not bothering to shut the door behind him.

Brodie sat up only to be assaulted by a wave of nausea. Food.

He needed food. A nice Dottie's Diner hangover breakfast and he'd be good as new.

He'd just have to figure out a way to postpone his conversation with Blake. That usually wasn't too hard these days. Blake was so busy being married and overseeing the main ranch business, Brodie had pretty much been left to his own devices down here at the hunting lodge. He kind of liked it. Except for the fact he couldn't seem to keep anyone in the kitchen. But he'd managed. There was cereal for the work crew, and Dottie's down the road in town. They were all used to fending for themselves.

Blowing out a breath and wincing at the stabbing in his head, he began to untangle himself from the sheets. He ran a hand through his hair, and shook himself.

Fuck it.

He shoved his arms into the worn terry. If Blake wanted to talk now, bring it on. But he wouldn't be coherent until he'd had a nice long shower. Maybe then, he could pick up where his dream had been so cruelly interrupted. Wiping the last of the fog from his eyes, he ambled down the hall to the great room that comprised the center of the hunting lodge they'd erected in record time late this spring. Blake was fully dressed and pacing in front of the fieldstone fireplace.

Brodie raised a hand in greeting, squinting against the early morning sun flooding the room. It was entirely too bright in here.

"'Sup, bro?"

Blake wheeled and stalked over, eyes sparking and a

muscle in his cheek twitching. "Are you kidding me? What in the hell do you think you're doing, Brodie?"

He took a small step back, but not too big of a step. He wasn't going to let Blake push him around. Even if it was ungodly early. "Whaddya mean what do I think I'm doing? I'm trying to run the lodge like you told me."

Blake's mouth flattened and he crossed his arms. "Really? When does going on a bender and bedding a bar bunny constitute running the lodge?"

God, he hated when Blake got on his high horse. After all these years, Blake still managed to make him feel like a dumbass and a disappointment.

He frowned at his brother, still trying to shake the cobwebs from his head. "There was no bar bunny. Only Brenda, the cook. And I didn't bed her." He'd tried, but had sent her home.

Kissing Jamey O'Neill had ruined him for other women. His balls were blue. As evidenced by his nightly dreams about the red-haired minx.

Ben snorted behind him. "*She* was a cook? Looked like the only thing she was cooking was your pants."

Goddammit. Now they were ganging up on him. "Shut up, Ben. Do you wanna be the cook?"

"Not if it means cooking your pants."

That drew a half-smile from Blake. Leave it to Ben to soften the tension that still occasionally arose between him and Blake.

"Joking aside, we've burned too much daylight," Blake continued.

"Wait." Brodie scrubbed a hand over his cheek. "What time is it?"

Ben looked at his watch. "Ten thirty. You've slept the day away lazy-bones."

Shit. Okay, maybe he'd overdone it just a bit last night.

A flush started up the back of his neck. He scrubbed his hand over his face again. God, he felt like shit. No more half-bottles of scotch on a weeknight. He took a seat in his favorite oversized leather chair while Blake returned to pacing in front of the large stone fireplace.

Brodie caught a glance exchanged between his brothers. "What's going on?"

Blake skewered him with a look – half angry, half concerned. "It's time for you to man up, Brodie."

"What the hell is that supposed to mean? So I got a little crazy last night." He shrugged. "Big deal."

Blake fisted his hand on the mantle. "Exactly. It is a big deal. When I put you in charge of the lodge two months ago, I expected you to step it up. Take responsibility and quit messing around. You're twenty-eight for Chrissakes."

That got his hackles up. Blake was his brother, not his Goddamned father. Not that Jake Sinclaire had been much of a father. He liked booze, brawling, and women. And not necessarily in that order. Jake had called Brodie a disappointment to the family name. Those words had cut like a knife twelve years ago. Hell, they still stung today.

Jake had put him in charge of the vaccination charts and he'd bungled the whole deal, causing some cattle to be vaxxed twice, and others not at all. He'd never forget the beating he endured, not to mention the public shaming. In short order, the whole town had learned about his mistake, and it had taken years for the ribbing to subside.

"Now wait just a second," Brodie sputtered. "You're the one with the MBA. You're the one who's running the family business. Let me ride the fence lines and look after the herd with Ben."

"Can't do that," Blake ground out. "Ben is working overtime on herd management because I'm front-loading my travel selling bison this fall. I need to be home when the baby comes. We can hire out fence repair. I won't hire out the lodge. This is a family business. We need you to step up and pull your weight around here." Blake shot a look over to Ben and sighed heavily. "I know how you hate spreadsheets, but they're a necessary part of running an operation our size. You can't hide out on the range forever."

This burned. "Come on. I'm pulling my weight."

"Not in the way we need. Don't think I don't know what's going on down here. You've already run us into the red, and we can't afford that."

"What the hell, now you're checking up on me?" That chapped his hide. He knew he was the family fuck-up, but he was honestly trying his best.

The cold hard reality of that churned his gut worse than the leftover liquor still sitting there. Things had been better recently with Blake. Since he'd married Maddie, Blake had been… gentler. He supposed it had something to do with their young half-brother, Simon, who was now spending half his time on the ranch. So experiencing the 'old' Blake – particularly when his head was pounding – hurt.

"Yes. And it's a damned good thing, too. You've gone through every cook in a hundred mile radius and your crew is starving and ready to quit. I can't have Mrs. Sanchez keep cooking them meals when you're supposed to be running the show down here."

Brodie scrubbed his face again, squinting to focus through the spiky pain in his forehead. Every time he moved his head, the stabbing intensified, adding to his general irritation. He blew out a breath. There was no way he could avoid taking his lumps this morning. Best to just take them, pop a few Advil, and go back to bed.

"Fine. I've fucked up. Sorry." He glared at Blake. "I'll find another cook."

Blake grunted, threading his hand through his hair and pacing again. "That's what you don't get. I can't afford any more weeks like this. You're breaking the bank, and that affects all of us. Me, you, Ben… Simon."

Brodie's heart twisted at the mention of Simon. He'd only found out that Simon was his half-brother this spring. Calling his reaction at the time 'a shock', was an understatement. Especially when he learned that Simon's mom was his ex-girlfriend, Kylee Ross. But Simon was a good kid. He genuinely enjoyed spending time with him.

Blake stopped and aimed weighted stare his direction. After a moment, he resumed pacing. "This is serious, Brodie. We've leveraged a lot to develop a hunting lodge as a second source of income. If you drive it into the ground before it gets off the ground, I'll have to sell the property back to Warren Hansen. And I'll be damned if I give that man the satisfaction of saving our asses twice."

"What do you want me to do?"

Blake paused midstep, and leaned on the heavy oak mantle above the fireplace. A pained look crossed his face. "I want you to grow the fuck up. I want you to stop carousing and letting everyone else do the hard work of running the ranch. I want you to think about the example you're giving Simon." Blake's eyes bored into him. "It's time to man up, Brodie."

Ouch.

He scowled back at his brother. "What the hell is that supposed to mean? Man up?"

"It means just that. It means step up and do the work necessary to make this place a success."

"I was doing that."

"You're failing. Do better."

He shot out of his chair. "Fuck you, asshole."

Blake crossed the room in two steps, standing toe to toe

with him, eyes blazing. "Do I need to remind you that I was supporting two families at your age? And had been for eight years? *And* I'd just finished my MBA? I know Jake was tougher on you than the rest of us, but you have to let that shit go. You are capable of more. We need you to do more. It's time to drop the perpetual chip on the shoulder you carry around. I can't let your failures pull us all under. You go down, you go down alone. Understand?"

"Better spell it out so it gets through my thick skull," he snarled back. There were times he hated his older brother. This was definitely one of those times.

"You have six weeks to get this lodge working in the black again. Got it? Six weeks. I don't give a shit if you do it yourself or you hire a business manager to tell you what to do. But I can't keep babysitting you. Whatever you do will be above board and you will turn around the mess you made."

"Or what?" The cobwebs were completely gone from his head now. Although his head was still in a vice, it somehow helped him focus.

"Or. You're. Out."

Brodie's hand involuntarily clenched and he consciously relaxed it. "What do you mean 'out'?"

Sweat beaded under Blake's nose, and his pulse throbbed wildly at his temple.

Shit.

He'd never seen his brother this mad.

"Out. As in off the ranch."

He jerked back as if he'd been punched in the gut. No way. He'd never do it. Blake wasn't that much of an asshole. "I don't believe you."

Blake's eyes looked bleak. "Don't try me. I'm done with your bullshit, Brodie. We have too much at stake. You step up or you can go waste your life on someone else's ranch."

A wave of nausea rolled through him, whether from the leftover liquor or the understanding that his brother wouldn't hesitate to kick him off the only home he'd ever known. He clenched his jaw so hard his teeth ground. He fisted his hand, not because he was in danger of losing control. He wasn't. He was in danger of breaking down, and he'd be damned if anyone, especially Blake, saw him give into despair.

Blake's eyes softened. "Against my better judgment, I'm throwing you a bone. Consider it your final bailout."

"I don't need a fucking bailout." He bit the words out.

"Don't be a fool. You're in so far over your head, you don't know what's down or up."

He snorted, crossing his arms.

Blake continued. "I hired someone reliable to run the kitchen. One less thing you'll have to deal with over the next six weeks. The *only* things you'll have to worry about are supervising the crew in finishing clearing the cedars in the bottomland, and booking guests."

The tightness in his gut eased a fraction.

"You'll need to keep clean books so I can track your progress. Understand?"

God, this sucked. But even he had to admit, he deserved it this time. He skated through life just like he'd skated through school as a kid. He relied on his charm and his easygoing personality while his older brothers shouldered the heavier burdens. And he'd let them. He'd never thought of it as taking advantage, it had just been… easier. Brodie nodded. "I can do that." *Liar.*

Blake clapped him on the shoulder. "I know you can. We're counting on you. We. Can't. Fail."

Shit. Then why were they counting on him? He could count his successes in life on less than one hand.

"One last thing…" There was still fire in Blake's eyes.

"What."

"Better get yourself cleaned up and out there with your crew. The new chef will be here for dinner." Blake stepped aside and over to Ben.

Ben gave Brodie an encouraging smile and a cuff on the shoulder. "You've got this. I know you do. Just dig deep. It's in times of crisis you discover your true self."

His brothers left without saying another word, leaving him standing in the middle of the great room.

He sat down as the breath whooshed out of him.

Well damn.

*Who do you think you're fooling? You can't run a ranch.*

He shut out the voice of doubt hammering at him. He was nothing if not resourceful. He'd figure it out. Come hell or high water.

## Chapter Six

*J*amey stepped off the plane and into the hot, muggy air that was the Flint Hills in August. Maddie had agreed to meet her at baggage claim since she'd had to check the bag with her chef's knives. Not that it mattered. The airport in Manhattan, Kansas, was so small that the waiting area and baggage claim were essentially the same space.

Jamey easily spotted Maddie's bright hair and hurried over, wrapping her in a huge hug. "Look at this bump." She couldn't help grinning as she reached out to feel Maddie's protruding belly.

Maddie positively glowed. No doubt that marriage agreed with her. Jamey's heart squeezed a little and she shoved her own thoughts of longing to the back of her brain. She hadn't been dealt those cards, so best move on and look at these next six weeks as a reset. After this, she could go anywhere she liked. Maybe California. The emphasis on healthy gourmet might mean a better fit for her. Certainly it would be better for her health. She'd read there were a handful of dedicated gluten-free bakeries in the Bay Area. A far cry from running her own place, but at least she wouldn't get sick on the job.

Maddie took a step back and narrowed her eyes. Concern peppered her features. "Jamey? Have you been sick? You look like you've dropped a lot of weight, and you didn't have much on you to begin with. Everything okay?"

Leave it to Maddie to not miss the details. Another pang of guilt pushed at her. "Yeah. I'm okay. I haven't been feeling well, but the doctor said it's manageable."

Relief flickered in Maddie's eyes. "So you've been to the doctor. Good. Well some good food and a few of Dottie's country breakfasts and you'll be back to yourself in no time.

She wrinkled her nose. "Not for me. I'm staying away from those grease bombs you call country breakfast." She reached down and grabbed her suitcase off the conveyer.

Not to mention, she wouldn't give that biddy the satisfaction. Dottie's ego was enormous, and she didn't need anyone else fawning all over her, especially when she couldn't accept that there was a whole world of incredible cuisine beyond diner food. Why couldn't you serve comfort food with a gourmet twist? And how was having more than one cook in a town a bad thing? It wasn't like she was going to go into the diner business. Not now. Not ever.

"I know you two didn't start off on the right foot at my wedding, but she really does mean well. She just doesn't understand you, that's all."

Jamey scowled at her best friend as they headed across the parking lot. "I never asked her to understand me, just respect that I might do things differently. She can do things however she wants, just as long as she doesn't tell me what to do."

"But that's the thing about Dottie. She's a mother hen. She looks at everyone like they're her daughters."

She snorted. "Thank you, no. I already have five brothers and my parents trying to boss me. That's seven people too many."

The drive back to the ranch was lively, as Maddie brought Jamey up to speed on all the aspects of her new job and life.

"I hope you're taking me straightway to the Trading Post. A feast of cowboys will be a sight for sore eyes."

Maddie slid a grin her direction. "Is that like a murder of crows? A feast of cowboys?"

Jamey waggled her eyebrows. "I'm a free woman this time, remember?"

Maddie hit the signal to turn under the Sinclaire and Sons arch that marked the entrance to their property. "I'm sure Brodie will be thrilled at the news."

"Pah. Don't speak to me of him. He may have inherited the Sinclaire hotness gene, but he's a gobshite."

"Put the Irish away for half a sec, Jamey." Maddie became serious. "So there's something you should know before I drop you off at the lodge."

Maddie's tone of voice put her instantly on guard. "What Mads? Is there a problem?"

"Not a problem per se, more like a heads up." She looked downright guilty.

"What is it Mads? What didn't you tell me the other day?"

Maddie gave her an apologetic glance as they pulled up to the back entrance of lodge.

"Blake put Brodie in charge of the business side of the lodge."

She threw her hands up. "*What?*"

"NOT the kitchen side. You're in complete charge. But Blake told Brodie he had to get the guest side running in the black or leave the ranch."

"Maddie Hansen Sinclaire. Are you out of your ever-loving mind?" Indignation roared to life with the same fire as her pussy. Damn her body. Always making its own decisions. She sat back in the cab crossing her hands across her chest. "I refuse. Absolutely refuse," she sliced the air in front of her, "to work with that half-crazed lunatic. I'd rather go home to Boston."

Not only did Brodie push every single one of her buttons, she couldn't trust herself to work with someone she was violently attracted to. Her track record was too bad on that front. How could she concentrate on making food-porn if she was having lascivious thoughts about a cowboy she'd love to lick from head to toe?

Maddie blushed to her roots and cringed. "I know, I know. I told Blake you wouldn't be happy about it. But he promised you don't have to work together. You just need to give him your weekly balance sheets. That's all."

She flattened her lips. "Fine. I can manage that."

"And one more thing."

"Maddie, I swear by all that is holy…"

"Ooh don't be mad at me, Jamey, please?"

"Just spit it out. What else is there?"

"Brodie's been living down here at the lodge since it was finished. Blake said Brodie'd do a better job managing the lodge if he was living here too.

Jamey couldn't think through the roaring in her ears. "So let me get this straight. I'll be living *and* working with Brodie for the next six weeks?" She couldn't do it. She'd explode. From complete and total irritation, or from suppressing her libido. Either way, it was a lose-lose situation.

Maddie flashed her a sympathetic smile. "Look, I don't know what he did to piss you off so badly, but he's really just a goof."

She snorted. "A goof with no verbal filter."

"Sounds like someone else I know."

Jamey narrowed her eyes at her best friend. "What exactly are you saying, Mads?"

"I'm saying that both of you can be strong willed. That's all." Maddie rushed on. "But I think you'd make a great team."

Damn it all to hell. If this didn't pour cold water on all her fantasies of spending six weeks in cooking heaven trying to reignite her food mojo. Now she'd have to deal with Brodie and his needling, pokey ways.

And his big strong hands.

And his hard thighs.

She squirmed in her seat. She'd die a thousand deaths before she'd ever let on to Maddie what had transpired between the two of them at her wedding. She'd just have to keep her libido well in hand whenever she had to deal with Brodie. That was all there was to it.

She expelled an angry sigh. "Fine. What's done is done. Let's get this show on the road."

"I've got to head back to the Big House, but everything's open. Kitchen is right through there. I think Blake said there are six crew here working on clearing out the cedars, so eight including you for dinner tonight?"

Jamey nodded, putting her game face on. "Okay. I'll check in with you two tomorrow?"

Maddie gave her a smile filled with gratitude. And leaned across the console to offer her a hug. "I'm so glad you're here, Jamey. If anyone can make this work, you can."

Jamey hopped out of the cab, grabbed her bags out of the back, and stood watching the truck barrel back onto the long drive and away to the Big House. Squaring her shoulders, she stepped through the door into the kitchen.

At first glance, she took in the large refrigerator standing next to a tall vertical freezer.

Nice.

Everything was stainless steel and tile. The range was a six burner Viking coupled with a flat griddle. They'd purchased the food service grade dishwasher like she'd suggested earlier in the summer, and had the proper number of sinks. In all, a decent layout.

But as she passed over the space again, cold fury rose up like a volcano.

Grease and grime covered every surface. Dirt had collected in the corners, and there were dirty dishes in the sink. A quick glance at the floor showed dark spots from spills not cleaned. Food remains lay crusted on the prep island along with a tipped-over box of Cocoa Puffs that appeared to be mostly gone.

Jesus, Mary, and Joseph.

What kind of slobs and derelicts had trashed this place? She prayed to the saints they hadn't attracted vermin. Clenching her jaw and dragging her suitcase behind her, she marched through the kitchen in search of a bedroom, barely pausing to admire the vaulted ceiling and large stone fireplace in the great room. The bedroom nearest the kitchen was blessedly open.

Good enough for now. She quickly changed into her work attire and stomped back to the kitchen hoping against hope there was at least a mop.

Two and a half hours later, she'd channeled most of her righteous indignation into a sparkling clean kitchen worthy even of her mentors' exacting standards. She'd have to shower again before starting dinner prep, but if she took stock now, she could menu plan while she was in the shower.

Jamey pulled open the cabinet she expected would have dry goods, and it was empty.

She tried the next.

Empty.

What on earth? Where in the hell was the food? Next cupboard. Empty. And the next and the next. She threw open the refrigerator. Empty, except for a half-used container of week old baloney. The fury she'd let go of while she'd been on her hands and knees scrubbing, came roaring back to life.

She glanced at the clock over the door. Three-thirty. There was no way she'd have dinner for eight ready by six. What in the hell kind of joint was Brodie running here? Was he ordering pizza every night? Whatever the case, she would have more than a few choice words for him over the state of the kitchen when they finally crossed paths.

In the meantime, how in creation she was going to get the four miles into town? Walking was out of the question. She thought she'd seen a truck parked out front when Maddie had dropped her off. With any luck, the keys would be in the ignition like they were up at the Big House.

"Oooh. You better have on your running shoes when I get my hands on you, Brodie Sinclaire, or you will find yourself trussed like a turkey and hung out to dry."

Spinning on her heel, she stalked out the front door. Sure enough, a big truck was parked cattywampus out front with the fob on the seat. Stepping on the running board and hauling herself up, she adjusted the seat and fired up the engine, gunning it so hard the tires spun. She barreled up the gravel and onto the long drive and turned the truck toward the ranch's entrance. Cursing the whole way.

## Chapter Seven

*B*rodie entered the kitchen through the back door, pulling off his sweat-lined straw hat. Wiping his forehead, he paused, relishing the cool interior and letting his eyes adjust to the dimmer light. His head still hurt, and he was still pissed as hell at about the turn of events.

Kicking him off his home?

Hell no.

He'd succeed come hell or high water. There was no way he was leaving the ranch. And if he was honest with himself, he didn't want to let Simon down either.

He scanned the kitchen through narrowed eyes. Someone had been in here. It was… sparkly. Hadn't looked this good since he'd moved in. New chef must be here.

"Hello?"

After a moment he moved to the entryway of the great room. "Anyone here?"

He glanced at the front door, which stood open a crack, and moved to shut it. But the sunlight flooding through the opening struck him and he opened the door wider.

Where in the hell was his truck?

Who the fuck had taken his truck?

He leaned on the doorframe for a moment, running a mental checklist. All the hands were with him... unless Ben had ridden this way and needed it for something... but in that case his horse would be tied to the post out back.

Anger twisted in his belly.

If the new chef had taken his truck, he'd have a word or two to say about it. No one took his truck. Especially not a new employee. Without asking.

As if on cue, his truck came careening up the dirt driveway too fast and pulled around back.

They were going to ruin his brakes, too.

Great.

He pushed off the doorway and made his way back through the kitchen, ready to have an argument he could win for once. Best to put the chef in his place from the get-go. He was the boss around here.

He threw open the back door, charging out and bellowing like a bull. "What in the hell do you think you're doing, stealing my truck?"

The body that popped around the front of the truck didn't belong to the burly chef he'd assumed Blake hired.

No.

Blake had gone straight to the top of the chef's chain.

Jamey O'Neill.

She gave him a scathing glance as she reached into the truck bed and started pulling out groceries. "Well don't just stand there, you great lump."

He stood there mesmerized by her muscled arms pulling out bags, trying to get his brain to register what he was seeing. Damn him for being this hungover. His brain couldn't keep pace with what was happening.

She brushed past him, sending a shock up his arm. He

tracked her through the door, still trying to process the redheaded whirlwind before him. She placed the groceries on the island, then spun around and marched back to the truck, her face a picture of fury.

He scowled at her. "You stole my truck."

"Did you think dinner was going to be shat out by magic unicorns?" She reached back into the truck bed for more groceries.

That spurred his legs into action and he crossed the distance to her.

"Here." She handed him a bag. "Make yourself useful."

"I am useful."

"Not when you're standing there gawping like a cow." She handed him several more bags, then grabbed more for herself. "Hop to it, cowboy. I can't afford to have this food spoil. Not for the retail prices I had to shell out."

She whipped around and hurried back into the kitchen. By the time he got to the island, she was halfway back out the door.

She called over her shoulder. "Put those on the island. There's another load to bring in."

"No need to be such a bossy mouth," he muttered under his breath. God, he hated the way she irritated him. Like an itchy rash he wanted to keep scratching.

"I told you before, I didn't get successful by letting other people call the shots."

Apparently her hearing was sharp as a tack, too.

She rushed back in. "Go get the last bags."

"Yes, Sir."

"That's *yes, Chef.*"

She was already bustling around the kitchen putting food into cupboards when he came back in with the final bags. He stood there, at a loss for what he should do next. "Should I be helping?"

Her head whipped around, copper curls flying. He was overcome with the urge to close the distance between them and wrap one corkscrew strand around his finger. But he was fairly certain in her current state that would earn him a slap. No thanks. He'd already experienced her wrath. Her glare kept his feet firmly glued to the floor.

"No. The help you could have provided *but didn't*, was to have this kitchen properly set up."

He crossed his arms over his chest. "What do you mean? You've got everything you need to cook."

She rolled her eyes. "And just what kind of leprechaun magic do you think I can concoct with half a container of baloney and a few cups of Cocoa Puffs? Even Jesus had more to work with than that."

"You have a phone. Pizza?"

"I'm a chef, not a delivery girl."

"Never trust a scrawny chef," he shot back. Come to think of it, she looked downright gaunt. Like she'd been sick or something.

She rolled her eyes. "Oh puh-leeze. I've heard that line my whole life. Try something original if you want to poke at me."

"I wasn't poking," he growled.

She snorted, unable to hide a hint of a grin. "Keep telling yourself that." She grabbed more items out of another bag and swiveled to the cabinet. Even though her chef's pants were baggy, the material stretched tight across her ass as she balanced an arm on the counter, reaching for the top shelf.

His balls tightened at the memory of that muscled ass under his palm.

"I'm serious about the kitchen, Brodie," she shot back over her shoulder. "The state of the kitchen when I arrived violated at least a dozen health department regulations."

"Aww come on. It wasn't that bad."

She spun back toward him. "Are you blind? Did you happen to notice the grease and grime on every surface? I *wasted* two and a half hours scrubbing this place from tip to toe. And *then* I wasted even more time in town paying full-price for groceries. This is a commercial kitchen, hotshot. Where are the wholesale vendors? Where are the daily deliveries?"

He shrugged. "Well it's only me and the crew right now."

She glowered at him, leaning over the island. "That's still no way to run a kitchen. You set it up right from the start."

A flush burned in his chest, spreading up his neck. What did she know about any of this? She was a city chef with no clue how things were done out here.

He threw up his hands. "Welcome to the boonies, darlin'. We don't do things like you're used to in the big city."

She slapped her hands on the island. "Well get ready because there are kitchen rules to follow, big city or not, and one of them is *making sure the chef has ingredients.*"

He leaned forward, placing his hands on the island and putting his face inches from hers. Quite possibly a mistake, given the way his pulse ratcheted up.

"Now just a stinkin' minute, lady. You want to talk rules? You stole my truck. Out here that's a firing offense."

She moved her face a fraction closer to his. "Then it's a good thing I don't work for you."

"Wanna bet?"

Her eyes flashed fire. And this close, he noticed gold flecks in her irises.

"I'd *never* work for you. I work for Blake."

He flexed his fingers on the stainless, every cell in his body going taut.

"My lodge. My rules."

"My kitchen. My rules."

She sounded breathless. Hell, was she as turned on as he was?

Only one way to find out.

Quick as a wink, he thrust a hand through her curls, tugging her head across the remaining few inches that separated their faces, bringing his mouth to hers.

Her lips were as soft and sensual as he remembered. Her mouth as hot. He flicked his tongue along her opening, demanding entry. With a soft noise in the back of her mouth that went straight to his cock, she opened, her tongue meeting his, continuing a physical battle where their verbal sparring left off.

He'd be damned if she bested him in this arena. Moving his other hand to her cheek, he caressed down her neck as his tongue slid along hers, tasting and sucking.

Goddamn.

Kissing her was so much hotter in person than in his dreams.

Like fire and lightning rolled into one. And as he deepened the kiss, she clutched his bicep, branding him with her touch. Need swirled in his groin, and if his crew wasn't due back any second, he had half a mind to haul her up on the island and fuck her silly right here.

Before he was ready, she groaned, her lips from his, and leaned back, panting. She stood there, eyes flashing with a mixture of lust and anger, hair swirling around her head like a red demon halo.

"Get. Out. Of. My. Kitchen."

He flashed her a crooked grin, still trying to get his dick under control. "Whatever you say, *Chef.*"

He spun on his heel and headed for the shower.

## Chapter Eight

*A*n hour later, he'd washed off the grime, but hadn't been able to wash off the sensation of their kiss. He could have taken himself in hand in the shower. Hell, he'd desperately wanted to. But not while the object of his desire was less than fifty feet away. He wasn't that desperate. He'd changed into clean jeans and a t-shirt, and the rest of his crew began to wander into the great room, also freshly clean.

It had been grueling work today, removing cedars from the river bottoms. Cedars were water hogs, and they squeezed out native vegetation that created ideal territory for hunting. They'd replanted with wildflower seeds and a dozen types of hardwood saplings. A century ago, the river bottoms had been full of hardwoods, but over time cedars had invaded. At Ben's suggestion, they'd started working to restore the river bottoms to their previous glory.

Jamey flew through the kitchen door holding a tub filled with ice and longnecks. "Enjoy some beers, gents. Dinner will be along shortly." She threw a glance Brodie's way. "I apologize for the delay."

One of his crew, a younger guy named Ernesto, spoke up. "Dang, Brodie. How come you never brought us cold ones after a hard day?"

"'Cause I'm not your mommy, you sissy. Get your own damned beer."

Ernesto grabbed a beer from the tub where Jamey had placed it on the hearth. "Thanks, ma'am."

Jamey laughed. A musical laugh for such a spitfire. He'd expected something harsher, rougher. Not the kind of sensual laugh you enjoyed after a thorough fucking. Hers was the kind of laugh that drove men to their knees.

Well damned if she would do that to him. No Sir-ee. He could ignore the fire blossoming in his balls.

"You can call me Jamey, or Chef." She smiled at Ernesto.

A tongue of jealousy snaked through Brodie's gut.

"You got it, Chef." Ernesto smiled back at her.

Oh no. This would not do. She was off limits to his crew. "No flirting with the help, Cruz," he growled, scowling at the younger man.

Jamey narrowed her eyes at him. "You're gonna have to work harder to insult me, cowboy. I've gotten worse burns from an easy bake oven." Then she smiled reassuringly at Ernesto. "Don't mind grouchy over there."

"Hey. I'm not grouchy."

Big Mike, another crewmember, let out a laugh. "Like hell you aren't, boss. You been actin' like you drank rattlesnake venom for breakfast."

"Maybe he did," Jamey added, "Given the state of the kitchen when I arrived."

Brodie narrowed his eyes at her. "My lodge. My rules."

Her eyes glittered as she smiled back sweetly. "Unless you can taste the difference between taco seasoning and dried camel testicles, you might consider a different approach with *the help*." She winked at the rest of the crew and spun on her heel, disappearing back into the kitchen.

Laughter erupted from his crew. "Looks like you've got a fireball there, boss," called Darwin from behind Big Mike, saluting him with his beer. "Who wants to play a round of cornhole before dinner?"

His crew filed out after a few more good-natured comments at his expense. Brodie stayed in the big leather chair, contemplating his beer. Fireball wasn't the half of it. She… *did things* to him. Made him want to thump his chest when other men were around. And after the kiss they'd shared, he wanted to toss her over his shoulder, take her back to his man cave, and kiss her senseless. How was he going to manage six weeks working next to her without going insane? Or having his balls explode?

Heavenly smells wafted from the kitchen. Aromas that transported him right back to childhood and sitting in the kitchen watching Mrs. Sanchez prepare a meal. He relaxed his head on the back of the chair and shut his eyes, concentrating on every detail…

A hand shook his shoulder. "Wake up boss, time to eat."

His eyes flew open to see Big Mike laughing down at him. "You were catchin' flies there."

Shit. Why the hell hadn't Jamey woken him up? Shaking the fog from his head, he rose to join his crew at the long table. Jamey stood at the head, tapping her foot impatiently.

"Thank you all for your patience. For the sake of time this evening, I went with a taco bar." She gave Brodie a sly smile. "You'll find seasoned ground bison in the hot chafing dish, hard taco shells, and a variety of toppings. The chafing dishes at the end contain pintos and cilantro rice."

"No camel testicles?" piped up Darwin.

She flashed him a grin. "Maybe. Maybe not."

Damn. She had more balls then most men he knew. Respect for her shot through him.

She gestured to the center of the table. "There's also a large chef salad, which you can dress yourself."

The men enthusiastically offered their thanks. How in the hell had she managed to charm all his men when she hadn't said more than three words to them?

She continued. "You can bring your dishes to the kitchen when you're finished." After shooting a glare at him, she marched back to the kitchen.

Before he could stop himself, he opened his mouth. "Aren't you going to eat with us?"

She paused at the door. "*The help* doesn't dine with the guests."

Damn.

He deserved that.

He glanced around the table at his crew. They were all looking expectantly at him.

"What are you waiting for? Eat." He glared at them and kicked back from the table grabbing his plate.

Quietly, they followed, piling food on their plates and sitting back down one by one. The silence grew heavy. Gone was the banter from previous evenings. The laughter, the insults.

Now they shifted uncomfortably, stuffing food in their mouths.

Damned good food, too.

Downright heavenly. Better than what she'd prepared for Blake and Maddie's wedding. The bison was savory and spicy. The toppings, fresh. He grudgingly admitted, to himself at least, this was supremely better than pizza and cold cereal.

His crew cast furtive glances to each other, but no one was looking at him.

Finally, he slammed down his fork. "What? What's the problem?"

"Well I'll say it, boss. Someone has to," Big Mike spoke up, looking him square in the eye. "This is the first square meal we've had, and we've been here near a month. You been barkin' orders like a drill sergeant today. We've worked our asses off for you without complaint, and I for one don't like how you're treatin' the lady."

There were a few mumbled agreements and nods. Hell and damnation. Now he had a full-fledged mutiny on his hands. He stared at his men in the tense silence, embarrassment prickling at the base of his neck.

Shit. Blake and Ben always hired the crew. He only came along for the ride. Or went off to work by himself. There was so much more to handling a crew than he'd realized. If word got out that he was a bad boss, he'd never be able to hire another crew for anything. If he failed to handle this the right way, he might as well pack his bags and leave on the midnight train.

He scrubbed his face. "Aw hell, guys." He blew out a breath. "I rode you too hard today, and that wasn't right." He looked at each of them again, making sure he held each of their gazes. "I'll make it right. With you. With Jamey." He nodded toward the kitchen. "Stick with me, and I'll make it worth your while. Bonuses if we wrap up early."

He had no idea if he even had the money for that, but what else could he say? If they walked out tonight, his goose was cooked.

They all looked at each other, then back to Big Mike. So he was their de-facto leader. How had he not seen that before? Mike nodded a fraction, and the rest followed suit.

The breath that he'd been holding whooshed out, relief flooding him.

"'Nesto, did I see you dancin' with some new lady at the Trading Post the other night?" Big Mike took over the conversation, and just like that, the table was alive with chatter again.

Brodie kept his head down and shoveled in a mouthful of salad. Maybe he could find Ben tomorrow and have a conversation. Ben always had the answer to everything. Maybe he just needed to stay the hell away from Jamey.

The conversation died down, and one by one the men took their plates to the kitchen and said their goodnights. Soon, he was alone at the table sitting in the fading light. He could hear Jamey cleaning in the kitchen.

Had she even eaten?

She was entirely too skinny.

Pushing back from the table, he grabbed a plate from under the sideboard, and filled it with two tacos and a salad. Taking his dirty plate, and the filled one, he hesitated in the doorway, watching her for a moment.

Her back was to him and she was humming something quietly as she scrubbed one of the pans. The dishwasher beeped, and with the grace of a dancer, she flowed from the sink to the washer, unclipping the door with flare and yanking the steaming dishes out.

Enchanting.

He leaned on the entryway and couldn't help but smile as he watched. He wasn't sure how long he stood trans-fixed, but on one pass, she caught sight of him and stopped short. The air changed from relaxed to charged in an instant.

"Don't stop on my account," he drawled lazily. He offered up the tacos. "Here. Best damn camel testicles I've ever had."

"Not hungry."

"You gotta eat, Jamey. You look like you could blow over in a stiff breeze."

Her eyes flared. "Since when are you concerned about my well-being?"

He pushed off the doorframe, bringing both plates to the island. "Since I'm pretty well screwed if my chef drops over."

He could have sworn he saw a flash of disappointment in her eyes. Whatever it was, though, disappeared to be replaced by cool assessment.

He cleared his throat, suddenly nervous. "I... ah... I'm sorry about earlier. I was out of line."

She nodded her acknowledgement.

Aww shit. He hated this. He should just talk to her instead of hovering like a star-struck teenager. "Jamey..."

She looked down, digging into her pocket, and thrusting a set of papers at him. "Here. These are lists of vendors and suppliers I need you to set up accounts with ASAP. You can't afford retail. And I need the name of a local egg supplier."

Disappointment deflated him a notch. He reached out and took the papers. "Jamey, I—"

"Stop gawping. Either pitch in or get out of my kitchen. I still have work to do."

"Will you let me speak?"

She opened her mouth, then snapped it shut, crossing her arms and raising her eyebrows at him.

God, this woman would drive him to insanity's edge. A slow smile lifted his mouth as he focused on her sensual mouth. She sucked in the corners when her brain was going a mile a minute, forcing her bottom lip to jut out the tiniest bit. Her mouth invited kissing.

Taking her in, all prickly and ready for a fight, set a

slow fire burning in his groin. He'd be dreaming about her again tonight, for sure.

"Spit it out, cowboy. I don't have all night."

"I just wanted to say, I don't regret kissing you. Either time."

He spun and left the kitchen. But not before he glimpsed her mouth drop open in surprise.

## Chapter Nine

The bleeping of the alarm at four a.m. pulled Jamey out of a restless sleep. Groaning, she rolled over and slapped it silent. "You can do this, girl."

She lay with her eyes shut another delicious moment, then shook herself and sat up, throwing the covers off the bed. Within seconds, she was dressed in her usual chef's attire and stumbling down the darkened hall through the great room and into the kitchen. She threw on the lights, taking a moment to adjust to the sudden brilliance, and moved to turn on the coffee pot. Grabbing her favorite knife and a bowl, she set them on the island, and started pulling ingredients from the cabinet for fresh granola.

Although it had been years since she'd interned as a pastry chef, and been up before the birds, she'd always enjoyed the stillness of early morning. In Paris, it had been the only time of day when the city exhaled. She found herself slipping into an old familiar rhythm of movement and thought.

As her hands moved, stirring and chopping, she dissected the events of the last twenty-four hours.

*I don't regret kissing you.*

That had been a shocker. She didn't know what to think. Brodie irritated the shit out her. Worse than any of her brothers. At the same time, when she was near him, her body went on high alert and the air charged with undeniable sexual tension. And he'd brought her a plate of food. His small gesture touched her deeply. In all the years she'd partnered with Jean Luc, even before they'd become lovers, he'd never once made sure she'd eaten. Not once. She shook her head, tossing off the sting of regret. She was a new woman now. She'd made changes.

The Jamey before Jean Luc would have stripped Brodie out of his ass-hugging denims and tasted that heavenly body without a second thought.

The Jamey after Jean Luc?

Not so much.

Jarrod had warned her repeatedly to keep business separate from love, and to date outside her profession. But had she listened? Of course not. Not only was it impossible to have a love life when you practically lived at a restaurant, but did she ever listen to anything her brothers said? Hell no. If she had, she'd still be in Boston living with her parents and slinging slop at the family pub. Not that she ever slung slop. She was an artist. Even when it came to pub food.

But that didn't matter right now. Her lack of sound judgment in men had made her beyond broke and struggling to start over. No matter how easy Brodie might be on the eyes, no matter how much their banter made her salivate, he was strictly off limits.

The beep announcing the oven pulled her out of her moping. Grabbing the sheet pan filled with granola, she placed it in the oven and set the timer, leaning her hip on the counter.

Radio.

She needed a radio in the kitchen.

That would help keep her mind off her problems and Brodie's hot-as-sin ass. Adding that to her mental supply list, she set back to her prep work, humming as she sliced fruit. At least singing all the tunes she'd learned around the pub kept her mind from wandering into dangerous territory.

Time flew as she bustled back and forth to the dining table, filling the sideboard with yogurt, fruit, fresh granola, juice, and coffee. She set a chafing dish filled with toast in the center of the table. It scared her to no end keeping sliced glutenbomb bread in the kitchen. But by meticulously cleaning her utensils, and by using an entire stick of melted butter, along with a parchment-lined sheet pan, she felt confident she wouldn't hurt herself.

She'd ditch the dangerous bread in a heartbeat if she could find a tasty replacement, but the gluten-free bread she'd tasted so far was… like cardboard building material. As soon as Brodie set up her vendor accounts, she could start doing breakfasts worthy of her training.

"Mornin'."

She glanced up to find Brodie leaning in the doorway, much like he had last night. His hair was sleep-mussed, and there was a hint of a shadow along his jaw. Just the kind of roughness she'd love to feel scraping along her flesh. Her body zinged to life at the thought. No doubt about it, one taste of him was definitely not enough to satisfy her.

She dipped her head, focusing on scrubbing an imaginary spot on the island. "Everything you need is out on the sideboard. Bring your dishes in when you're done. I'll have a couple of coolers ready for you to take when you head out."

"What if what I need is in here?"

She eyed him sharply. The lazy smile on his face gave every indication what he meant.

Ignoring the delicious tingles running straight to her pussy, she pointed to the dining area. "Out. I'm trying to run a kitchen in here."

Laughing, he pushed off the door and disappeared... only to reappear a few seconds later, frowning. "That's sissy food out there. Where's real breakfast?"

Oooh.

The nerve.

In a flash, she stalked around the counter, hands on her hips. "Sissy food. That's what you call a gourmet breakfast made with real ingredients? Sissy food?"

His eyes flashed and narrowed. "Yeah. I do. My men need food that will stick to their ribs, not fancy, pretty stuff that makes you feel good about yourself."

"You think that's why I'm doing this? For an ego trip? You have a lot of nerve, buddy."

"You have a lot of nerve serving this frou-frou to my crew."

"It's a helluva lot better than Cocoa Puffs."

He leaned in closer. Close enough, she could glimpse the different colors of blue that made up his eyes.

"Where's the real food, *Chef*? Where are the bacon, eggs and biscuits?"

"Where are my chickens? Fresh eggs and bacon don't just magically appear out of thin air. Do you think for a second I will *ever* serve factory eggs and meat? This is supposed to be a high-end lodge. If you want slop, go to Dottie's. I will not serve crap." She spun on her heel, striding around the counter to make more coffee.

"You calling Dottie's food *slop*?" His voice held barely restrained laughter. "I doubt she'd take kindly to that."

Spinning back, she glared at him. "Unless you're here to offer help, or something constructive – Get. Out. Of. My. Kitchen."

He opened his mouth like he was going to say something more, but then shut it, and leaving her with a look that was part triumph, part laughter, returned to the dining room.

She slammed her hand on the counter, focusing on the sting to bring her temper back into check. She wasn't an idiot. She'd grown up with five bottomless pits for brothers. She *knew* what big men needed to eat. But she'd be damned if she made excuses to Brodie. This was her kitchen, her call. Frou-frou, her ass. He wouldn't know frou-frou if it hit him upside the head.

She pulled three loaves of bread from the cupboard, and launched herself into gathering sandwich fixings. For the next half-hour while the men ate, she worked furiously, pulling together roast beef and horseradish, turkey tomato and pesto, and ham with spicy jack cheese sandwiches. She piled together bags of chips, oranges, and today only, store-bought cookies. She'd make some this afternoon for tomorrow, provided Millie Prescott at the organic grocery had any eggs today. Yesterday she'd been sold out.

By the time the men started bringing in their plates, she'd stacked two coolers by the back door with enough food and drink to last them until dinner.

Brodie was last in. "Jamey…"

She held up her hand, shooting him a glare. "You've got plenty of food to last the day. Dinner will be at six, and if you want manly food for breakfast, get those accounts set up."

He stood across the island with his arms crossed over his chest, assessing her through hooded eyes. His biceps stretched the cotton of his shirt, bringing the outline of his

71

hard muscles into bold relief. She forced her eyes away before he caught her drooling.

"It doesn't have to be this way."

Her eyes shot back to his face. "What's that supposed to mean?"

"You. Me. We could try being a team."

"You don't know the first thing about running a kitchen."

He sighed, nodding. "You're right, I don't." He opened his mouth to say something else, then snapped it shut, shaking his head. "Never mind." He grabbed the coolers and left without a backward glance.

She'd won that round, but the victory somehow felt hollow.

She couldn't team up with him, could she? How could she team up with someone who didn't respect her skills as a chef? As an artist? She'd tolerated that more times than she'd cared to, over the years. She certainly wasn't going to accept it in a kitchen where she was supposed to be calling the shots.

In the meantime, though, she had more important things to worry about. Like how in the name of all that was holy was she going to figure out how to make a decent gluten-free biscuit?

Three hours and six disasters later, she was no closer to answering the question. Hot tears of frustration pricked her eyes as she tossed yet another rock hard batch of drywall into the trash.

It rankled her to the core.

Not just the failure, but the reality that she could no longer work with flour. Make magic with it. She'd just have to keep at it. Learn how to make magic a different way. And the food waste pissed her off. An operation like this should have a few hogs. Although she wasn't sure that what she'd just tossed was suitable even for hogs. But some of the finest green restaurants in California had achieved zero food waste through composting and raising their own meat. There was no reason with all the space on the ranch that the Sinclaires couldn't be doing the same. The practice would make them a destination spot for foodies and locavores from all over.

As Jamey wiped down the counters, she added hogs to her list of items to bring up with Brodie. But in the short term, she'd have to solve her biscuit problem. If the men wanted biscuits, then by God, she'd give them the best damn biscuits they'd ever had. And until she figured out what she was doing, that meant going to Dottie.

She hated to admit it, but the woman made biscuits that rivaled her own. Flipping off the lights, she stepped out the back door to where she'd parked Brodie's truck the previous afternoon.

## Chapter Ten

*F*ifteen minutes later, she pulled into the gravel parking lot next to Dottie's Diner. Jamey understood the appeal. In many ways, the diner functioned like her family's neighborhood pub back in Boston. Folks came in to share the news, have a bite, and get a lift to their day. The diner was no different.

Steeling herself for the triumphant look in Dottie's eyes when the Cordon Bleu chef humbled herself to beg for biscuit batter, she pushed open the door. Fortunately, she'd timed her visit perfectly and the diner was quiet, with only a few men at the counter.

"Jamey?" The man in the cop's uniform slid off the stool, approaching her.

She immediately smiled in recognition. She'd spoken with him at Maddie's wedding. A tall man, about Brodie's size but leaner, and with light brown hair and light hazel eyes.

"It's Travis, right?"

He nodded, taking her offered hand and eyeing her quizzically. "What are you doing in town?"

"Always the officer, I see."

He flashed her a grin. "I'm in the business of paying attention. You here for a visit?"

"More or less. I'm here for about six weeks, helping Blake and Maddie get their hunting lodge off the ground."

His eyes lit up at the confession. "Great. That's great. Maybe I'll see you around then?"

"Of course. Take it easy, Travis."

She gave him a smile and scanned the diner for Dottie. She must be in the office. Wiping her suddenly sweaty hands on her chef's pants, she marched back to the door marked 'Office'. Nothing about this conversation would be easy or pleasant. Knocking on the door, she turned the handle and leaned her head in. "Dottie?"

The older woman wheeled around, not disguising the look of surprise followed by suspicion that settled on her features. "Jamey O'Neill. I assume this isn't a social call?"

Yep.

Not going to be easy at all. She plastered a bright smile on her face. "How's it going, Dottie?"

"Just dandy. To what do I owe the honor of a visit from the great French chef? Come to critique my pie?"

"Now Dottie, you know I think your pie crust is great."

The older woman flattened her lips and let out a little huff as she swiveled back to her desk, effectively dismissing her.

Gritting her teeth at what she knew she needed to say next, Jamey slipped into the office and shut the door behind her. "I… ah… was hoping you could help me with a problem I have."

Dottie swiveled around in her chair. "You think *I* can help you with a problem?" She threw her hands up in the air. "Land sakes, the sky is about to fall."

Jamey bit back the retort on the edge of her tongue. If

Dottie turned her down, she was screwed. Gulping and smiling, she continued. "I don't know if you know this, but I've agreed to come down for six weeks to help Blake and Maddie get the hunting lodge running."

Dottie narrowed her eyes at her. "I thought that was Brodie's set-up."

She nodded. "Well, it is… but it's been a bit rocky."

Dottie's featured softened a bit. "Don't I know it? That boy is headed for a whole lotta trouble if he doesn't get on the straight and narrow." She shook her head, tutting. "But I tell you, underneath his bluster is a heart of gold. He's had a tough time of it." She looked up sharply. "And he's by far the best looking of the bunch."

"Riiiiight." She'd just ignore that last comment. "So, I'm here to help get things running. But I think Brodie and I could use your help." She wasn't above playing on Dottie's love of the Sinclaire men to get what she needed today.

Fighting the gall at what she was about to do, she plunged ahead. "The oven at the lodge is brand new and hasn't been calibrated. I got it on a waiting list, but it's going to take a few weeks. The men love your biscuits, and with the oven being wildly inconsistent, I don't want to risk ruining their breakfast. If you're willing, I'd like to arrange to purchase four dozen biscuits from you every day we have guests, until I can get the oven business sorted out."

There.

She'd done it.

She hadn't told a bald-faced lie like that since she was thirteen.

Dottie's eyes lit up with glee, then immediately narrowed. "Are you going to try and pass my biscuits off as yours?"

*Hell yes.*

She let her eyes go wide and shook her head, putting her hand over her heart. "Heavens no, Dottie. Chef's honor." Maybe she was laying it on a bit thick, but she needed those damned biscuits.

Saints forgive her for what she was about to say next. She lowered her voice conspiratorially. "But that's not all. You know how things can get between Blake and Brodie?"

Dottie nodded sympathetically, all ears at the hint of juicy gossip.

"Well, Blake told Brodie he had to figure all this out on his own. And he's determined to do it. But if word got around you were supplying Brodie with biscuits… well… it might be a point of… conflict between them. And for Maddie and the baby's sake…" Silently apologizing to Maddie, she let her voice drift off, letting Dottie's imagination to fill in the blanks.

Dottie sat tut-tutting, a frown pulling at her mouth. "I would do just about anything for that child. But I just don't underst–"

"It's only for a few weeks, Dottie, and it would be a help to everyone."

Dottie shook her head, a full-blown frown now present. "I don't know… I smell somethin' rotten. I didn't raise four girls only to have the wool pulled over my eyes by a skinny hoity-toity chef from up north."

Desperation churned through her gut. "Dottie… please. You're right. There's more to the story… but I'm not at liberty to say. Please? Help me?"

It gutted her to beg this way. Especially to Dottie.

The silence spun out between them and her breath caught anxiously in her throat as Dottie stared her down.

After what seemed an endless wait, Dottie blew out a breath. "Fine." She speared her with a blistering glare. "I don't know what you're playing at young lady, but the truth always comes out. In the meantime, you'll have your biscuits."

Relief whooshed out of her. "Thank you, Dottie. This means a lot to me. I really appre—"

Dottie threw up her hand. "Don't need your gushin'. Let's talk brass tacks. Twenty dollars a dozen."

Leave it to Dottie to stick it to her. "That's highway robbery and you know it. Why should I pay more than what everyone else pays? Twelve."

Dottie raised her eyebrows. "That's not all you're payin' for sweetie pie, and you know it. Fifteen."

Damn.

"Twelve-fifty."

"Fourteen and that's my final offer."

Dottie had her over a barrel. "You drive a hard bargain. Fourteen then." She stuck out her hand to shake. The triumphant smile on Dottie's face was as distasteful as the one she'd imagined on the drive over.

A half-hour later, she pulled up to the back door of the lodge, hoping that Brodie was back. The lodge didn't have an outdoor grill or smoker, and with the plans she'd conceived while wrapping up her errands, they'd need to be purchased right away. With the right certifications, they could start selling smoked meats online. She also wanted to check the calendar for the next full weekend. If she could smoke the meats in time, she could try them out on the next guests. Passing through the kitchen, she paused outside the office door.

"Brodie?" She rapped twice and the door swung open to reveal a small office in total chaos.

Papers were strewn everywhere, and a laptop balanced precariously on what looked to be a pile of bills.

"What on earth?" She stepped in to catch the handle

and process what she was seeing. She'd seen messy offices before, but this… it–

"What in the hell are you doing in my office?"

She whipped around.

Brodie stood blocking the doorway, eyes on fire.

## Chapter Eleven

"I'll ask again," Brodie grated, working to keep his temper in hand. "What in the hell are you doing in my office?" First she invaded his kitchen, now his office? What was she going to do next to drive him crazy?

Her eyes widened in startled surprise. "I came to talk to you about some equipment to purchase, and to see our events calendar."

His heartbeat grew loud in his ears. "Events calendar?"

"Yes. So I can see what's going on?"

"There's nothing to see. I tell you what's going on."

Her eyebrows rose at his raised voice, then indignation flickered across her face as she rolled her shoulders back. Damn, the way her face wrinkled when she was pissed. He fisted his hand at his side to keep from rubbing the creases between her eyes.

"I need to see when guests are coming... how many, and who they are... so I can tailor my menus. We have to look ahead. You can't just spring things on me and expect me to make magic." She lifted a stack of paperwork. "I can help you get this all organized. It won't take much. You need a calendar on the wall, a receipts file, delivery file, inventory, payroll on your laptop, banking…" her voice trailed off.

God he hated lists.

Drove him nuts when people gave him a list. "I'm not an idiot."

"I didn't say you were. But this kind of chaos can mean things fall through the cracks and important bills don't get paid… or clients get double booked." A look of determination shone in her eyes. "Trust me. I've made mistakes before. Serious mistakes. You don't want to run a business this way."

The telltale flush of humiliation began to prickle at the base of his neck, spreading forward and further agitating him. He didn't need chastising. Especially from her. He'd endured enough of that everywhere else in his life.

"I can run a business just fine," he barked. "What I don't need is your bossy mouth telling me how to do it."

Her head snapped back as if he'd slapped her. Pressing her lips together, she stepped forward into his space, poking him in the chest.

Jesus.

She smelled like cookies.

"Let me tell you something about my bossy mouth, bucko."

*That it's perfect for kissing?*

She narrowed her eyes at him. "I've run a multi-million dollar restaurant. Until recently, I was one of the top chefs in Chicago. I've had successes *and* failures. And an office like this is a red flag." Her eyes softened. "Keep your bedroom chaotic, not the office. Mine is." She gave him a wry smile. "Bad things will happen if we don't stay on top of things. I can help—"

Something in him snapped. "I'm *not* going to fail." His voice rose a notch.

"Yeah?" She stood glaring at him, eyes full of challenge. "Then show me. Because so far all you seem to be good for is posturing."

"I'm good for a helluva lot more than that, lady," he growled.

The air charged between them. She felt it, too. He could see it in the way her breathing subtly shifted, and the way her tongue darted out to wet her lips.

He didn't care how mad she made him, what he wanted more than anything was to fist his hands through her curls and find out if her mouth tasted like cookies, too.

His belly tightened at the thought of tasting her again. He leaned forward, unable to help himself. Recognition dawned in her eyes and she stepped back, putting what little space there was in the office between them.

"Then if you are, you need to get this office under control or ask for help." She waved at the laptop. "We just need to enter the bills, put a calendar someplace, and..."

There she went with another list.

How in the hell was he supposed to remember everything she was saying?

"*Are you even listening to me?*" She poked him again. Harder this time, eyes flashing fire. In that moment, he believed she could call down lightning if she wanted.

"Oww. Yes." *No.*

"Then, *please*, address this," she swept her hand over the sea of papers. "Or you'll sink both of us." She narrowed her eyes, piercing him. "And I don't want to sink. Now let me pass. I've got dinner to prep." She pushed past him, and her footsteps faded.

His stomach twisted as he surveyed the chaos. He'd never admit it to her, but she was right. Blake and Ben had sat with him, and tried to help him set up a system, but he couldn't keep the piles straight. No matter how hard he tried. It irked the hell out of him that he was in this position. But he was in no mood to fix it right now. Right now he needed to check in with the crew and sweat off his anger. If it looked like they could finish clearing tomorrow, he'd spend the evening dealing with the office and prove to Jamey and everyone else that he was fit to run the lodge.

He spent most of dinner head down, hardly tasting the food. Jamey made chili using the leftover meat from the previous night and brought steaming plates of buttery, cheesy cornbread to the table. The men devoured it as if it was their last meal.

He'd avoided meeting Jamey's eyes as she moved in and out of the dining room, drowning in a sea of memories. His father's hand beating him at age nine, calling him an idiot for mixing up the bags of alfalfa and oats. An angry teacher's sneer in high school, calling him stupid.

Did Jamey think he was stupid?

His heart twisted at the thought.

He wasn't stupid.

He knew it.

He just didn't do books. And why should he? He was a rancher, not a librarian. The kind of stuff he was good at didn't count at school. He could tell which way a steer was going to turn, and have the rope ready to catch him. He could fix anything on the ranch, and better than anyone else. He could see structures in his mind, and build them with no plans. So what if the letters sometimes floated off the page? He could still take care of things. Hell, maybe his father had clocked him one too many times in the head as a kid.

"Boss?"

Big Mike stood at the end of the table, eyeing him

intently. The others had already cleared their places, and disappeared.

"We're turning in. You need anything?"

*Besides another hit on the head?*

He shook his head. "Nope. I'm good. See you early."

Pushing back from the table, he made a bowl of chili for Jamey, stacked his dishes and brought everything to the kitchen. Again, he hesitated at the door, watching her. She'd taken off her chef's coat, and was furiously scrubbing pots in a tank top, her curls sticking out every which way from underneath her bandana. Her muscles rippled as she lifted and scrubbed.

He frowned at the way her elbow bones stuck out when she bent her arms. She could use a little more meat on her bones. But not too much. He admired the strength in her body. It… intrigued him. Made him want to run his hands all over it the way he'd run his hands over a horse's withers, just to feel the muscles bunch underneath his palm. Seeing her in her element fueled a slow burn deep inside. The kind of burn that wouldn't be satisfied with just a roll in the hay.

He wanted her to see him like that.

In his element.

Shaking himself before he did something stupid like ask her on a date, he quietly placed his dishes and her chili on the island and went to the office, shutting the door behind him. Leaning back against the door, he surveyed the mess. Where to even begin?

Calendar.

There was a calendar in here somewhere. He started shuffling papers, moving most of them to the chair. He grimaced when he found the calendar at the bottom of a pile of envelopes. A topless beauty stared back at him. Jamey would have a few tart words to say about that. He tossed it in the trashcan, making a note to grab something with horses and flowers the next time he was at the five and dime.

He grabbed the stack of mail lying unopened. Flipping through it quickly, he kept anything that looked like a bill and trashed the rest. See? He could do this business stuff just fine.

*Who you foolin', man?*
*You're an idiot.*

Shaking his head and blowing out a breath, he opened the laptop and turned it on, opening a few envelopes while he waited for it to boot up. He clicked on the bookkeeping icon, and drummed his fingers impatiently on the desk while the file opened. The spreadsheet opened before him, a bunch of boxes and columns.

Squinting, he hunted on the keyboard for the button to make the text bigger. He ground his teeth in frustration. God, he hated computers. As far as he was concerned, the only thing they were good for was as a doorstopper.

Giving up, he refocused on the boxes and columns. After several minutes in which anxiety built and roiled in his belly, he slammed the laptop shut and pushed it across the desk.

Fine.

He didn't do computers.

But he could do it the old fashioned way.

He stared at the envelope in front of him, willing his eyes to focus. Grabbing it and ripping it open he pulled out an invoice. He placed it on his left, and grabbed the next envelope in the stack.

Letter. On the right.

Fighting the anxiety that had morphed into dread, he grabbed the next envelope and ripped it open.

What in the hell was this? He had no fucking clue.

He crumpled the paper and beat it against his forehead, squeezing shut his eyes, and momentarily giving into the waves of panic assaulting him. Tossing the paper against the wall, he picked up another set of envelopes, skimming through them. What was this shit?

It was all too much. He threw the envelopes and swept the papers off the desk, letting out a grunt of despair. Flinging open the door so hard it bounced against the wall, he stalked down the hall to his bed.

He was a fucking failure.

And the whole world would know it in less than six weeks.

## Chapter Twelve

*T*he men finished clearing the cedar a day early. Brodie waited until they'd all finished breakfast before handing them their final checks, including the bonus he'd promised them for wrapping up early.

Paying them, especially the bonus, felt… good. Really good. Like he'd accomplished something significant. He was good at running things. He knew it. He just needed to figure out the office. Maybe now that the men would be out of his hair he could figure it out.

Johnny Benoit and his twin brother, Jimmy, were the last to leave. "So you ropin' at the fair?" Johnny asked as he took the envelope Brodie handed him.

The county fair was ten days away, and while he and Ben hadn't practiced much this summer, the two of them worked intuitively, and had won team roping three years running. He wasn't about to give up his title this year. Not if there was a chance Jamey would be there to watch him.

He flashed a cocky grin. "Hell, yeah. Prepare to get your ass whupped again this year."

"Case of beer says Jimmy and I take you two down."

"Make it two and you're on. Winner picks the beer."

"Fair enough." Johnny stuck out his hand. "You ever need us again, you know where to find us."

Turning, Brodie paused in the office only long enough to grab the four-pack of Guinness he'd picked up yesterday at the liquor store.

At the kitchen door, he stopped to admire Jamey from behind. She'd stripped out of her chef's coat again, and was busy running dishes through the washer, singing along with the new radio to ACDC. It fascinated him, watching her move through the kitchen. Like every movement was made for maximum efficiency.

"Did you dance as a little kid?"

She spiraled around, surprise in her eyes.

Shit.

Why in the hell had he gone and blurted that out?

She laughed, shaking her head. God, his teeth could rot from the sweetness of her laugh. His belly warmed at the sound. She'd laughed for him. Not at him, or at someone else's joke, but for him.

"Ah. No. In fact, I ended up in the kitchen because I was too awkward for dance class."

"There's nothing awkward about you."

Her eyes narrowed suspiciously.

"In the kitchen," he backpedaled. "I mean there's nothing awkward about you in the kitchen. You move like you own it."

She cocked her head at him, smiling slowly. "I do."

Oh God. He was digging the hole of a verbal idiot. He lifted up the box of Guinness and stepped toward the island.

"Uh. Here." He didn't know what to say next. "Thanks for your help... And... I'm sorry I was a jerk the other day." The last bit came out in a rush.

Jamey's eyes widened, and her mouth quirked. "I've been thinking…"

*That you'd like to go to bed with me?* Desire settled in his balls as his eyes raked over her.

Shit.

She wasn't wearing a bra.

He could see her nipples protruding through the fabric of her tank top. Damn if that wasn't the hottest thing he'd seen. Ever. He wanted to throw her on the island and devour her head to toe.

She looked at him quizzically. Had he given something away?

"You okay, Brodie?" Her voice came out a little breathless, and she licked her lips.

He swallowed hard. "Uh. Yeah."

"So I was thinking… I could take over some of the office duties. You'd still have to pay the bills, but I'll go ahead and set up all the vendor accounts. And help you balance your sheets. That should take some pressure off you. You'll still have to schedule and handle guests, and all I ask is at least three days notice so I can prep properly."

"Uh. Yeah. That sounds great." He made himself look her in the eye. He really wanted to stare at her tits. Touch them. Work them into hard pebbles and cover them with his tongue. But he didn't want to get slapped… She would undoubtedly slap him. Maybe that's what he needed to get his dick under control.

Or not.

Tendrils of lust snaked through his belly.

She waved her hand in front of his face, snapping her fingers. "Brodie. What's going on?"

"I… nothing. Nothing's going on."

"This is serious and you look like you're on another planet."

He shuddered out a deep breath, allowing himself to drown in her irate gaze. "I'm here."

"You better be. You're not the only one who can't fail. I have a lot riding on this, too."

"So are you suggesting we start over as a team?"

She crossed her hands over her chest, assessing him coolly. After a moment where he found himself heating under her direct gaze, she answered. "Yeah. I am."

"For the record, didn't I suggest that a few days ago?"

She rolled her lips together, but they pulled up at the corners. Her chin dipped ever so slightly.

He pounced, not bothering to keep the glee out of his voice. "A-*ha*. Admit it. I was right."

She shook her head, still trying to keep the smile from her face, and losing the battle. He placed the Guinness on the island and leaned across, grinning openly. "C'mon, Jamey, let me hear you say it."

A breathy giggle escaped and she tried to glare at him. But there was too much laughter in her eyes. Her cheeks turned the sweetest shade of pink, and she rolled her eyes. "Fine. You're right. We're better off working as a team." She covered her smile with her hand and shook her head again.

He should gloat. He should remind her that he won. But he only wanted to celebrate this tiny victory. He tore into the cardboard packaging and pulled out two cans. "Then we should drink to that."

"At seven in the morning?"

He shrugged. "Why not? Don't you Irish have a reputation for starting early?"

Her brow furrowed. "Don't you cowboys have a reputation for being wildly misinformed?"

"Aww, come on, Jamey. This at least deserves a toast."

The smile she gave looked anguished, and she shook her head. "Sorry. I don't drink Guinness."

He stepped back, deflated.

Damn.

He should have asked. He'd just assumed after all her talk at Blake and Maddie's wedding. Flames prickled at the back of his neck. He'd never come off looking anything like an ass in front of her.

"But, thank you for the thought. It's... ah... just bad for my girlish figure."

He snorted, half laughing at her, half embarrassed at himself.

Her eyes softened. "But we could toast with a little magic of the leprechauns." She moved to the cupboard and grabbed two glasses.

"What the hell is that?"

She grinned at him. "Irish whiskey, silly. Made with magic of the leprechauns."

"Did anyone ever tell you you're full of shit?"

"Magic leprechaun shit, that's me."

He laughed out loud. God, he wanted to kiss her. She was funny when she was relaxed. And fun.

Then he opened his mouth before he could stop himself. "You're beautiful."

She snorted back, half-laughing, as she poured amber liquid into each glass. Pink tinted her cheeks, highlighting some of her freckles. "Riiiiight. You called me scrawny." She gave the glass a push and sent it flying across the island to him.

"You need to eat more. Not watch your weight." It wasn't his business. He knew that. But he couldn't help himself. He worried about how skinny she was. "You look like you're... not well."

Her eyes softened a fraction. "You sure know how to lay on the charm."

He waggled his eyebrows at her. "You ain't seen nothin' yet, darlin'."

Silence fell between them… and grew heavy. He cleared his throat and raised his glass. "To teamwork."

"New beginnings," she added, tossing back her shot. Then she spun back to the dishes in the sink, dismissing him.

But he didn't want to be dismissed. Not yet, at least. He remained at the island, fixating on her arms as they moved the pans from one sink to another. Then to her ass. The baggy chef's pants she lived in pulled tight every time she bent, revealing round, shapely muscle. Muscle he imagined sinking his fingers into. He shifted his weight as the familiar tightness in his balls surged to life. God he'd love to bend her over the counter…

"I'm sure you have work to do?" Her voice jolted him out of his very pleasant fantasy involving the two of them pantsless.

"Ever been to a rodeo?"

She snorted and kept washing dishes.

"County fair's in ten days. Ranch'll have a crew."

She placed the pans in the washer. "We better have a crew of visitors or we'll be out on our asses before you know it."

Damn, she was a tough nut to crack. "Say you'll go, Jamey."

She finally swung around and leaned back on the counter, eyes teasing. "Why? Don't have enough skirts to ogle you while you rodeo?"

He winked at her and grinned. "Never hurts to have one more."

Her sweet mouth flattened grimly. "Let's get one thing

straight, cowboy. I have never been, nor will I ever be, *a skirt.*" She leaned forward, placing her hands on the island.

The way her tank top stretched across her nipples made his throat go dry. "You have to stop doing that," he croaked hoarsely.

"Doing what?"

"Standing there, looking so Goddamned delectable."

Her breath hitched, and the air sparked with electricity. Standing there, with the island between them, not even touching her, his knees nearly buckled from the wave of hot desire that crashed over him. Her eyes darkened as she held his gaze. Her nipples hardened to peaks underneath the cotton, further stretching the fabric.

"I dream of you at night, Jamey. Of fucking you."

Her pupils dilated, and he could see her chest rising and falling with shallow breaths. The fingers splayed across the island clenched.

"I dream of tasting you. Of pushing into you, and hearing you cry my name underneath me. I dream of holding your sweet, tight ass in my hands." The knot of need that remained a constant reminder of her presence, clenched deep inside him. His cock throbbed against his denim. He'd never been so turned on just looking at someone. Just talking.

Her tongue flicked out to wet her bottom lip. He wanted to suck on that lip. Nibble it, devour it in little bites until he she moaned for him.

"You have to stop talking." Her voice sounded breathy and high. Why wouldn't she just give into this electricity that constantly thrummed between them?

"Why? I know you feel it, too." His own voice came out rough with need. He didn't care. At this moment, he was beyond caring.

She seemed to shake herself and the light went flat in her eyes. "We work together. This. Can't. Happen."

Her words acted like ice water.

He clenched his hand, forcing his blood back up to his brain. Away from his cock.

She was right.

He needed to put her out of his mind and focus on not getting his ass kicked off the ranch.

But still... something niggled at him deep inside. This was... different. He'd regret not finding out what was between them.

He nodded his assent. "Fine. You're right." He could have sworn he saw a flash of disappointment in her eyes.

He stepped back, breaking their connection. "I've got errands to run in town. Need anything?" He wasn't sure his voice sounded quite right.

Averting her eyes, she shook her head and returned to her dishes.

Motherfucking shitballs.

## Chapter Thirteen

*J*amey leaned into the oven and pulled out her latest batch of scones. The sound of hammering drifted through the open window. Brodie and his young half-brother, Simon, had been working on a project out back for the better part of the week. It looked like it could be a fancy chicken coop, but they refused to tell her. Even after bribes of her kitchen sink cookies.

She pulled apart one of the steaming scones, trying not to burn her fingers, too impatient to wait until they'd cooled. The last batch, and several before, had been abject failures. She'd tried them out on Brodie, who'd been very polite, but she could see in his eyes that he was swallowing his thoughts along with the dried out, crumbly dough.

She popped a piece in her mouth. The flavor was right, but it was a little on the gummy side. She'd have to check it when it cooled. She set the timer for ten minutes and went about straightening the kitchen.

The last week had been... tense.

She and Brodie had slipped into a pattern of careful

avoidance peppered with accidental skin grazes and stolen glances. Their chemistry was undeniable. She'd paused at the back door on more than one occasion this week, just to admire him sawing and hammering without a shirt. The man had serious muscles, honed from hard labor, not sculpted in a gym like Jean Luc and the rest of the chefs she knew.

And oh my, was there a difference.

Imagining those muscles corded under her soaked her panties through in a heartbeat, and set her internal temperature to broil.

He knew the effect he had on her, too, damn his arrogant ass. The knowing smile he'd thrown her way when he'd caught her staring the day before, had been half conceit, half invitation. Invitation that was becoming harder and harder to deny.

Especially when he was so damned cute with Simon. He wasn't just playful with the boy, he was gentle. More like a parent than an older brother. Brodie treated Simon like an equal, letting him do all but the most challenging work at the lodge. When she'd asked about it, he'd brushed it off. "I was driving a tractor and wrestling steers when I was his age. The sooner he learns, the better he'll be at all of it."

"What if he doesn't want to ranch?"

"They're life skills, Jamey, just like what you do." He'd narrowed his gaze on her. "Not everyone who's smart is good at school. If he's good at school, great. But he'll always have work if he knows how to ranch."

The timer sounded, pulling her back to the present. Grabbing some glasses, and the fresh lemonade she'd made, she took the scones out to where Brodie and Simon were working. She paused in the yard to watch as Brodie threw down a stack of two-by-fours like they were toothpicks. Shooting her a grin, he called out. "Break time, Simon. Chef's got some more experiments."

She crossed over to the two, setting the lemonade pitcher on an upended log. She handed Brodie the dishtowel she'd tucked into the waist of her chef's pants. "Here. You're covered in sweat."

He grabbed the towel, slowly raking his eyes over her. Her skin, already on fire from her thoughts, flushed and prickled. Her nipples tightened as the ache at her clit grew. She should leave now. Head back to the safety of the kitchen and bury herself in work.

She spun away, but his hand snaked out and caught her arm. "Wait."

She met his heated gaze, her breath catching in her throat. His hand scorched her skin like a hot poker. And his sky blue eyes held a light that made her pulse go all thready. Like he was undressing her in his mind.

"Stay a sec. Don't you want to know what we think?" He tilted his chin toward the scones.

Swallowing hard, her throat suddenly dry, she could only nod. Simon had already stuffed half a scone in his mouth.

Brodie reached out and ruffled his hair. "Easy there, kiddo, you don't want to choke."

"Mmmupmhf." The kid nodded vigorously.

She poured out a glass and handed it to Simon. "Here. This will help wash it down."

"Thanks. Better than yesterday." Simon grinned and took the glass, gulping down the contents.

Brodie hadn't stopped staring at her during the whole exchange. Keeping his eyes locked on her, he spoke. "Simon. Can you hike over to the Big House and ask Blake or Ben to bring up the posthole digger?"

"Can I take Captain?"

"No way. If you want to ride, saddle up Sunny. I'll check the cinch before you go."

The boy scampered off to the stable.

Brodie snagged a scone off the plate. Breaking off a chunk, he popped it into his mouth.

Jamey couldn't stop staring at the crumbs sticking to his lip. She must have gasped, because lust flared in his eyes and his tongue flicked out to capture the crumbs. Then he slowly scraped his thumb across his lower lip, catching the remains.

Her stomach dropped to her ankles while an ember flared to life in her ribs. Before she could stop herself, she reached a finger out to his lip. "You missed a spot." Her voice came out breathy.

Electricity arced between them as she ran her finger over the corner of his mouth. Blood buzzed in her ears, and it registered that his body had gone tense. His hand whipped up, capturing hers and keeping it there. He slanted his mouth and captured the digit between his lips, tonguing and sucking on the tip.

Jesus and all the saints.

Flames licked up her arm and straight down to her clit, as her knees started to shake. There were a dozen places she wanted those lips right now. She fixated on his mouth as he licked the tip of her finger again before dropping her hand.

The air between them lay heavy and thick.

"Delicious," he breathed, his own voice rough at the edges.

"They taste okay?" she finally asked when she could find her voice again.

A devilish, all too knowing smile curved his mouth. "I might need another taste."

He was *so* not talking about the scones. Taking a shaky

breath, she offered another bite, breaking off a piece and bringing it to his mouth. She was playing with fire, but the sensations he was causing were too yummy to stop. He made her feel... womanly. Keeping his eyes on hers, he took the bite she offered.

He looked like he was going to say something more, but Simon walked up leading Sunny, and the moment fizzled.

With a regretful look in his eye, he gave his attention to Simon, and checked the cinch. "Looks good, kiddo. You're getting better." He gave Simon a leg up and sent him on his way.

"You're good with him, you know." Jamey tilted her head toward the retreating form of Simon astride Sunny.

Brodie shrugged. "Why wouldn't I be? He's just a kid."

"A lot of people your age wouldn't take the... care you do with him."

Brodie's expression hardened. "It's adults who fuck up kids. Simon's a good kid. Least I can do is make sure I don't fuck him up."

She stood rooted to the ground, thunderstruck. She'd have been less surprised if a meteor dropped out of the sky.

Brodie grimaced. "What. Does that surprise you?" The edge in his voice dared her to admit it.

She wasn't sure how to answer. He was acting like she'd just caught him with his pants down. But... seeing him gentle with Simon like that was... a total turn-on. She shook herself and moved to gather the lemonade. "You're sweet, Brodie," she tossed over her shoulder. "I don't know why you try and convince everyone you're not."

She needed to get out of Brodie's sight before she dropped her pants and jumped on him in the middle of the yard. She was halfway back to the kitchen door, when his voice reached her.

"Jamey, wait."

She stopped, heart pounding like a teenager. What exactly was she hoping for here? A relationship between them was impossible. Imprudent at best. She could hear Jarrod's voice in her ears scolding her about mixing work and love. And yet...

"Help me?"

She shook her head. "I should really..."

He puffed his chest and grinned slyly. "Afraid you might not be able to control yourself, darlin'?

"Cocky bastard." If only he knew how close he was to the truth. Hell. Who was she kidding? He did know and that's why he was challenging her. And she was already moving back his direction. She put down the lemonade and continued toward him, steeling herself. "All right, I'll help. But no funny business."

"Wouldn't dream of it."

"You gonna tell me what you're building?"

He grinned. "Nope. You'll figure it out soon enough." He handed her the pair of work gloves Simon had been using. "These should fit you."

"So I'm not just the beauty bonus? You really want me to help?"

His gaze raked over her again, leaving pricks of attraction pebbling over her skin. "You're definitely the beauty bonus." He gave her a funny smile. "But I do need your help. Take these nails and hold this post." He popped a few extra nails in his mouth, and set to work hammering.

"Why the second layer of fencing?" She'd seen chicken coops before, but not like this one. And she'd bet her bottle of Redbreast that's what they were building.

Brodie chuckled. "Patience, grasshopper."

"Why the secrecy? Why not tell me what it is?"

He shot her a sidelong glance. "What is this, *twenty questions?*"

"You *are* a cocky bastard."

He winked at her, then refocused on the post. The way he teased her warmed her insides. Set her nerve endings alight. The sexual tension between them grew daily. It was a delicious distraction. But one or both of them was bound to get hurt, and then working together would become impossible. There was no way she'd ever do that again.

She offered him a nail.

"Don't need it yet."

"Yes you do. You missed a spot."

His eyes bored into her. "You bossin' me?"

She met his gaze without flinching. "Just pointing out you missed a spot. Don't be so touchy."

"I'm not."

She snorted. "You are."

He moved to the next post. "I need an extra pair of hands, not a foreman."

"Well I'm a forewoman. So there."

His arm swung the hammer, and she took a moment to enjoy the curl of his bicep as he moved.

He grunted out a laugh. "Like what you see?" He didn't miss a thing.

But she didn't either. It was like she had hyperaware-ness radar whenever he was nearby. "Maybe. Maybe not." She handed him another nail. "Don't you need to brace this post before moving on?"

Instead of taking the nail, he put down the hammer and stood, bringing his body toe to toe with hers so that she was nearly eye-to-eye with him. He studied her intently, his blue eyes honing in on her mouth. "You keep tryin' to boss me."

The air sizzled between them. A breeze floated through the yard, ruffling his dark hair and bringing with it the clean tang of his sweat. And musk. God, she could lick him like a popsicle right now. Trace her fingers down over the light scattering of hair to where it disappeared into his denims. She wet her lips at the thought, her breathing coming more shallowly.

Lust flared in his eyes. "I don't need bossing." His voice ran over her skin like sandpaper.

"What do you need then?"

His mouth pulled into a sinfully sexy smile. "You can boss all you want in the kitchen, but out here – this is my territory. I do the bossing."

It wasn't a threat. There was no antagonism in his voice. Only pure confidence and the undercurrent of sexy promise.

"Where else do you boss, Brodie?" she blurted before she could stop herself. "Who bosses in bed?"

His eyebrows rose in surprise. "You don't want me to answer that."

"What if I do?"

Every cell in her body vibrated in anticipation. He tilted his head forward, eyes daring her to stop him. He was going to kiss her and end this crazy weeklong dance of touch and retreat.

This time, she was ready.

The rumble of a truck turning into the drive snapped the invisible cord between them, and Brodie stepped back.

The breath she was holding whooshed out of her body, as heat flushed her face. Embarrassed, she gathered up the lemonade and scones as Blake hopped out of his truck. "Hold up, Jamey," he called. "This concerns you, too."

She glanced over to Brodie, whose face was a mixture of curiosity and worry.

"What's going on?" Brodie's tone was even, but she could see how tightly he held himself.

"You've got guests coming," Blake said, surveying the two of them.

"We do. This weekend." Brodie crossed his arms, shifting his stance.

Blake tipped back his Stetson. "Just giving you a heads up. Mason Carter, his foreman and two ranch hands will also be here this weekend. I need you to put them up here. He's coming to purchase fifty head of bison, but he also wants to see how you're running the lodge."

Brodie scowled. "So he can spy on me for you?"

"No," Blake shook his head exasperatedly. "I told you, this is your gig. I'm not going to babysit you. Mason wants to see the set up so he can do something similar at his spread in Montana."

A little of the tension left Brodie's shoulders and he glanced at Jamie. "No can do, bro. Sorry."

Blake fisted his hands on his hips. "Why the hell not?"

Jamey glanced between the two men. Not good. Not good at all. "Umm. Blake?" She felt awkward interfering, but the way Brodie had looked at her seemed like he was asking for help. "We're already full this weekend. Ben has some college friends coming up for the county fair. We've only got one bed left."

A look of surprise crossed Blake's face, quickly followed by pride. Brodie shot back a look of triumph.

Her mind was already in problem solving mode. She'd been overbooked before at the restaurant. "I'm sure we can come up with a solution." They could manage this. Hell if they pulled it off, they'd look great.

"We could put the foreman in the homestead. It needs a cleaning, but would be fine for sleeping," Brodie offered.

Blake nodded. "I can make sure that's taken care of. What about the other two?"

"Can they stay in one of the bunk houses? We can feed them here." Brodie looked to Jamey for confirmation. She nodded, mentally reformulating her dinner plan.

Brodie stood a little taller. "I won't boot paying customers. Even if they're Ben's friends. *Especially* if they're Ben's friends."

Blake grimaced. "Of course not, but it's less than ideal."

"Well if you were expecting a little Luck 'O the Irish, you waited too long. Last minute surprises like this send us assways downstream with no paddle. You of all people should know better, Blake," Jamey chastised. "I don't have unicorn magic stored in my cookie jar. I have to reformulate my menu planning and pay retail for last minute groceries."

Blake's mouth quirked as Brodie's laughter erupted behind her. "Shoulda known better than to set off her Irish, brother. I can tell you all about it."

Blake threw his head back, laughing. "You're right. I apologize. Mason only called this morning. I'm sorry I've put you in a bind."

"We'll make it work," she and Brodie spoke in unison.

"I sure appreciate it," said Blake, his voice filled with gratitude.

Jamey nodded, toeing the dirt. "Did you bring the post-hole digger Brodie sent Simon for?"

"It's in the back of the truck." Blake moved to grab it, and she risked a glance at Brodie.

He met her gaze head on, a mixture of triumph and admiration in his eyes.

He lowered his voice. "You're... good."

She winked, giving him a saucy smile. "Teamwork."

Admiration was quickly replaced by a stare so hot, her mouth turned to dust. Her ears buzzed. Not from the August locusts, but from the speed at which lust ignited her insides, making her pussy clench with want.

*Bad Jamey. Bad idea.* No… very good as far as her body was concerned.

"Jamey… I—"

"Menu. Gotta go fix the menu." Clutching the lemonade for dear life, she swung around toward the kitchen, mentally revising the weekend's menu as she walked, and failing miserably to banish the idea of rubbing up against the solid mass of cowboy hotness she'd left standing in the yard.

## Chapter Fourteen

*B*rodie sat stewing in the office, tapping his fingers on the desk. How was he going to come up with two more mounts for the weekend? Especially during the county fair, when everyone's horses were in use? Mason's ranch hands could use the extra horses at the Big House, but that still left him needing two more horses and tack for Mason and his foreman.

His only hope was talking to the Hansens to see if they could work something out for the weekend. Not his first choice, but things had softened enough between the Hansens and Sinclaires when Blake and Maddie had married, that asking them for help wasn't so bad.

Ultimately, he'd have to see about purchasing two more horses. That was an expense he hadn't counted on. His eyes slid to the closed laptop. He needed to buckle down and figure out the spreadsheet. Keeping loose track of expenses in his head wasn't working anymore. But every time he opened the damned laptop the numbers seemed to float away and take on a life of their own.

"We have to talk."

He swiveled the chair to see Jamey lounging in the door. She'd taken off her bandana, and her curls stuck out every which way. There was a streak of flour across her arm, and more at her cheek. Like she'd wiped her face with the back of her hand. The urge to pull her into his lap and brush the flour off her and then some had him clutching the chair arms.

"Breaking up with me so soon?"

She rolled her eyes. "I need a second pair of hands in the kitchen this weekend."

Shit. Another unexpected expense.

"Nope. No can do." He spun back to the desk and opened a drawer looking for a pencil.

"What do you mean 'No can do'? I need a second pair of hands."

"You were fine with eight of us, what's a few more?"

She let out an exasperated sigh. "There's a big difference between eight ranch hands and paying guests. Especially when one of them is a billionaire with a discerning palate."

"Then don't go high falutin'."

"You think my food's too snobby?"

"I think it's a waste of money to hire help."

"It's an investment. Besides, at some point I'm going to need a day off."

"Why? Ranchers never take a day off."

She fisted her hands at her hips. "Maybe you would be a bit more pleasant if you took a day off every now and then."

"What do you mean?" he said, glancing up and grinning. "I'm Prince fucking Charming."

She rolled her eyes, stifling a laugh. "Is that what you think?"

He waggled his eyebrows at her. "That's what I know."

"Don't think you can distract me, Captain McCharmypants." She narrowed her eyes. "Where are we at financially? Is that what this is about?"

He spun the chair back around. "That's my business."

"It becomes mine when I can't do my job."

"Then do your job better," he growled. Why in the hell did she have to be so pushy?

"Brodie. I need a second pair of hands this weekend. It's just temporary."

"I don't care if it's for thirty seconds. Answer's still no."

Her eyes sparked. "Why the hell not?"

"'Cause I said so."

"That's a bullshit answer and you know it." She narrowed her eyes at him. "You don't know where we're at, do you?"

"'Course I do." He spun the chair to face the laptop, avoiding her persistent glare.

"You don't." She stepped up beside him, bending to reach for the computer. "Just let me take a look. It's not that hard."

Her movement launched him to action. In one fluid motion, he pushed out of the chair and, coming to stand behind her, pinned her hands flat to the desk.

Wrong move.

Now the base of her neck was exposed to him and he was overwhelmed with the scent of her. How in the hell did she manage to smell like sex and cookies all wrapped up into one?

"Brodie. You should... let me go." Her voice had gone velvety and sweet, sending ripples of craving straight to his cock.

He should.

But right now his cock was calling the shots and he wanted a taste of her.

Just a little taste.

He lowered his lips to her neck, lightly brushing the skin just below her hairline. She shivered underneath him, the skin on her neck pebbling. She exhaled a tiny sigh, letting her head fall farther forward, and exposing more of her neck to him.

He took another taste, flicking his tongue out and savoring the slightly salty tang of her skin. She gasped, rolling her hips. Grinding her ass that way against his straining cock was torture. He'd fantasized about this and more, for weeks. Sucking in a steadying breath, he ran his hands up the length of her arms, pausing where her biceps bunched under his palm.

There was nothing soft about her.

Just strength and fire.

Goddamn if that didn't turn him on more than anything in his life. An all too familiar ache throbbed deep in his balls, begging for release.

"Tell me to stop," he muttered into her neck, his breath ragged from holding back.

She whirled, leaning back into the desk, her eyes glittering.

Everything slowed.

Then sped up again as she placed her hands on either side of his face and pulled his head the remaining few inches to meet hers.

Hell, yes.

His mouth crashed into hers, his tongue diving into her recesses, tasting and savoring. Her tongue slid into his mouth, twisting and curling against his, pulling him into her mouth, then parrying and thrusting into his.

She moved, rising and pushing him backwards against the wall. He spun them around, pinning her as she raked her hands through his hair.

Never in his years of Casanova antics had he wanted a woman as much as he wanted Jamey.

He ran his hands down to her waist, slipping his fingers underneath her tank to rest on the silky skin above her waistband. Moving his hands up, he traced her ribs, reveling in the way her muscles tightened under his fingers.

As his fingers reached the curve under her breast, she groaned in the back of her throat and rolled her hips.

He tore his mouth from hers. "God, Jamey, I've been dreaming about your tits for weeks. It's the fucking sexiest thing, you walking around with no bra."

Her lips smiled against his. "You noticed."

He growled, taking another taste along her neck. "God, woman. How could I not? You set my balls on fire."

"Tell me how you really feel."

Her low giggle thrummed through him and settled in his nuts. Holy fuck, she made him blind with need. "I just did."

He captured a peak between his thumb and forefinger, rolling it to a hard point, reveling in the way she threw her head back against the wall. He moved his hand to her other breast to do the same. Her breath came in fast pants now.

"Your tits are perfect."

A wry smile twisted her face. "They're too small."

He growled in protest. "Whoever told you that should get pounded into the dirt. I love the way they fit in my hand." He gave her a little squeeze for added emphasis before pushing up her tank and bringing his lips to the rosy peak. He sucked it in, rolling it with his tongue, then scraped his teeth gently over the tip.

Her hips bucked, and she stopped her perusal of his chest to clutch his shoulders.

"Jesus, Brodie."

He lifted his head, surveying her flushed face through hooded eyes. She was soft and pliant under him. A contradiction to the tough as nails firebrand who kicked ass and took names in the kitchen.

"Is that a Jesus Brodie stop now? Or a Jesus Brodie you love this?"

She pushed his shirt up giving him a sly smile. "I know you've seen me givin' you the glad eye."

"Not following. Is that Irish for I'm hot?"

"No, you arrogant bastard. It's Irish for fuck me now before my head explodes."

Raw lust thundered through him. He yanked her tank over her head, baring her. Then reached for his own shirt, throwing it next to hers.

"You sure?" He brought his mouth to the base of her neck, sucking and nipping, half afraid of her answer. He didn't know why hearing her say she wanted him meant so much to him. It was only sex.

"You want me to spell it out?" She panted, running her fingernails over his chest, and holy hell… She sucked on the hollow at his neck, scraping her teeth over his collarbone. Her antics sent a jolt of electricity straight to his balls, building on the ache that had kept him awake nights the last few months. If she kept this up, he'd lose control before his pants dropped.

"Yes, dammit," he gritted out between breaths. "Say it."

He needed to hear her say it. Grabbing her ass, he hauled her up against his rigid shaft, not that he had far to pull. She was so damned tall, he only had to tilt his head to kiss her.

"Fine, then." She raised her head, spearing him with

dark lust-glazed eyes. His insides scorched, and he locked his knees against the onslaught of craving that crashed over him.

"I want you, Brodie Sinclaire. Right here in this office. Pants off."

## Chapter Fifteen

*S*he didn't need to ask twice.

Releasing her, he fell to his knees, fingers tugging on the elastic of her chef's pants.

"Wait."

Goddammit. She'd gone and changed her mind. Fuck him for being the idiot.

He glanced up at her, working to bring his breathing under control, but what he saw wasn't the face of a woman who changed her mind. A hungry glint lurked in her eyes, as a crooked smile curved her lips.

"My boots."

Jesus fucking Christ.

He attacked the laces of her ridiculous purple patent leather Doc Martens with a ferocity normally reserved for fighting with his brothers. He was all thumbs working at the ties. As the laces loosened, she kicked her foot out and used it to push on the other boot he was madly working to remove.

As soon as her foot was free, he reached up and unceremoniously jerked down her pants and panties in one swift motion.

Finally.

He breathed a sigh of relief and appreciation all at once, as she stood completely exposed to him. He'd never seen anything like her.

Red curls only slightly obscuring glistening pussy lips just waiting to be tasted and claimed by him. This was better than fucking Christmas Day. Peering up, he could see her mouth parted and her head thrown back against the wall. Her breathing came in shallow pants, and her tiny breasts thrust out, standing at perfect attention.

God, she was gorgeous. Like some wild ethereal Irish sprite.

Running his hands the length of her thighs, he gently pushed them out, silently demanding greater access. She shifted, spreading her stance. He slid his thumbs up the inside of her thighs and paused, resting at her apex, caressing the link between torso and leg and reveling in the strength of her.

Slowly, he slid a thumb the length of her slit, eliciting a high moan as he encountered her silky wetness. The scent of her arousal assaulted him and only served to deepen the ache in his balls.

He brought his other thumb up and traced the length of her, spreading open her lips, baring the deepest part of her to him.

Leaning forward, his breath stuck in his ribs.

How long had he been dreaming of this moment? Fantasizing about her? Her scent, her taste?

He couldn't breathe.

The reality was so much better than the fantasy.

She reached down and slid her fingers through his hair, urging him forward. Coming forward on his knees, he bent his head to her pussy. All pretty and glistening pink. Keeping himself back from diving in and devouring her, he nuzzled her lips, reveling in the sweet tangy musk of her desire.

"Quit. Toying. With. Me." Her command ended on a high gasp as he flicked his tongue out to taste her, moving on the same path his thumbs had. Her cream ran over his tongue, filling him with her taste. Salt and sweet and... her. He was ruined for anyone else.

Ever.

She clutched at his hair as he took his pleasure with his tongue, swirling her clit, then sliding his mouth down the length of her pussy lips to plumb the depths of her honey.

There was only her, and the taste he could never have enough of. Over and over, he dove into the recesses of her hot silky sex, licking along her cleft, and circling her clit as it stood higher and harder with each pass. Digging his fingers into her ass, he pulled her forward, his tongue diving deeper and flattening to sweep the length of her. She was keening now, muttering profanities under her breath as her hips undulated beneath him.

He covered her clit with his lips, then sucked in, allowing his teeth to gently graze her peak. Crying out, she went rigid. He continued suckling as her body shuddered, slipping one finger, then two, into her hot, wet, channel so she could fully ride the waves that shattered her.

He swallowed hard, working to keep himself in check. Every sound she made went straight to his cock, heightening his own desire and practically wringing out what little control he had left.

He slowly rose to his feet, drawing her nipple into his mouth and curling his tongue around it before moving his lips to her neck. She slid her fingers inside the denim at his waist, running along his belly and pausing where his cock was jammed ramrod straight, confined against the zipper. Grazing a nail over the head of his cock, she laughed low and velvety.

A groan ripped from his throat and he crushed his mouth to hers, his tongue demanding entry. She eagerly opened and he thrust in his tongue, letting her taste herself. Her answering moan had him fumbling with the button and jamming down his jeans.

Pressing into her, he lifted her thigh to his hip and in one fluid motion thrust into her slick entrance.

God, she was a piece of tight, hot heaven. His breath caught in his throat as he settled into her. The sensation of her skin gliding over him, surrounding him, nearly undid him right there.

Her breath came out in a little moan as she twisted her hips against him. Pulling back, he angled himself so he slid against her clit as he pushed back into her. She threw her head back, fingers digging into his shoulders and gasping for breath.

Again, he pulled out and buried himself into her, lifting her off her toes and reveling in her tightness, her heat. His own inferno grew and pooled in his belly, winding him tighter with each thrust.

She rocked with him, crying out as he drove into her, her voice pitching higher with each movement until she clenched his cock in waves as her release shuddered through her. Her ecstasy surrounded him, coming in ripples down his hard shaft and squeezing his own climax from him in a blinding bolt that ripped a shout from his throat. He threw a hand up against the wall, bending his forehead to hers as their breathing slowed to normal.

Panic started to creep into the edges of his awareness as they separated. "Fuck, Jamey. I'm so sorry."

She gazed at him with glassy, sated eyes. "What do you

mean?" A slow, satisfied smile lifted the corners of her mouth. "You're feckin' magic, you know."

"Condoms," he rasped out, his heart in his throat. "We didn't use a condom." He'd never ridden bareback before, and he'd been so far gone, he hadn't cared.

Blake had basically drummed into him the summer he'd dated Kylee Ross that his dick would fall off if he didn't use a condom. He bit back a laugh. His dick hadn't fallen off, not by a long shot. Being inside Jamey had been heaven.

She rolled her head, eyes wide. "Shit." She let out a breathy laugh. "I don't think I've ever been so carried away I didn't pay attention."

"So it was good for you, then?"

Her eyes softened for a moment. "Didn't you hear me? You're magic."

His chest swelled with pride. He might be a mess everywhere else, but at least he knew how to satisfy a lover.

The softness about her was only fleeting. All too quickly, what he'd come to think of as her business face was back in place. Damn. He liked her soft around the edges.

She slapped his arm. "Well, I'm on the pill. And clean. So no worries about making little Irish babies."

The comment jarred him. Not that he wanted baby Sinclaires anytime soon. But the vision of a little redheaded girl loomed over him and his heart thumped a little bit harder against his ribs.

"Brodie. Snap back." She waved her fingers in front of him.

"I get tested every six months."

Her eyes registered surprise. "Really? How... responsible of you."

Her astonishment rankled him. "Why wouldn't I be?"

Why did everyone just assume he was a reckless fuck-up? Maybe because he'd always let them.

Jamey's eyes narrowed. "Are you some kind of a man-whore?"

Heat flushed the back of his neck. "Umm… no," he hedged. Maybe? What constituted a man-whore? "Blake drilled safe sex into all of us. You?"

"I'm not a man-whore either," she answered with a wink. Her voice still held a hint of the breathy quality he'd come to associate with her level of arousal.

He drew a finger down her cheek. "What are you then?" He grinned back, already starting to get half hard.

She brought her hands up to his chest and pushed him back, her smile turning into a smirk. "Trouble, cowboy. My middle name's Trouble."

"I thought it was Irish Whis – Hey. What are you doing?" He scowled as she sashayed to the desk, hit the space bar, and brought the laptop to life.

She tossed him an open grin over her shoulder. "What does it look like I'm doing? I'm finishing what I started." She shifted her attention back to the computer, punching a few keys and bringing up a spreadsheet.

He stiffened as if he'd been sucker punched.

Shit. If she saw that his numbers were all jumbled, that his spreadsheet was a mess…what then?

"Let it go, Jamey," he spoke sharply. She made quite a picture, bent over his laptop, studying his numbers, buck naked and freshly fucked. She had nerve. And why the hell did she have to swish her ass so tantalizingly as she did it? Grumbling, he bent to retrieve his jeans, jamming in one leg, then the other.

She glanced back at him, eyes filled with concern. "Brodie? What's going on with these numbers?"

"What the hell is that supposed to mean?" He ground

out the words, yanking up the zipper and buttoning his pants closed. She seemed remarkably oblivious to the fact she was naked.

She gave an exaggerated sigh. "It's supposed to mean these numbers are all off. Let me see—"

"I've got it under control."

She stuck out a hand as the spreadsheet scrolled. "Hand me my shirt will you?"

That brought him up short. This wasn't how people behaved after mind-blowing sex. Sex between them had *meant* something. Hadn't it? It was the most powerful damned orgasm he'd remembered experiencing. Disappointment crashed through him.

The printer started to make noise, and she glanced at him sharply as she reached for the papers. "What is it?"

He glowered. "I can handle the books."

"Let me help you." She pulled the papers off the printer. "I don't know what's going on here, but once I figure it out, I can fix—"

"No," he bellowed.

Her eyes widened, filled with hurt. "Don't be an ass, Brodie."

"I'll take care of it." Couldn't she see that he *had* to figure this out on his own?

She stepped up to him, tall and fierce. So close, her nipples brushed his chest. "What happened to teamwork?" Her lips thinned to a straight line.

"I run the office, you run the kitchen."

"But you're…" Her eyes flashed anger, followed by worry. "You need help. Brodie… I know you don't want to hear this, but the numbers aren't that hard."

Ha.

Maybe not for her.

"You need to charge enough to cover your costs and a

little extra. Do you know which columns are which?" She flicked the papers she held.

"Of course I do," he blustered, covering the pool of shame building in his belly. "I'm not an idiot. I can do this." Panic twisted in his stomach. Why couldn't she just let it go?

Compassion filled her eyes. "Of course not. I–"

"I don't want your goddamned pity. And I sure as hell don't need you telling me how to run this place." Anger and humiliation swirled through him, clouding out reason. Jesus. How had the best sex of his life collapsed to this? "Let's keep this clear. You worry about the kitchen. I've got the rest under control." He pivoted on his heel and stalked out, slamming the door shut behind him.

He'd figure out the numbers if it was the last thing he did.

If only he knew where to start.

## Chapter Sixteen

*W*hat in the saints had she been thinking? The thwack of Jamey's butcher knife resonated across the kitchen as she separated a pheasant wing from its carcass. She'd been up since dark early prepping food. Three days of food for nineteen heads would be a feat without prep help. She scowled and separated the next wing with an extra hard thwack.

Brodie was nothing but a flirt. Clearly, sex between them had meant nothing. Not only had he avoided her entirely since their crazy encounter, but Mr. Host with the Most had turned on the sugar with the female guests as they'd arrived this afternoon. He was gifted. She'd grant him that. He could charm the panties off a snow queen in winter.

Jamey kept forcefully separating the pheasant wings. Was Brodie the popover she'd accused him of being at the wedding, or the man who made sure she had a plate of food waiting for her every night at the end of dinner service? The life of the party, or the man who treated Simon with such kindness? He paid attention to every word she said. Repaired something the second she mentioned it in passing.

Who was he? Mr. Superficial? Or Mr. Super Amazing?

She should never have caved and had sex with him. It… complicated things. But damn, it had been electrifying. Her body tingled at the memory. She wanted more. So much so, if she didn't take great pains to avoid him in the future, she'd shamelessly rip his clothes off and run her hands over his magnificent body until they both exploded.

She'd do best to remember they were a business team. And if he refused to let her help him, he was going to run this place into the ground. She needed to get something lined up at the end of her six weeks and move on. She couldn't afford to be out on her ass for a second time in one year. Whatever was going on with him, he'd made it clear he didn't want her help. His behavior didn't add up, but she wasn't going to force her expertise on him. Especially after watching him fall all over the lady guests.

"Thinking about the other night?" Brodie's voice drawled from the threshold.

Her head snapped up. He stood propped against the doorframe, beer in hand, a sexy grin on his face.

She frowned, giving the pheasant wing an extra, extra hard thwack. "We're overbooked and have six more people arriving in the next hour, and the only thing you can think about is your pants around your ankles?"

His smile flickered a fraction. "I'm all set for them."

"How lovely for you. I'm in the weeds. Now if you'll excuse me." She threw the final wing into the prep pan and covered it with plastic wrap. Later she'd confit them in duck fat.

Grabbing a new knife, she began breaking down the pheasant breasts, tossing them in a separate prep pan.

Out of the corner of her eye, she could see Brodie still

lounging in the doorway. "What?" Did he have to watch her that way? It was positively unnerving the way her tracked her movements. She glanced up again, then shrieked as her knife slipped and sliced her thumb. "God*dammit.*"

He lunged from the doorway, eyes full of concern.

"Are you okay? What's wrong?" He crossed around the island to where she stood, putting pressure on her thumb. It was a deep cut, but not so deep it would need stitches.

"I'm fine," she snapped. "Just get me the first aid box next to the sink." She moved behind him, turning on the water and letting the stream clear out the cut.

Yeah. The cut was a good one. Total rookie move.

"What happened?" Was that an edge of fear in his voice?

"I'm fine. I wasn't paying attention, and my thumb got under my knife. Hand me an alcohol wipe."

He tore the wrapper, his hands shaking slightly.

"Oh God. You're not one of those people who faints at the sight of blood, are you?"

"Me? No."

"I don't have time for you to pass out on me today."

He handed her the wipe. She hissed in as the alcohol sunk into the cut and pain shot up her hand.

"You sure you okay?"

"Only a flesh wound. Stop hovering."

He cracked a small smile at her joke, but his eyes remained full of concern.

"Band-Aid. I'll need two." She pinched her thumb hard while she waited for him to open the first one.

He handed the first one to her, and she wrapped it as tight as she could stand it. There. That should staunch the bleeding for the moment. He handed her the second, and she covered the rest of her thumb.

"Finger condom?"

"*What?*"

She smothered a grin at his expression. "Finger condom, in the corner of the box."

"What the hell is that?"

"What the hell does it look like? Keeps everything clean and tidy."

He handed the small package to her, a flush coloring his neck.

"See?" She tore the package. "Just like the bigger version, minus the spermicide." She winked at him as she rolled the latex down her thumb.

"Well I'll be damned." The laughter left his eyes. "Jamey."

The silence stretched between them.

"Is there something else you want to say, Brodie? I've got prep work to complete, or dinner will be late."

He remained where he was, looking down, shuffling his feet. Why in the hell did this sudden awkwardness hurt?

A voice giggled from the doorway. "Brodie sweetheart, watchya hidin' out in the kitchen for? Brandi and I need you for cornhole."

Brodie coughed, guilt flickering in his eyes.

Jamey plastered on a smile and peered over his shoulder. "It's Cami, isn't it? He'll be out in a sec."

The young woman assessed her coolly, tossing her bottle blonde hair over her shoulder.

He coughed again and flashed Cami a brilliant smile. The kind of smile that slid panties right off bottoms like they were greased with Crisco.

"Be right there, darlin'. You gals get the game set up."

Not that a smile like that would work on her. Ever. *It didn't have to. You practically threw yourself at him.* The realization she was nothing more than a notch on a belt buckle stung. Her own damned fault for letting her hormones get the best of her.

What did Maddie like to call them? Pheromones? Maddie had teased her about them the last time she'd popped over for a chat. Heat flushed the base of her neck. Regardless of what they were called, she wouldn't be making *that* mistake again anytime soon. The other night had been a blip. A physical way to let off steam, like the steam valve on a pressure cooker. Nothing more. She couldn't let it be anything more.

Taking a deep breath and keeping her professional smile in place, she waved her thumb.

"Thanks for the help. I'll put the appetizers out by six, dinner at seven."

She grabbed her knife and resumed breaking apart the pheasant breasts. The sooner she finished, the sooner she'd be able to move to the next item on her laundry list.

"Jamey." He put his hand on the top of her arm.

She froze. "Don't *ever* touch me when I have a knife in my hand," she bit out through gritted teeth.

He dropped his hand, but remained behind her.

"Out." She risked a glance over her shoulder, glaring. His blue eyes were filled with confusion and a little hurt. "Out. Of. My. Kitchen."

He clenched his jaw, eyes flaring. "I don't know what just happened, but we'll talk this through later."

He stalked off through the door to the dining area. Like he had any right to be mad at her. He was the one flirting with the guests.

She redoubled her efforts on the pheasant, jamming the unproductive thoughts back to where they came from. The last thing she needed was to get twitterpated over a hot cowboy in tight jeans. Too much was riding on this weekend. She needed it to go well.

Brilliantly, really.

With the kind of circles Mason Carter ran in, who knew what chef or restauranteur he might be able to introduce her to? She needed to focus on making art this weekend and securing her next gig. That meant keeping her mind off Brodie's luscious ass in a pair of denims. And his thick cock pushing into her. And the scrape of his stubble across her nipples.

Giving herself a shake, she tossed the last breast in the prep pan. She covered it and put it in the fridge. Next, she gathered the carcasses and tossed them into the large stockpot on the back of the stove. The stockpot was already filled with her signature mirepoix, a mixture of onions, carrots, celery, sea salt, thyme sprigs, and her secret ingredient, celery root. Popping the lid on, she set the gas to low. By this time tomorrow, she'd have a velvety stock ready to make magic.

Jamey glanced at the clock. Ninety minutes until the appetizers needed to fire. Once the polenta was prepped and spread on a sheet tray, she could start on the venison and pork belly meatballs. Venison was too dry for a meatball on its own, but with a little fat and flavor from the pork belly, the combo would be perfect.

Grabbing a clean knife, she settled into the rhythm of prep work. Slice, dice, measure, stir. The repetitive action settled her nerves and sharpened her focus. Everything faded except the tactile pleasure of creating a feast.

An hour later, a throat clearing pulled her out of her zone. She popped her head up to see Mason Carter hovering in the doorway. "What is it with you men lurking at the door? In or out."

He flashed her a grin and held up a bottle of her favorite twelve-year Redbreast and two glasses. "I come bearing gifts."

He was a big man. A little taller than Brodie, but leaner, and an intelligence in his eyes that indicated he never missed a detail. His mildly unkempt sandy hair gave him more of a boy next-door appearance than a billionaire with a killer instinct.

She couldn't help but smile back. "A man after my own heart, Mason. I'd shake your hand, but you can see I'm a bit messy." She lifted hands from the meatballs she'd been rolling.

He stepped over to the island, placing the bottle on the counter. "What are these?"

"Venison and porkbelly meatballs." She rolled a ball in cornstarch before placing it on the parchment.

"Can I help?"

She smirked at him. "You mean the billionaire cooks?"

"Hell yeah. Dad's third wife was a self-styled Julia Child. She made sure my sister and I knew our way around the kitchen."

"Don't you want to relax with the other guests?"

He shook his head. "My crew are getting settled across the way, and I don't care for small talk. Besides, Brodie seems to be doing an excellent job of entertaining the ladies."

She didn't miss the admiration in his voice. A flash of jealousy stabbed through her. "I can't imagine you need lessons with the ladies, Mason. But yeah, Brodie takes his hosting seriously." Too seriously.

*Stop it, Jamey. He doesn't belong to you.*

Mason shrugged. "Charm seems to be a Sinclaire trait. One that doesn't run in my family... So how 'bout it, chef?" He waved his hands. "Or are these hands too pretty for you?"

She snorted. "I hope you like taking orders."

"Keeps me humble."

"Then wash your hands, grab a dish towel, and get over here."

She showed him how to ball and roll the meatballs in cornstarch and took the first tray to the stove for frying.

"Don't most people use flour?"

Jamey winked at him. "I'm not most people."

"No foolin'. Seriously. Why not flour?"

"Crisps better than flour." *And I have this tiny issue with gluten.*

"Why'd you leave the restaurant in Chicago?"

"Enough with the questions."

Mason rolled a meatball in the cornstarch. "Just curious. I was surprised when Maddie mentioned you'd taken over the kitchen here."

"I needed a change."

"Is that code for a bad break-up?"

"You never miss a thing, do you?"

"It's why I get paid the big bucks."

Jamey lowered the first batch of meatballs into the hot oil and covered the pan with a spatter guard. She leaned her hip on the counter behind her. "I hear from Maddie you're working on a similar concept in Montana."

Mason moved to the sink to wash his hands, then reached for the dishtowel. "Sure am. I have about eighty-thousand acres in the Paradise Valley." He moved around the island and poured them each a measure of the whiskey.

She transferred the meatballs to a cooling rack, and lowered the next batch into the oil. Taking the glass he offered, she took a long sip, relishing the way it warmed her insides. The same way Brodie did when he gave her one of his scorching hot looks.

Huh.

Even Jean Luc had never heated her like a taste of twelve-year Redbreast.

She glanced up to see Mason studying her thoughtfully. "What would it take to for you to come set up shop in Montana?"

Jamey rolled her eyes, grinning. "I told you at the wedding. All the money in your bank account won't convince me to leave the big city."

"But you're here, aren't you?"

She shook her head, pushing away the pang of regret. "Nah. Just until the lodge gets on solid footing. It's a favor, that's all."

"If you ever change your mind, put me at the top of your list."

A throat cleared and they both looked up. Brodie stood, bracing an arm on the doorjamb, the cool assessment in his eyes at odds with the easy smile he wore. "Since when are you recruiting the guests for help, *Chef*?"

## Chapter Seventeen

*W*hy in the hell was Mason Carter trying to woo away his help? And what in the hell was he doing with his sleeves rolled up in *his* kitchen?

Mason cracked a cautious smile. "Just lending a hand."

*Trying to steal my help is more like it.*

Jamey glared at him before taking a sip of her whiskey. "I'm happy for the help."

"Why didn't you ask me then?" A wave of hurt coiled through him. He'd have stopped entertaining the guests to help her. All she'd had to do was ask.

She clenched her jaw and smiled frostily. "Mason, would you please excuse us? I can take it from here."

Mason's eyes filled with concern as he looked back and forth between the two of them, a frown lurking at the corners of his mouth. "Everything okay?"

Jamey tossed a dishtowel into the dirty linens bag under the island before turning back to the stove. "Nothing I can't handle."

Mason finished his drink and placed the glass on the counter. "If you need anything—"

She waved him off. "I'll handle it."

Brodie kept his smile in place as Mason brushed past and into the dining area. Mason was a good guy, even if seeing him all chummy with Jamey made him see red. Jamey whirled around, eyes flashing fire.

"Why'd you do that? Piss on a fire hydrant?" She grabbed the tray of meatballs from the island and moved it to the stove, slamming it down hard.

"Maybe I don't like it when other people start honing in on my territory."

Clenching a fist at her side, she carefully removed the meatballs from the oil, and lowered in another batch. She grabbed her glass, drained the remaining amber liquid, and raked her gaze over him, eyes glittering. "Is that what you think I am? Your territory?"

Aww shit. That hadn't come out right. "No. Not exactly."

"Not exactly?" The air between them charged. "Let me make this clear. The only territory you need to worry about is the territory between your legs which will be sorely lacking if you don't get out of my kitchen right this second."

Dammit if her temper didn't stir something devilish in him. He wanted to poke at her some more. See the fire that blazed so strongly inside of her. He shook his head, tutting, and stepped around the island, invading her space.

"You catch more flies with honey, bossypants."

She flushed and turned back to the stove, removing the last batch of meatballs and turning off the gas. "You're presuming I want to catch flies."

"Don't you?" He reached out and captured her hand, bringing it up to inspect her injured thumb, and placing a kiss on the palm of her hand. She sucked in a breath, but didn't move away.

"So fiery. So feisty." He murmured the words into her hand, relishing the tendrils of desire that rippled through his abdomen. This verbal dancing was torture. At the same time, it sharpened his awareness. Made him hyper alert.

"Brodie…" She leaned in, green eyes darkening.

"You captivate me."

She yanked her hand away, eyes full of doubt. "Until the next guest sashays along. Now out." She waved her hand toward the door.

He wasn't leaving yet.

Not by a long shot.

He settled himself against the stove, stretching out his legs, blocking her passage as realization hit him.

"Wait… are you *jealous?*" He was an ass for not keeping the glee out of his voice.

She eyed him warily as she grabbed a dozen eggs from the fridge. "I have nineteen mouths to feed this weekend, and you refused to let me hire help. Now you want to have a heart to heart in my kitchen?"

He shrugged, grinning. "Don't avoid my question."

A blush inched up her neck. Holy smokes, she *was* jealous. A little thrill coiled through him. He lowered his voice. "Why are you fighting this, Jamey?"

She rolled her eyes, shaking her head. "Out. Now."

He pushed off the stove and came to stand next to her. "Your temper doesn't scare me."

She glanced over, momentarily pausing her egg cracking.

He reached out and caressed her cheek, running his thumb across her full lower lip. "You're going to have to do a lot more than yell at me to get me to leave."

The hungry look in her eye made his cock stand at full attention. God he wanted more of her. One taste… one naked moment, was far from enough.

Her tongue flicked out nervously and brushed against his thumb. He bit back a groan as his cock jolted from the electricity.

"What do you want, Brodie?"

He grinned slowly. He couldn't help it. "You darlin'. Hot and bothered underneath me. Beggin' me to love you."

Her eyes widened and flared. "I don't beg."

"You will. And I promise you. You'll love every damned minute of it."

He brought his mouth to hers, his tongue invading without invitation, sweeping through her sweet, whiskey-tinged mouth.

She made a little noise in the back of her throat as he wrapped his arm around her back, pulling her against him. She clutched his sleeve and deepened the kiss, her own tongue sparring with his.

He growled, rolling his hips against hers, then pulled his mouth from hers, steadying himself. If he didn't stop this second, he'd throw her down on the floor right now. Guests and dinner be damned.

Her hand flew to her mouth as she took a step back. Her face contorted in pain and she dropped her focus to her bowl. "Don't toy with me, Brodie Sinclaire."

Frustration overwhelmed him. "I've never been more serious," he bit out, clenching his jaw.

Her mouth flattened in obvious disbelief. Did she have to be so stubborn? He'd never worked so hard for a woman's attention.

Ever.

"Don't believe me? Watch me rope at the rodeo tomorrow afternoon. Then let me take you out to the Trading Post tomorrow evening. Everyone will be eating at the fairgrounds tomorrow night, so you won't have to cook."

There. He'd asked. The air thickened between them as she stared at him through narrowed eyes.

Letting out a breath, she nodded once. "Fine. I'll go."

Relief whooshed through him as he flashed her a grin. Once she saw him in his element, she wouldn't think he was such a fuck-up. "You'll have a great time. Promise."

A small smile tugged at the corners of her mouth.

He stepped close again and tilted her chin. Brushing his lips against hers, he murmured low. "For the record, your prickly act doesn't fool me for a second. You're sweet as honey on the inside." He kissed her harder, allowing himself just one more taste of her lips. "And I love your taste."

Her quick intake of breath warmed his insides. He shifted back and winked at her before she could smack him, or say anything. Then wheeled and strolled out of the kitchen, whistling "Home on the Range".

## Chapter Eighteen

*J*amey wiped a bead of sweat off her brow. She'd be toasting herself after cleanup. Nineteen plates to fire, and no sous. She'd achieve rock star status, at least in her own mind, if she pulled this off without a hitch tonight.

Ben, his friends, and Mason's ranch hands sat at the long table in the great room. Blake, Maddie, Simon, Mason, and his foreman sat at a table on the front patio. Her biggest challenge would be getting the mains out fast enough that the first plates weren't cold by the time the last plate dropped. She'd opted to serve the salad family style, which irked her. Presentation always made the food taste better. But she knew her limits. She was pushing them as it was.

Brodie strode in, a determined look on his face. "Let me help."

She shook her head, stacking the plates in three piles on the island. "I've got it. You go entertain."

He started opening drawers until he found a large flour

sack dishcloth. "They're talkin' just fine without me." He tied the dishcloth around his waist.

Jamey covered a laugh. "You look like a dork."

"Then get me a coat like yours."

"Oh no. You have to earn that."

Earnestness replaced the humor in his eyes. "Then let me earn it, Jamey, please? We're a team, remember?"

She paused her rushing to glare at him. "Yeah? Then why won't you let me help you with the ledgers?"

His eyes instantly became guarded. He let out a heavy sigh. "That's... I... That's different. Something I need to take care of... for me."

She reached to pull a pan of polenta out of the oven, shutting the door with her hip. "Are you aware of how razor thin our margins are? Probably as razor thin as a ranch's. We've got no room for error."

He scrubbed a hand across his face. "You think I don't know that?"

"Then why won't you let me help?"

He put his hands on his hips, and stared hard at her, inner conflict playing out on his face. What was it? What was he holding back? And why wouldn't he tell her?

Throwing caution to the wind, she crossed around the island, bringing her bright purple Docs toe to toe with his Tony Lamas.

A wry smile played at the corners of his mouth. "Your boots are hideous."

She flashed him a grin. "Yes they are. And the best damn pair of kitchen shoes I've ever owned. I can stand for fourteen hours and not ache."

His eyes widened a fraction. "You work fourteen hour days?"

"Ranchers aren't the only profession with long hours

and little pay. We don't fanny about the kitchen in miniskirts and frilly aprons, waving a magic wand."

Desire lit his eyes. "You'd look mighty fine like that," he said suggestively.

She snorted. "I'll remember that when we don't have nineteen mouths to feed." She grabbed his hand, studying the callouses that crossed his palm. She traced one with her finger. "Brodie... whatever it is..." She risked a glance his direction. His blue eyes locked on hers. "You can tell me..." she swallowed hard, suddenly feeling very exposed.

His fingers closed around hers, encasing her in warmth and strength. Words played over his face, and he opened his mouth, then quickly shut it again, mask back in place. "Nothin' to tell." He flashed her his Mr. Charming smile. "You don't worry about a thing, darlin'."

Her heart twisted in disappointment.

Fine. If that's how he was going to play it. "It's Chef, cowboy." She dropped his hand, all business. "Lay out the first five plates. We'll serve the patio first."

She retreated to the other side of the island, professional armor back in place. He was her business partner, not her boyfriend. She must remember that at all costs.

Taking a pizza cutter, she ran it through the toasted polenta, making thick rectangles. The familiar adrenaline rush of running a fast kitchen seeped into her veins, sharpening her focus to a laser point. Keeping her eyes on her work, she rattled off orders like she was back home at Frenchie O'Neill's. "Polenta at six o'clock. Line the left side with brussels. I'll add the pheasant and sauce the plate. Got it?"

"Brussels?"

She nodded at a pan on the stove. "I'm going to fire these in about 30 seconds. I'll put them on the island. You'll want four to six on each plate." She gave him her most intimidating chef's stare. "You ready? This will go fast."

"Not faster than a calf tearin' outta the chute. I got this."

"Let's go then." She turned back to the stove and upped the flame on the brussels. Grabbing a spatula, she lifted the first piece of polenta out of the tray, and laid it on the plate. "I'll do this first one so you get a visual. Then you're on your own. Any questions, ask. Don't assume."

"Got it, chef."

She could have sworn she detected a note of humor in his voice, and glanced up sharply.

"You laughing?"

"Nope. Just admiring."

She gave him a little smile. "So long as it doesn't slow you down." She spun back to the sauté pan and gave it a shake. Opening the stove, she grabbed the tongs with her free hand, and reached in for a prosciutto-wrapped pheasant breast. She placed it at an angle over the polenta, then grabbed the brussels pan and brought it to the island. She laid out six in a row alongside the polenta. Next, she ladled a little demi glace over the meat, and finished with a squeeze bottle she'd filled with a balsamic fig reduction. "Drizzle it across the plate like this," she demonstrated. "Not too heavy. Got it?"

"Yup."

Jamey handed him the spatula and reached back into the oven for another pheasant breast. Brodie's big hands worked rapidly and with surprising facility for someone who'd never worked in a commercial kitchen. In no time, he was carrying the plates out to the table.

"Remember to serve from the right," she called after him.

Five down, fourteen to go.

Now came the tricky part. With only two of them, they'd have to work furiously to get the plates to the table while the food was still hot. Grabbing a second pan, she divided the remaining brussels from her prep area between the two pans. Firing them both, she spun and started laying out the last of the plates.

Brodie returned, and relieved her of plate duty. She started plating the polenta. As soon as Brodie finished laying the plates, he reached for her spatula. She whipped around and gave the brussels a toss. They worked in silence, focused on the getting the plates built as rapidly as possible. She brought the brussels around behind Brodie, brushing him as she passed, and laid them on the island.

"I'll get the pheasant," Brodie offered. He moved to the oven and, grabbing the potholders, brought the pheasant to the island.

For a kitchen novice, he sure caught on fast. She hid a smile as she laid down the brussels. They worked from end to middle, meeting at the last plate.

He darted a glance her way before concentrating on the plate again. "You're good, Jamey."

Warmth bloomed in her chest. "You're catching on."

"I mean it."

She scooted around him, reaching for the demi glace. "Grab the drizzle. Food's getting cold." She sauced the meat and Brodie followed behind with the glaze.

Grabbing two plates, she bustled around the island, calling over her shoulder as she went. "I'll start with Cami, then we put them down clockwise."

Brodie followed, and in short order, the table had been served while the food was still hot. Wiping her hands on her pants, she stepped to the sink and began rinsing the stack of salad dishes. A hand snaked out and grabbed the sprayer. "Let me."

She refused to release it. "Nope. You go entertain. I made enough for you, too."

"What about you, Jamey? Who takes care of you?"

*No one.* She lifted a shoulder. "Stop acting the mother. Go be Mr. Charming."

"What if I'd rather stay here?"

So he could charm the pants off her? Brodie would scorch her like a hand on a hot stove. And yet... she liked him. He pushed her buttons. Hell, she pushed his. And it was... *fun.* Before she could stop herself, she flicked the sprayer at him, wetting his shirt.

He leapt back in surprise. "What the hell was that for?" he yelped.

Laughter bubbled up. Laughter like she hadn't enjoyed in... forever. And she couldn't stop. God, teasing him was better than pulling one over on all her brothers at once. A feat she'd only managed twice in her life.

His hand closed over hers. "Two can play this game, lady."

She valiantly tried to fend him off, but he was too strong, and in no time had the sprayer aimed at her face. She shrieked in laughter. "S-s-s-STOP."

"Hell no, woman. You're going to pay for that." Laughter tinged his own voice as she tried to twist behind him and use him as a shield. He pivoted, grabbing her waist, and pulled her back against him. She was soaked. And so was he.

Then, using a move her brother Jarrod had taught her, she swept his foot, tumbling both of them to the floor, leaving the sprayer swinging wildly. She landed stretched out on top of him, gasping for breath. His hand snaked around her back, clasping her close. His chest shook with laughter underneath her, and they locked eyes.

Instantly, the mood shifted, and Brodie lifted his head off the floor, capturing her mouth. He brought his other hand to the base of her neck, gently holding her in place as his tongue flicked across her lips. Giving her hips a roll, she opened her mouth, meeting his tongue with her own. The laughter they'd shared set off a fire inside her that could only be quenched with his kiss. God, his kisses set her body buzzing like a whole bag of chocolate espresso beans. He caressed her back… and lower, cupping her ass and squeezing her tighter against him.

"Jamey? Everything all right?" Maddie called.

Shit.

Caught making out on the floor of her kitchen. He'd charmed the pants right off her.

*Again.*

She popped up, knowing her face was bright red.

Blake and Maddie stood just inside the entrance, the picture of concerned parents to be.

"Hi," Jamey said brightly. Too brightly. "Everything's fine. Just a little spill." She nudged Brodie with her boot. He stood up.

Maddie and Blake stared at the two of them. The start of a scowl formed on Blake's face, while Maddie looked confused.

Brodie coughed. "There was ah … water on the floor. Tripped."

Blake's eyes narrowed and darted between the two of them, but understanding dawned in Maddie's eyes. She never missed a thing. Maddie'd be back later asking questions. No doubt about it. If not tonight, then at the fair tomorrow.

"Just so long as no one's hurt," Blake said cautiously.

Jamey spread her hands. "All good here. How was your meal?"

"Perfect," Maddie answered quickly, giving Blake a sideways glance.

Blake nodded. "Everything I expected. You're good, Jamey. Mason was impressed, too."

Jamey filled with warmth at the compliment. Nothing made her happier than when people were happy and filled up on her food.

"I was looking for Brodie, though," Blake continued, aiming a look at his brother. Brodie tensed beside her.

"I'm proud of you, little brother. You've got the hospitality part of this down. You're a natural. Get the numbers back on track and I think this is going to be a successful venture for all of us."

Brodie nodded. "Thanks."

"And Jamey, when we get this turned around, I'd like you to consider staying. You'd be an asset to the ranch."

Whoa.

That put a new twist on things. But was it the right choice for her, long term?

An awkward silence descended on the bunch. Maddie reached for Blake's hand. "We should go."

"Don't worry about bussing the dinner plates. We'll take care of them." Jamey met Maddie's eyes. "And thanks. I'm glad dinner was everything you'd hoped for."

Maddie's eyes narrowed slightly. Yeah. Maddie would definitely be back with questions. More importantly, would she have answers?

## Chapter Nineteen

*J*amey pulled Brodie's truck up to the back door, cut the engine, and grabbed the box of steaming biscuits from the front seat. Pink clouds streaked the early morning sky as she hurried into the kitchen. She had just under an hour to prepare early breakfast for Mason and his crew before they headed out to survey the bison herd with Blake. The rest of the guests would want later breakfast before they left for the county fair.

Placing Dottie's biscuits in the warming oven, she set to work on her newest scone formula. If these passed Mason's taste test, then maybe she could stop sneaking out to Dottie's every time she needed decent pastries. The woman's gloating smile irked her to no end. And this morning, Dottie made sure to point out that last year she won all three baking categories at the county fair.

As if Jamey gave two hoots about who won a baking contest at a county fair. Not when she'd trained in Paris. In her old life she'd have baked circles around Dottie. She quashed the wave of bitterness that hit in the back of her throat. Her old life was never coming back. She could wallow or move on. And if she didn't move on and figure out how to help Brodie keep the lodge afloat, she'd be out on her ass and homeless in a month. Blake's offer or not.

She patted her scone dough into a rough log and began slicing in zig-zags down the log. Grabbing a silicone pastry brush, she swept the top with a wash made from eggs, sugar, and cream, then popped them into the oven.

She'd slept terribly last night. What had she been thinking, *playing* with Brodie? Playing with fire... And the second she let her guard down, without fail, she tumbled right into his arms. Or pushed him against a wall. Her libido seemed to run unchecked as soon as he was within arm's length.

She blew out a long slow breath as she dumped the prep dishes into the sink and grabbed a sponge. Brodie was bad for her. Bad. Bad. Bad. His kisses were an aphrodisiac in the worst way. She burned hot when he was around. Hell, she burned hot when he *wasn't* around. That kind of chemistry would inevitably flame out, and she'd be left with nothing. Again. Her brothers were right. She needed to be with someone less hotheaded, less like her, more... boring.

She grimaced, furiously wiping at a sticky spot on the island. Too bad the idea of that left her as cold as aspic. She shuddered. She'd just have to do a better job of separating work and... not work.

Turning to the fridge, she grabbed the half 'n half and poured it into a pretty ceramic pitcher, placing it on a tray alongside a bowl of butter pats, strawberry preserves, and a jar of honey. Brodie stepped into the doorway as she rounded the island with the tray, blocking her in.

Without a word, he reached for the tray, his hands brushing hers. Even at this early hour, her body jumped in awareness. Electric currents spiraled up her arms, leaving a trail of tingles and settling into her sex.

"Can I take this?"

Keeping her distance would be so much easier if he was just an ass all the time. But noooo. He kept trotting out Hotcakes McCharmypants. She nodded mutely and retreated behind the island, trying to ignore the flush emanating from her breastbone. Thank God for her chef's coat. At least he couldn't see what his gaze did to her nipples. They pushed out against her tank, begging to be brushed with something harder than cotton spandex.

She was safely tucked behind the island, beating a bowl of eggs into submission, when he returned.

"Do you have a minute?"

Professional distance. She must keep professional distance. "No time. I'm right in the middle of breakfast prep." Damn, her voice sounded breathy and expectant.

He stepped up to the island, undeterred. "I promise, it will only take a few minutes."

She put down her whisk a little too forcefully. "Fine. You have four minutes. Mason and his crew are heading out with your brother this morning. I don't want to keep them waiting." She could do this. She could be the cool professional.

"Scout's honor."

"Why do I think that means nothing to you?" She rounded the island and followed him out the back door.

He crossed the yard to the structure he and Simon had completed two days before. On the ground in neat rows were several pallets of plant starts. And inside the structure were… chickens. Lots of them.

She stopped short. "I knew it! You *were* building a chicken coop."

He looked at her half expectantly, half nervously and jammed his hands into his pockets. "Is that okay?"

Her mouth suddenly wouldn't work. She opened it, but no sound came out. Her pulse started thrumming in her ears. "Of course. But I can't figure out why."

He rolled his eyes. "Why? You blasted the pants off my ass about not having stuff for the kitchen."

"You did this for me?"

He frowned uncertainly. "I sure as hell didn't do it for the livestock. Chickens are dirty and a pain in the ass."

Her heart slammed against her ribs. Nobody did nice things for her. Not like this. Not even her overprotective brothers. She opened her mouth again, but still couldn't form words.

He studied her intently. "Did I piss you off?"

She shook her head. "No… *no.*"

"You look like you swallowed a crawdad."

Her ribs ached as if she had.

He cleared his throat.

God, what was wrong with her mouth? She couldn't string two words together right now.

His eyes crinkled and softened as he smiled at her. "Go take a look." He nodded toward the door.

She stepped up to the structure and clutched the wire fencing. Peering through, she began to count. Three dozen. Perfect for a small kitchen. *If* she was staying.

Behind her, he cleared his throat again. "The hens probably won't start laying heavily 'till spring. But I figured it was a good investment. I picked up some greens and broccoli starts for later in the fall. You can plant them in the second fenced area, and the chickens will eat the bugs."

So *that's* why he'd built the second fence. She pivoted around, staring at him.

"I… ah have some pots out back by the barn that I'll plant with herbs, too. You can—"

Jamey closed the distance between them, covering his mouth with her fingers. "Stop. Just… stop." She couldn't handle this. This thoughtfulness. It left her off-kilter. Uncertain.

He stiffened at her touch, eyes wary.

But now she was touching him, she couldn't stop. Didn't want to. She moved her fingers from his mouth, caressing the stubble along his jaw and reveling in the rough sensation tickling her palm. Fuck professional distance.

Her own breath caught somewhere in the back of her throat. She gently scraped the pad of her thumb across his full lower lip, her thighs clenching at the sound of his sudden intake of breath. His eyes darkened and narrowed.

Slowly, as if something else was guiding her move-ments, she threaded her fingers through his hair, pulling his head the few inches to hers. His hands came to rest on her hips, searching for and finding the bare skin underneath her chef's coat.

She brushed her lips against his, murmuring against him. "Thank you."

His whole body shuddered and relaxed into her as he deepened the kiss, flicking his tongue across her lip. She sucked him in, and pulled him closer, pouring the words she didn't have into his mouth. The ache between her legs built as his fingers skittered across her bare flesh. But then without warning, he stepped back and she felt the loss of him immediately.

He flashed her a somewhat sardonic smile. "You're past your four minutes. Thought you didn't have time for me."

*Oooh.* His comment lit a spark in her, and an embarrassed flush crept up her neck. How did he manage to be all sweet one minute, and completely infuriating the next?

"Right. I'll be in the kitchen." So much for professionalism. She'd gone and thrown herself at him again. She spun on her heel and marched back across the yard to the kitchen door, shutting it extra firmly behind her. Only then, as the buzzing registered in her ears, did she remember the scones.

Flying to the oven, she yanked down the door and pulled them out.

Great.

She'd nearly burned the scones, too.

Maybe she needed to ban him from the kitchen. Or ban herself from him. Did he always have to be so damned cocky? What was she thinking, opening herself to him? Sex between them had been a blip. A consensual release. Nothing more. The quicker she got that through her skull, the safer she'd be.

"Everything okay?" Mason paused in the doorway, a concerned look on his face.

"Yes, yes. I'm fine. Grab some coffee. Eggs will be out in a sec. Try a scone will you?" She waved a hand toward the basket of scones on the island.

He raised an eyebrow. "Am I allowed back in here?"

"My kitchen. My rules." She threw him a smile. Banter with Mason was so much easier.

Probably because he didn't turn her insides into quivering custard the way Brodie did.

He approached the island and peeked under the cloth covering the scones. "These look great, but I'll pass."

She jerked the egg pan a little harder than she should have, flipping him a quizzical glance. "What do you mean?"

"I mean I don't do carbs anymore." He winked at her. "I need to keep my girlish figure."

She groaned. "Please don't tell me you're a paleo."

"In the flesh."

"And you waited until now to tell me?" Disappointment rushed through her. She needed someone with a developed palate to try them. Without knowing they were gluten-free. Maddie would automatically tell her they were wonderful, and she sure as heck wouldn't give Dottie the satisfaction of criticizing her baking. She plastered on her best professional smile and scooped the eggs out into a chafing dish.

"What was there to tell? Your food is great, and there's plenty for me to eat without you putting yourself out on my behalf."

"Puh-leeze." She rolled her eyes and gave the chafing dish a little shake. "I don't know whether to thank you or smack you."

"You're not bothering my chef are you?" Brodie stepped through the back door, his eyes narrowed at Mason.

"Back off, cowboy," Jamey snapped. "Or the only thing you'll get for breakfast is shoe leather." Why did his charm disappear the second Mason was around?

Brodie grabbed a scone from the basket and broke it apart, popping a corner in his mouth. He raised his eyebrows, grinning. "Mmm. That's good. Maybe now you'll stop sneaking out for Dottie's biscuits."

She opened her mouth then snapped it shut, her face flaming with embarrassment.

"Here." She shoved the egg pan at Brodie. "Make yourself useful and take these out to the sideboard."

Brodie took the pan and slipped through the door, giving Mason the stink-eye as he passed.

She heaved a sigh, shaking her head. "I'm sorry. He's got cactus prickers shoved up his ass."

Mason shot her a knowing smile. "I don't think that's his current problem."

"Oh?"

Mason shook his head. "You're one of a kind, Jamey. I think he's smitten."

Her insides clenched and flamed again. She shook her head vehemently, and pinched her nose. She hated that her emotions showed on her skin. But she was a redhead. There was no way to avoid it. "Just. Stop."

"Shall I quote you Shakespeare? Something about protesting too much?"

She pointed toward the door. "Out. Go eat your eggs."

Mason paused at the door. "It's obvious there's something between you." He took a breath like he was going to say more. Then he stopped, shaking his head. "Brodie's a good guy once you get to know him. You should give him a chance." He disappeared into the dining room, leaving her more flustered and confused than ever.

Should she give Brodie a chance? They had chemistry for days, but was that enough? Could she trust him? With her heart and her business?

## Chapter Twenty

*B*rodie waited for the signal to maneuver Captain into the box for his final team-roping round. He adjusted his grip on the rope one last time and rubbed his lucky competition buckle.

So far, he'd sucked.

He'd never been more embarrassed. Especially in front of Jamey.

The last two rounds, he'd missed the steer's heels entirely. He and Ben had slid from reigning champions in team roping, to town laughingstocks.

Hell, he'd have to get out of the fairgrounds fast if they didn't make it out of dead last. He hadn't brought a change of clothes and had no intention of participating in the ritual dunking that all the last place losers endured. It had been easy to go along with the ritual in years past, because he never lost.

Ever.

"Hey, Sinclaire," Jimmy Benoit called down from the fence. "I can taste that beer already."

Ben rode up alongside him, also checking his rope.

"Don't let him rattle you." He spoke low. "Jimmy's right though, you need to get your head in the box and off a certain lady."

Brodie shot Ben a little scowl. "What's that supposed to mean?"

"We've all seen how you can't keep your eyes off Jamey. Blake know you're involved with the help?"

He bristled. "She's not the help and you know it."

"You know what I mean. Blake's always insisted we stay away from anyone on the payroll."

"It's none of Blake's damned business what I do in my off time."

Ben's mouth flattened and he fixed him with a stern look. "You're not thinking with the right head, brother. Blake put a lot of faith in you with the lodge. Hell, I vouched for you. We can't afford a repeat of the vaccination fiasco."

Even though it had been more than fifteen years since the vaccination fiasco. Shame still gnawed at him. His whole life, everyone had assumed the worst about him, and he'd let them. It had been easier to hide behind a façade of clowning than to explain why he kept making mistakes. But he was gonna prove himself this time, or die trying. "Are we gonna rope or are you gonna sit here and lecture me?"

The cowboys motioned for him to enter the box.

Ben's eyes softened a fraction. "Be careful, okay? And for God's sake, keep your head up and your ass in the saddle. I don't wanna get dunked."

Brodie shook himself. Ben was right. His head wasn't in the box at all. He wheeled Captain around and backed him into the corner of the box, blanking his mind. He had to get this right, at least.

He loosened his grip on the rope and rolled back his shoulders, squeezing the saddle with his thighs. The steer came bursting out of the chute and Captain's muscles bunched beneath him.

Quick as lightning, they were off and through the barrier, ropes swinging. Ben's rope landed around the steer's horns and tightened, swinging the animal away and leaving a clear opening for him.

This time his rope sailed through the air, encircling the steer's hind legs. At his signal, Captain wheeled, and backed up. People could give him all the shit they wanted, but he had a damned fine horse.

Five and a half seconds.

Not great, but enough to move them up from dead last.

Ben cocked his chin, grinning as he circled Sergeant Pepper around. "Guess we dodged the bullet, huh? Good work."

"You still owe us a case of beer, Sinclaire." Jimmy's voice carried across from the fence.

"Yeah, yeah. You'll get your beer."

First things first. He wanted to see Jamey. He looped his rope over the saddle horn and trotted Captain out of the arena.

Jamey and Maddie were waiting for them. "You're a little rough around the edges today," Maddie chided with a soft smile.

He dismounted. "What do you expect when you're stuck working a lodge instead of livestock?" He should be grateful. Instead, he was just irritated.

"Could have been worse, Mads," Ben jumped in. "He could have gotten us dunked."

Jamey hung back, a little smile playing on her lips.

Brodie zeroed in on her. "What did you think?" The question was out of his mouth before he could stop it. A bundle of nerves settled in the pit of his belly. It shouldn't matter what she thought. She was just... what *was* she?

He didn't like where those thoughts were taking him. And yet…

"Yeah, Jamey," Maddie elbowed her, smirking. "What did you think?"

She shrugged, color tinting her cheekbones. But she met his gaze dead on, like she was really seeing *him* for the first time.

"Well?" He rocked back on his heels, waiting for her answer.

Maddie didn't wait. "I think her exact words were 'Jesus and the saints, that's hot. Like sex on a stick with chocolate sauce, hot.'"

His brows shot up, heat pooling in his groin at the thought of one or both of them covered in chocolate sauce. "Yeah?"

The pink in her cheeks transformed into a full-scale flush that started well below the scoop of her white shirt. His mouth went dry at the thought of her tits exposed and flushed like the rest of her.

"Hey. Eyes up here, cowboy."

He dragged his eyes back to hers and liked what he saw. Her eyes filled with appreciation… and invitation.

"So you liked what you saw?"

Her lips twitched. "You? On horseback? You were good."

"Wait 'til you watch the tie-down roping." He didn't want to brag or set up false expectation, especially after his piss poor performance in team roping, but a burst of confidence shot through him, expanding his chest. Hell, he could beat Captain America if she'd just keep looking at him like that, her eyes lit from within, and her wide mouth turned up at the corners.

"Enough with the heated stares, you two," Maddie

interrupted. She tugged on Jamey's arm. "Come on. I want to get a corn dog."

Jamey wrinkled her nose, still staring at him. "Eww. You shouldn't put carney food in your body Mads. Especially in your condition."

Was she telling him she would rather stay?

Shit.

He'd never been good at reading signals. Especially from women. All he knew was that he didn't want her to walk away. "Ben could take you, Maddie. Just as soon as he puts up Sergeant Pepper. I want to give Jamey a behind-the-scenes tour while I walk Captain."

That wasn't all he wanted to do, not by a long shot.

He'd hardly seen her out of her chef's clothes, and here she was, wearing a short skirt and a pretty white shirt, looking downright edible. He could overlook the hideous purple patent leather Doc Martens on her feet because he wanted nothing more than to pull that shirt up and run his fingers over the creamy skin at her waist.

Yeah.

Getting her alone would be a step in the right direction.

"That line work on all the skirts, cowboy?" Jamey winked at him.

He winked back. "Nope. Good thing you're not a skirt. Although you look mighty fine in that one."

Maddie arched a brow his direction. "I recognize that look in your eye. You be a gentleman, Brodie." She shot a look over to Jamey. "I'll be expecting a full report later."

Jamey reached out and patted Maddie's arm, a hard glint in her eyes. "For feck's sake, Mads. Do I look like a virgin about to be devoured on the way to confession? Have you forgotten my brothers?" She smirked and winked at him. "I could take Brodie in my sleep with one hand tied behind my back and the other mincing onions."

The picture of her bent over the kitchen counter, skirt rucked up and ass bared, swelled his cock to full mast. He could practically smell her arousal mixed in with the scent of barnyard and sweat. He held out his hand. "Come on."

## Chapter Twenty-One

$\mathcal{H}$e couldn't quite keep the rasp out of his voice. He swallowed hard, willing his tongue to form words. "I'll show you around."

"Be good, you two." Maddie's voice floated in the air behind them as Jamey slipped her hand into his.

"A little naughty's okay, though." Jamey glanced over at him, a sly smile playing at the corner of her lips.

"Not a lot of naughty?" His pulse quickened as he pictured her bent over a hay bale in some out-of-the-way corner. He led her away from the crowd toward the back-side of the fairgrounds. "Tell me, what's the naughtiest thing you've ever done?"

She raised an eyebrow. "Is this confession time?"

He shrugged, giving her a mischievous smile.

Her eyes filled with speculation. As if she was assessing him. He stood a little straighter as they wove through the rodeo contestants and he tightened his grip on Captain's reins. Lord, he hoped he measured up to whatever standard she was setting in her mind's eye. Finally, her silence moved him to speak. "Well?"

She gave his hand a little squeeze. "I'm trying to decide how much to tell you."

He leaned over and nuzzled her ear. "Don't worry darlin'. Your secrets are safe with me."

Her scent tantalized him. Sent little tingles across his chest, settling neatly in his balls. A man could get drunk on her just by breathing her in.

She hummed in the back of her throat and began to face him. But she pulled back. "You tryin' to butter me up?"

He drew her close, wrapping his arm around her back, bringing his mouth to within a breath of hers. "Would you let me? Butter you up?"

Her eyes lit, and she gasped a little, rocking her hip against his. Her free hand splayed across his chest, but she didn't push him away.

"Hmmm…. tempting."

He'd never played cat and mouse like this. Had never worked for a woman's affection. It frustrated him and, at the same time, was the hugest turn-on. He couldn't remember being this worked up from a conversation.

Ever.

He'd always scoffed at the notion that half of sex was in the brain, but maybe there was something to it. She made him want to keep pushing the verbal stakes higher. How far could he go before she'd blush and turn away? Or they'd finally kiss and burn up the energy between them?

A slow smile curved her lips. "All right." Her voice had gone low and husky. "You go first."

He stepped back. "Wait. What? You want me to go first?"

Shit.

The naughtiest thing he'd ever done was have sex against the wall of his office with her. The second naughtiest thing he'd ever done was lose his virginity to Kylee Ross in the back of the family pickup truck after the homecoming dance when he was sixteen.

Tangling with Kylee had brought him nothing but years of bitterness, culminating in the discovery last spring that she was the mother of his little half-brother Simon. It had taken him years to get over her veiled barbs about his inexperience their first time, something he'd set about remedying immediately. Thanks to her, he always made sure the lady he was with was satisfied. Problem was, he'd never liked a woman well enough or been driven crazy enough by a woman to care about sexual adventure.

That is, until Jamey.

She drove him wild.

Rutting stag wild.

He suddenly understood how two-thousand pound bulls could bash down a fence to mount a cow in heat. Every lascivious and naughty thought that entered his head he wanted to bring to life. With her.

He cleared his throat and swallowed. "Ahh. Okay…" He waited a moment, letting her anticipation build. "Back of the family pickup truck after the homecoming dance."

She raised her eyebrows, eyes laughing. "You have some catching up to do, cowboy."

He lifted a shoulder nonchalantly. "Usually takes two to play naughty."

"So it does. So it does."

The air charged between them like the atmosphere right before a big thunderstorm. "So you sayin' you like to play naughty?"

Her tongue darted out, wetting her lips before she captured the bottom one in her teeth. She looked at him straight on, her eyes hungry and hot. "Maybe…"

God, if that didn't just send his libido into overdrive.

His cock pushed painfully against his zipper, eager to be let out. Even though it wasn't as crowded where they stood, there were still too many people around. Especially for all the images that filled his head of the two of them, sweaty and tangled.

He shook himself. He had one more event in less than an hour. He needed to be sharp when he leapt off a horse going thirty, not sex drunk and slow. He reached up and slid his thumb across her lower lip.

Keeping her eyes on his, she captured the digit gently in her teeth and sucked. His balls squeezed hard.

Christ.

He was already buzzed and he hadn't even kissed her.

"Your turn, darlin'. You still haven't confessed." His voice came out all rumbly in an effort to hide the unbridled desire stampeding through his veins.

Her tongue swept across the pad of his thumb, and she gave him a little nip before releasing it. "Hmm... Yes... Indeed. You sure you want to hear?"

Was she toying with him? Some kind of feminine form of torture? Pink crept across her cheeks as she looked away briefly before bringing her eyes back up to meet his. "I've never even told Maddie this."

His chest inflated with satisfaction at her little confession. No one had ever entrusted him with a secret before. Sure, he had plenty of his own. Big ones. But that wasn't the same. "Spill."

Her cheeks were bright red now, but she didn't look away. Her eyes contained a hint of defiance. "The first orgasm I ever had was on the pool table of my pop's bar... while my brothers were in the storeroom counting inventory."

Damn.

Double damn.

Heat rose through his own body at the image of her splayed out and open for him on top of a pool table. In the Big House, at the Trading Post, hell... anywhere.

"Jesus, Jamey." His breath hissed out as straight up lust took hold of him and settled in deep in his belly.

His balls were going to burst if he didn't start walking again. Moving his arm to her elbow, he steered her and the horse to behind the farthest outbuilding.

Sliding a glance at her, he had to ask. "You really did that?"

Her saucy grin was enough of an answer.

"Hell. That's the hottest damn thing anyone's ever told me."

"You really need to get out more, Brodie."

"No. What I really need is a taste of you."

They were finally alone. Alone as they were going to get at the county fair, and he couldn't wait one second longer. He dropped Captain's reins and captured her face in his hands, driving his fingers into her silky curls. Bending his head, he paused one last time, brushing her lips with his and savoring the ache that would surely kill him if he didn't relieve it.

She sighed, and closed the remaining distance between them, opening her mouth to his.

Fire burned through him like a kerosene trail, and he grunted in return, reveling in the sweet taste of her tongue curling against his. There was so much more of her to taste, to savor. Her hands grasped just under his shoulders, squeezing. Fingernails digging through the thin cotton of his shirt.

Regretfully, he broke their kiss, breathing raggedly. "God. I want to taste all of you. And I don't have time. I want to do it right."

Her eyes glazed and widened. "I don't care about

proper. You should know that by now." She nipped at his lower lip.

He groaned, kissing her again and sweeping his tongue into the sweet recesses of her mouth. His cock pounded at his zipper. Riding a horse this worked up would only end in ridicule and disaster. He stepped back, willing his rocketing pulse to slow down. "I'm going to find out you're some kind of an Irish witch, aren't I?"

She rolled her head back against the rough painted wall, smiling like a self-satisfied barn cat. Reaching out, she captured his pants at the belt buckle, and pulled him against her. A feral light lit her eyes as she slid her hand over his arousal.

"You sure we don't have time to take care of this?" She gave him a little squeeze, nearly dropping him to his knees. "It wouldn't take long for me to turn around and lift my skirt. No one back here but us and the angels." She grinned devilishly.

He allowed himself one grind into her palm, his need for her rolling back his eyes. He bit back a moan. "Goddamn, Jamey. If I was done roping I'd strip you down to those hideous purple boots and make you holler my name."

A breathy giggle escaped her lips.

"But I can't just yet. I have to show you I can do this. What I'm good at."

Her eyes softened. She reached up and caressed his cheek, her voice thick with emotion when she spoke. "You don't need to prove anything to me, Brodie."

The conviction in her voice unleashed something hot and thorny inside of him. It swelled and rolled through his belly. He couldn't name it. Whatever it was, it was so foreign, so powerful, as it slammed into his chest, he nearly fell back.

"I see you," she whispered so softly he barely heard her.

His chest ached at the expression on her face. He had to get out of here, or his head wouldn't be in his next event. He wouldn't make a fool of himself twice in one day. Not in front of her.

He brought his hand up to cover hers. The swirl of emotion roughened his voice. "One more kiss for luck?"

She nodded and lifted her mouth. He liked she didn't have to stand on tiptoe to kiss him. Where the previous kisses they'd shared had been hot and unbridled, this one was painfully sweet. Feeling enveloped them, and she wrapped her arms around his neck.

He poured himself into her, silently thanking her for her faith in him.

He'd show her he was worthy.

He'd win, then take her home and make love to her until the birds started chirping.

## Chapter Twenty-Two

*J*amey shot an impatient glance at the clock on the wall above the pool table.

Nine o'clock.

Where in the hell was Brodie?

After he'd claimed his winnings from the tie-down roping contest, he'd suggested they meet at the Trading Post a little past six-thirty. She'd gone back to the ranch with Maddie, endured an hour of her pointed questions about the state of her relationship with Brodie, completed a little prep work for the next day's meals, and then hiked back to the Big House to catch a ride back into town with Maddie and Blake. And while the two of them had gone out of their way to include her, it was obvious she was a third wheel this evening.

"Earth to Jamey. It's your shot." Maddie peered at her over her soda. "You okay?"

Jamey scowled and made a shot, hitting Blake's ball into the center pocket.

Damn.

Under normal circumstances she was a decent pool

player. But getting stood up by the man you'd made out with at the rodeo didn't constitute normal. The last time she'd been stood up, she was sixteen and her brothers had chased off Jimmy O'Rourke, her homecoming date. And he hadn't even kissed her.

"Jamey." Maddie's hand pressed on her shoulder. "What's wrong?"

She shook her head. "Nothing. I'm fine. Long day."

What was she supposed to say? 'The man you've been teasing me about ditched me?'

She should have known better than to get all touchy feely with Brodie. She'd let him charm her yet again. And she should have double known better than to allow herself to start developing feelings for a business partner. Especially one who refused her help and insisted on struggling to keep the business afloat by himself.

Maddie studied her, obviously concerned, and clearly not buying her brush-off. "You know you can tell me anything, Jamey. I'm always here for you."

"I know." She forced herself to smile. "I've had a great day." Except for the last three hours.

She deserved every bad feeling she was experiencing. Hadn't she learned anything from Jean Luc's shenanigans? Maybe she should consider taking Mason Carter up on his offer. He knew how to run a business. Too bad she had no desire to live in the nether reaches of Montana.

Prairie was remote enough. At least here, she had friends, and a decent food scene to explore in Kansas City. Plus, Chicago was only a short flight away. Prairie might be small, but it wasn't the far end of the universe like Montana.

What she wanted, coveted, really – was to become a managing partner at a place like the lodge. She could make it something special. An environmentally friendly, local food, hunting mecca. She didn't care about the hunting necessarily, but the variety of game and fowl would keep her on her culinary toes.

Maddie elbowed her. "Axel and Gunnar just walked in. You should go dance with them."

"They're cute and all, but not my type, Mads." She circled the table looking for another shot, one that she could actually sink this time.

"Yeah, you like those bad boy types… like Brodie. Deny all you want, but I saw the way you were looking at each other today. You were practically making out with your eyes."

"Oh?"

"Yeah. And I don't know what Blake and I walked in on in the kitchen last night, but I don't believe for a second you were cleaning up a spill."

Ah, yes. The inevitable second round of questioning had begun. She shrugged, and chalked her cue.

"Your nonchalance doesn't fool me for a second, Jamey." Maddie sighed heavily and rubbed her burgeoning belly absently. "Look. Brodie may have his flaws… heck, Blake does. But he's got a good heart. And I don't think he'd hurt you on purpose. Not the way Jean Luc did."

Maddie didn't know the half of it, and would be hurt when she found out. Jamey'd had ample opportunity to tell Maddie about the celiac diagnosis today, but it had never felt right. She was managing the kitchen just fine, and if she and Brodie could get the lodge going in the right direction, then she'd feel better about spilling the beans to Maddie and Blake. She wanted to prove she could still cook five-star food first.

Jamey flashed her friend a tight smile. "Thanks for the advice, but I meant what *I* said, too. I can take care of myself."

Her brothers would disagree. If they had their way, she'd move back to Boston and settle down with a nice, boring, unadventurous Irish Catholic boy from the 'hood. The thought of that churned her stomach. But maybe they had a point. Maybe boring was better. Less excitement. *Less heartache.*

A hand tapped her shoulder.

She whipped around, hoping. But the hand belonged to Travis Kincaid.

"Care for a dance before I report for duty?"

Her heart sank as she flashed him a smile. "Sure." She'd rather be dancing with Brodie. Damn his sorry ass.

Travis took her hand and led her onto the dance floor. "What'd you think of your first rodeo?" He spun her around the floor, keeping time with the music.

"Oh, I had fun." She kept her smile carefully in place.

"What was your favorite part?"

This was why she *hated* dating. She was socially awkward and was happier perfecting her craft in the kitchen than making small talk with strangers. Even nice strangers like Travis.

"My favorite part?"

Travis looked at her quizzically. "Yeah. Most women like bull riding and bronc riding the best."

She had a favorite part all right, and it wasn't the bull riding. It had been watching the fierce determination in Brodie's eyes as he focused on roping a steer. It had been the way he'd launched himself off his horse and whipped the calf's legs together. And his triumphant smile when he'd realized his time was fastest. But she'd never admit that to anyone, let alone Travis.

So she injected enthusiasm into her voice. "Oh yeah. Bull riding. So exciting. Those guys are crazy."

Travis's eyes clouded for a brief moment. "Yeah. Bull and bronc riders are a special kind of crazy. I know."

"Why do you say that?"

"My brother, Colton. He rides broncs for a living. I've seen that kind of crazy up close."

He kept his voice light, but his eyes held a glimmer of pain.

"Was he here today?"

"Oh no. He stays far away from Prairie."

"Why?"

His smile didn't quite reach his eyes. "Prairie is small beans. Not for pros."

"Ahh. I see."

The music filled the silence between them as they continued to circle the dance floor.

Travis moved smoothly, was good looking and personable. But there was no… zing.

No flutter in her belly.

No smoldering glances.

Was this the best she could do?

If all she had to look forward to was boring on one end or hot but unreliable on the other, she'd rather die a spinster chef and get eaten by the rats that lurked by the dumpster.

## Chapter Twenty-Three

*B*rodie strolled through the doors of the Trading Post in high spirits. Half his winnings were in his pocket, the other half in the bank. He'd dutifully paid Jimmy and his brother their two cases of beer for having lost at team roping and had stuck around the grounds to enjoy a few with them and some of the other local ranchers.

He scanned the crowd for Jamey. He couldn't wait to pick up where they'd left off this afternoon. The whole drive over from the fairgrounds, his mind had traveled a very naughty road, one that ended with the two of them tangled in the sheets on his bed.

Blake, Maddie, her cousins, and some of the lodge guests, including Mason Carter, were grouped around one of the pool tables in the back, but he didn't see Jamey. Until he caught a flash of red hair on the dance floor. Where she was dancing with Travis Kincaid.

What. The. Ever. Loving. Fuck?

Jealousy shot through him, and he ground his teeth together.

His vision hazed as she laughed at something Travis said when he leaned his head in close.

Un*fucking*believable.

After everything that had happened this afternoon, she was spending *their* date in the arms of another man? *Laughing*?

A low growl rumbled up from his belly as he clenched and unclenched his fist. He strode over to the dance floor, ignoring the urge to lay Travis flat, and tapped him on the shoulder.

Jamey's eyes widened when she saw him, then immediately narrowed. "Nice of you to show up, cowboy." She crossed her arms, glaring.

Not the welcome he was expecting. "What's that supposed to mean? Why wouldn't I show up? I wanna know why you're spending our date dancing with him?" He tilted his head at Travis.

Jamey's eyes flashed fire... and hurt. "Why wouldn't I? I was sick of waiting around a second longer for your sorry, skeeving ass to show up. I waited *over three hours*."

Travis cleared his throat. "Ah, I'll see you around Jamey. I gotta get to work soon."

She shook her head vehemently. "Stick around, this won't take long."

"You two look like you need to talk. I'll see you around." Travis disappeared into the crowd.

Brodie took a step closer. "I don't understand. It's just a little after six-thirty. I'm right on time." Brodie spoke with bravado he was rapidly losing.

"Really?" Her eyes shot daggers. "Check again Jizzle McShinglepants. The clock says it's after nine-thirty. Did you happen to notice it getting dark?"

Dread pooled in his gut.

It couldn't be after nine-thirty.

He hadn't spent that long with the guys out at the fairgrounds. Had he?

"In trouble with time again, Brodie?" Kylee Ross had sidled over, a tray of empty beers in her hands. "You never did learn how to tell time, did ya?" Her eyes glittered in mean triumph.

"Shut up, Kylee," Jamey spit out, not taking her eyes off him. "This is between me and Cowboy Careless here."

He shook his head, shame surging through him, heating the back of his neck. "Now just a big fat second. This can all get cleared up–"

She shook her head, lips pressed into a thin line. "There's nothing to clear up, Brodie. I made a mistake. One that I won't make again."

Dread morphed into panic.

No. *Nononono.*

He reached out a hand to stop her. "Wait. Jamey. I can explain."

She shrugged him off, shaking her head. "There's nothing to explain." Her eyes were pools of sadness. The recognition he'd caused that made him feel sick. A sharp pain sprouted and twisted in his chest. "Jamey. *Please.*"

Desperation rushed through him. She couldn't turn on him. She couldn't. This had been an honest mistake. Hell, it wasn't like he'd cheated on her. *She* was the one dancing with someone else.

Travis returned, placing a hand on Jamey's shoulder. "Everything okay?"

"Everything's fine, Travis," Brodie ground out, glaring at the other man.

Jamey flashed Travis a smile, igniting a punishing arrow of jealousy that coursed through him like wildfire.

"Brodie and I were just coming to an... understanding."

Like hell they were. "We'll talk about this later, Jamey."

Her eyes narrowed again. "There's nothing to talk about. *Nothing.*"

The pain in his chest squeezed harder. He opened his mouth to respond, but she had already whirled away, leading Travis back to the dance floor.

He locked his knees as the urge to punch the daylights out of something, or *someone*, overwhelmed him. Clenching his jaw and stretching his fingers, he marched over to the bar, dug out a twenty, and tossed it on the worn wood. "A shot of Jack, double. And a beer chaser."

It wasn't scotch, but it would do. Anything to numb the anguish that bounced around his ribcage. He still wasn't exactly sure what had happened. So he was late. Really late, apparently. Was that the end of the world? He swore when he'd looked at his watch it had said six-thirty.

The bartender placed the shot and the beer on the counter before him. Brodie took the shot glass and downed the contents in one gulp, feeding off the burn. He shook it off, then chugged the cold beer.

Fuck her.

She wasn't his type anyway.

Too damned scrawny.

He scanned down the bar looking for someone pretty to talk to. There were a handful of pretty faces to choose from. The county fair always brought in new people. He should get right on it. Right after he had another shot.

Blake stepped up next to him, eyes furrowed. "How many shots you had?"

Brodie had no idea. Or how long he'd been sitting at the bar. "Only a couple."

Blake arched an eyebrow. "Only a couple."

"S'what I said."

"Hhmph."

Why in the hell was Blake always checking up on him? "There something else you wanted to ask?"

"Why don't you come shoot a round with us? Maddie went home to bed."

He shrugged and slid off the barstool. The world tilted a bit, but quickly righted itself. How many shots had he had? Not nearly enough. He could still see Jamey's face every time he shut his eyes. A few more rounds and she'd be the furthest thing in the world from his thoughts.

Mason smiled and handed him a pool cue. "Great roping today. I could use someone with your talent if you ever want to come to Montana."

He scowled. "What. You think I'm not good enough to run the lodge? Be a big businessman like you?"

A look of exasperation crossed Mason's face. "Hey, I don't know what your problem with me is, but be cool."

Something dark and ugly inside him snapped. He charged Mason, pinning him up against the pillar with his elbow across his throat. "You wanna know what my problem is?" He growled, feeding off the anger that had been building since Jamey had turned her back on him. "I'll tell you what my problem is. You come in and throw around your money and your advice. You try and steal my help."

Two sets of hands yanked him back. He staggered as the room spun, then fought to break loose from the bodies dragging him toward the door. At least that's where he thought they were dragging him. He wasn't sure because the room kept moving.

A boot connected to a door with a thud, and the warm night air caressed him as the ground rushed up to meet his face.

"What in the *fuck* do you think you're doing?" Blake bent toward him, roaring in his ear. "I'll be goddamned if you ruin my business by attacking one of my guests."

Brodie rolled over digging an elbow into the gravel in an attempt to rise. "Oh. So it's my business until I fuck it up, and then it's yours?" He hurled himself forward, bringing himself to his knees and slowly to his feet. Since when did the world feel so jiggly? He raised his hand, leveling a finger at his brother. "Wait. I get it. You're just looking for an excuse to kick me off the property now. Is that it?"

Blake glowered at him, arms crossed.

He took a step forward, focusing on Blake's hard expression. "That's it, isn't it? I've never been good enough, have I? I'm the dumb one. Can never do anything right. Well fuck this. I'm outta here." He waved his hand, dismissing Blake. "Don't mean nothing anyways."

"Don't get in that truck, Brodie."

He stopped, drawing his hands into fists. "What else you gonna tell me to do, brother? Gonna tell me when to piss and take a shit too?"

"You're in no condition to drive."

"Leave me alone. I'm fine."

Blake's boots crunched on the gravel behind him. "I mean it. I won't hesitate to tell Travis to haul you in."

"Fuck you, asshole."

Blake spun him around, eyes harsh under the cold light of the lone parking lamp.

"You know what your problem is, Brodie? You're a spoiled punk. No one ever took a strap to you when you were a kid. Ma felt sorry for you because you struggled more than the rest of us. She wouldn't lift a hand. I hate to tarnish her memory, but she did you a disservice."

The ache he'd worked so hard to eliminate came crashing back, pushing against his ribs with the force of a raging bull. "She did not." He knew he was shouting, but he didn't care. "You have no idea what it was like. You were… perfect. And never home."

Blake threw back his head and laughed harshly. "It's time for you to grow up and start taking responsibility for your actions. Ma never gave you tough love. I don't have that problem."

"Shut up. Just. Shut. Up." He pinched his nose, breathing in and out through his mouth and trying to focus on the toe of his boot. But it kept moving.

A vehicle rolled to a stop just behind him, boxing in his truck. Great. How in the hell was he supposed to get out of here now?

The car door slammed, and footsteps crunched across the gravel. "There a problem here, Sinclaire?"

Blake's face shuttered. "Take his keys, Travis. He's six sheets to the wind." He turned on his heel and stalked back through the door into the bar.

Travis placed his hand on his service belt and extended his hand. "I can drive you home tonight."

"I don't need your damned help," Brodie snarled, adjusting his stance.

"No need to get belligerent. I can't let you get in your truck."

Brodie took a step forward, placing his hands on his hips. "What are you plannin' to do about it, Kincaid?"

Travis shook his head, studying the gravel. "You're gonna back down right now."

Brodie growled, taking another step closer. "Or what?"

Quick as lightning, he was face down eating gravel, the

breath knocked out of him with a big 'oomph'. Travis's knee pressed painfully between his shoulders. "Don't ever fuck with an officer, Sinclaire," he ground out. "You'll always come out on the losing side." Travis shook him hard for emphasis. "Now I'm gonna do you a favor. I won't press charges. And you're going to get up and crawl into the backseat of my vehicle without saying a word."

He grunted.

"Not a word. Understand?"

He nodded, his cheek scraping along the pebbles.

"You can sit in the drunk tank until you can find someone to come get you. Give me *any* guff and you'll have a record so fast no one in town will hire you for anything."

He nodded again, the world spinning, and despair leaking out of him like the ooze from a broken toilet bowl.

## Chapter Twenty-Four

*B*rodie woke up shivering in the corner of Prairie's lone cell. The stench of stale urine, vomit, and sweat dripped from the pale green walls. Why in the hell was he here? The last thing he remembered was pleading with Jamey in front of Travis.

"Travis? Travis." He winced at the sound of his voice echoing off the walls. Was this some kind of a sick joke? Had Travis arrested him to get him out of the way?

Nah. Travis was pretty stand-up. He liked Travis. Except when his paws were all over Jamey. Then he wanted to break him to pieces.

He dropped his head back to the cool cement. How much energy would it take to move his body to look out the window in the door? Heaving out a breath, he pushed himself up, then locked his knees as the room spun.

Damn.

He'd really fucked up this time.

Squinting and breathing deeply, he willed himself to focus on the door.

A picture of his arm across Mason's neck came to him.

And Blake yelling at him. But that wasn't unusual. Until Maddie, Blake usually yelled at him for something. Maybe he shouldn't have gotten into it with Mason. He peered out the dirty window. No Travis.

Damn, he was thirsty. His mouth felt like the inside of a cat box.

Fuck it.

He had to get out of here. What time was it anyway? Had he slept here all night? His sense of time was just plain off. Jamey had made *that* perfectly clear. He'd set his alarm for six-thirty and had left the fairgrounds when it had gone off. Did she think so little of him that after what they'd shared, he'd blow her off?

The realization that she did, twisted in his gut.

And thanks to his idiocy, he was sitting his sorry ass in the drunk tank trying to piece together the remains of his night.

"Travis. Come on, man." He drove his fist against the glass, flinching with each blow as the echo triggered stars behind his eyes.

After what seemed like ages, Travis slowly walked around the corner, hands thrust in his jacket pocket. He'd known Travis for years and had never seen the steely look in his eye before.

"Step back from the door, Sinclaire."

Raising his hands, he stepped back into the corner of the small cell.

"Stay where you are. Don't move."

"Jesus… fuck, Travis." He thrust his hand through his hair. "Do I look like a criminal?"

The vein in Travis's temple throbbed visibly as his jaw tightened. "Threatening an officer is a crime. So yes. You do."

His stomach dropped to his toes, making the room

spin. Panic filled in the void where his stomach used to reside. He'd done lots of stupid shit in his life. Too much, if he was honest with himself. But he'd never cross the line and assault Travis while he was on duty. Off duty was another story.

"I gotta know, man. Did you arrest me?"

Travis's mouth thinned. He shook his head once. "You were this close." He held his thumb and forefinger together, glaring at him. "If a stranger had pulled what you did, he'd be in the clink at county."

Relief washed over Brodie. A lump formed in his throat as the gravity of what he'd avoided, sunk in. He swallowed, not trusting his voice to work. He braced his hand against the cool concrete and tried again to piece together what had happened. "So… ah… how bad was it?"

"Bad enough you're here. Your brothers can fill you in."

He nodded. Blake would skin him alive. No doubt about it. A new realization dawned as he considered Blake.

Oh, God.

Was this it?

Would this be the straw that broke the camel's back?

What if Blake kicked him off the property? Told him to get out? Hot tears pricked the back of his eyes as loss swept through him.

*OhgodOhgodOhgodOhgod*

Where would he go?

He brought a fist to his forehead, squeezing his eyes tight. Prairie was the only place he knew. He'd never worked off the ranch, never gone to college like his brothers, never dreamed of living anywhere else. He staggered to the stainless steel toilet and wretched the remaining sour contents of his stomach. He would do anything to stay. *Anything.*

"Feel better now you have that shit outta you?"

He shook his head, swiping his mouth across his sleeve. If anything, he felt worse.

And scared.

Brodie coughed, clearing his throat. "Can I, uh… make a phone call?"

Travis tossed him a cell phone, but he was too slow to catch it. The phone clattered by his boots, skidding behind him. He bent slowly, the room still wobbly. There was only one person he could call. He prayed to heaven she'd answer. If she didn't, he was screwed six ways to Sunday, and more than likely, out on his ass for good.

Only he didn't know Jamey's number.

Fuck.

He'd had her punch in the numbers then taken her picture. Everyone in his phone was findable by picture. Bile rose in the back of his throat, threatening to choke him in a flood of despair. He clenched the phone in his fist. "Uhh… you mind if I use my own phone?"

Could he be any more pathetic?

Travis studied him intently. "Sorry, man. You know the rules. No personal possessions on the inside."

Panic fluttered at the edges of his conscious. "Aww, come on, man. Just one call."

Travis shook his head, his face hard. "You're already on thin ice. Use the phone or don't." He held out his hand silently demanding the phone.

There was no faking his way out of this. And it irked him to no end that Travis Kincaid of all people would learn it first.

Godfuckingdamn his worthless life.

His throat swelled from the ache, and he swallowed

hard before tearing his eyes away from Travis's outstretched hand.

"Can you call her for me?" His voice came out in a mumble.

"Come again?"

Brodie cleared his throat, trying to see through the film of shame clouding his vision. "Would you mind calling Jamey for me? I… ah… didn't memorize her number."

Travis glared at him. "You're a piece of work. Know that, Sinclaire? A fucking piece of work. Gimme that phone."

He tossed it back to Travis, who caught it easily and punched a few buttons, bringing it up to his ear. Shit. Travis had her phone number? Now would be a good time for the earth to swallow him up. Shame radiated off his body in waves, taking the chill out of the cement walls for the first time since he'd stuttered awake.

Travis's voice cut through his fog. "Jamey? Yeah, it's Travis. Sorry to wake you… no… nothing's really wrong… No… no one's hurt… I'm here with Brodie… No… no. He's more… incapacitated than injured… Will you talk to him?"

Brodie snuck at look at Travis out of the corner of his eye. Asshole had a smirk the size of Texas.

Travis nodded, glancing at Brodie, as her muffled voice drifted out of the phone. No doubt about it. Travis was enjoying this extra bit of humiliation, and Jamey was pissed as hell. Brodie unclenched his fist, taking a shuddering breath.

"Well, you'll have to ask him that…" Travis extended the phone. "Five minutes." He stepped back, and slammed the door behind him.

The reverberation set off another round of daggers poking behind Brodie's eyes. He pinched the bridge of his nose, bracing for the worst. "Jamey?" His voice came out hoarse.

"Is there a reason Travis is calling me at let's see… three-thirty-seven in the morning?"

"Look. I know I messed up. Big time."

She harrumphed in agreement.

He swallowed hard. "And… I know I have a lot of explaining to do, which I want to, but not over the phone."

Silence stretched between them.

"But please… I need your help right now…"

The silence continued.

Hell, he deserved every bit of her wrath and then some. If he was going to have to beg, so be it. "Please, Jamey. There's no one else I can ask."

Her snort told him exactly what she thought.

"Okay, no one else I want to ask. Please?"

"If you're calling me because your twisted brain somehow thinks you'll be in less hot water than if you call one of your brothers, you are sorely mistaken."

"No. No. It's not that at all." His throat hitched as a shot of emotion spiked in his chest. "I owe you the most. And I… and I… want to… no, I *need* to explain to you first."

Oh, God.

He'd made such a mess of things. He'd been faking things so long, hiding behind bluster, booze, and one-night stands, that the thought of shedding it all and exposing the real Brodie, scared him shitless. And yet, if he didn't, she'd walk out and never come back. He was certain of it. The realization punched him square in the gut, taking his breath away.

She was important to him.

Her approval was important to him. More important than anyone else's. And he'd crawl over broken glass to make things right with her. "Please, Jamey. Please, will you hear me out?"

His heart squeezed tighter with every second of silence. Finally, after what seemed like minutes, her breath whooshed into the phone. His own breath released with hers.

"Fine. Where are you?"

He braced himself for the onslaught of anger. "I'm... ah... down at the station." Might as well get through it fast, like tearing off a Band-Aid. He rushed on, hearing her quick intake of breath. "There was an incident at the Trading Post."

"An incident?" Sarcasm dripped from her voice.

Ouch. He deserved that. He nodded. "Please, Jamey. Give me a chance? I promise I'll explain everything. Answer any question. All of them. Just please come get me?"

He would never drink like that in public again. Hell, ever again, if it meant having her stay in his life.

"Fine."

His knees gave a little, and he leaned against the wall as relief washed over him. It didn't matter she'd hung up on him before he'd been able to say thanks. He'd make it up to her a hundred times, and more.

## Chapter Twenty-Five

*J*amey tugged the coat tighter around her shoulders as she trudged up the darkened road. It was still a few hours before sunrise, and the air held just a tinge of the coming fall.

Damn Brodie's sorry ass.

She should be trying to get a few winks, not hiking into town to fetch him from the drunk tank. She'd wasted enough time and tears on him already.

Her feet crunched along the dirt as she passed the Big House, looming in the moonlight. At least the sky was beautiful. She'd never experienced skies like this, living in Boston and Chicago. Even with the half moon sinking down to the horizon, stars littered the sky overhead, their white points sparkling like glitter over spun sugar.

Was she making a mistake betting on Brodie?

If Jean Luc had pulled this, she'd have kicked him out on his ass and that would have been that.

So why was it different with Brodie?

Was it because he was her best friend's brother-in-law?

She chewed on her lip as she trudged the last leg down to the road. Nope. That wasn't it.

It was something about them... *him*.

The way she caught him staring when he thought she wasn't looking. The way he listened to her ramblings, then did things like build a chicken coop. It wasn't romance, but it was startlingly thoughtful.

He had way too much swagger for his own good. But she got the sense he was trying to put her first, even if his words came out wrong. And they were hot together. Jesus and the saints, did they burn hot. She'd never experienced the sensation of being broiled from the inside until she'd kissed him.

Somehow, around him, she felt more herself. That was new.

Different.

Unsettling.

Exhilarating.

So yeah... here she was before the ass-crack of dawn, heading into town, on foot, to bail him out. "You better be worth it." Her voice cut through the dark, jarring her ears. Even the birds weren't awake.

She paused underneath the large wrought iron arch that announced the edge of the Sinclaire property as headlights in the distance moved steadily closer. They slowed, and she recognized the patrol car that wheeled around on the empty road.

Travis.

The passenger window lowered.

"You didn't have to come back. Brodie can wait on me," she chastised as she leaned into the window.

"I wouldn't be a gentleman if I knowingly let a lady walk into town. Hop in."

She opened the passenger door and slipped in. "I won't

turn you down. Not when I've got mouths to feed later this morning."

"How's it going out there?"

"The lodge? Pretty good, actually. We're making progress."

Travis's made a noise in the back of his throat.

"What? Did I say something wrong?"

He shook his head. "No, no... It's nothing."

Realization dawned on her. "Wait. You're pissed at Brodie."

"I just don't like to see a lady like you treated poorly."

"And you think he's a fuck-up." She found herself getting defensive on Brodie's behalf. Yes, he'd fucked up... big time. But he wasn't a fuck-up. Not by a long shot.

Travis shrugged. "He has a track record."

"You know how to beat around the bush."

Travis's face looked grim in the dashboard light. "Life's too short for innuendo." He pulled into the Trading Post parking lot and stopped behind Brodie's truck. He jammed his hand into his coat pocket and pulled out a set of keys. He looked her in the eye as he placed them in her hand. "Have dinner with me."

She held his frank gaze for a moment. "Why?"

"You look like you need a friend."

She didn't get the tingles when Travis touched her. Not even an extra thump from her heart. Certainly no pulse racing or mental distraction. Travis was good looking. And nice.

Was there something wrong with her?

Was she truly out of her mind when it came to Brodie? Did she have feelings for him, or did she just have crazy?

She slid out of the car. Her hand trembled a bit as she pulled open the door and hopped into the cab of the truck. She liked Travis. But if she was honest with herself, whatever dance she and Brodie were embroiled in, she wanted to see where it led.

Longing for her brother, Jarrod, shot through her. Not that she'd *ever* take his dating advice. She just wished she could… talk with him. Maddie was too close to the drama. She jammed the truck into reverse and spun out of the lot, following Travis the six blocks to the station.

Travis stood waiting outside the squad car when she pulled up. He opened her door and helped her out of the cab. Placing an arm at her elbow, he led her into the station, all business. "He's in rough shape, just so you know. And headed for one helluva hangover."

All the anger toward Brodie that had simmered down since the night before, resurrected in mammoth proportions.

Damn Brodie.

Damn him for standing her up. For leading her on. For not coming home and worrying the heck out of her, then waking her up at an indecent hour. For confusing the ever living fuck out of her.

She stopped, pulling Travis to a stop with her. "About dinner. Yes. Tonight."

His eyebrows shot up. "Yeah?"

"Yeah. Now let me see him." She steeled herself, letting her anger burn white-hot.

Travis unlocked the door and pushed it open, letting her through first. It was a modest holding area. Not like the big one she'd visited in Boston where her brother was an officer. It still smelled the same, though.

Then he unlocked the holding cell door and pushed it open. "Your ride's here."

Brodie shuffled out, a crooked smile not quite reaching his bloodshot eyes. He nodded at Travis and coughed. "Appreciate it, man."

Travis caught him by the arm, glaring. "You got a pass this time. You won't get one again."

Brodie nodded. "I know. I'm sorry." He shifted his attention to her, smiling tentatively. "Jamey, sweet–"

Fury spotted her vision. The hurt he'd inflicted, the worry, the confusion – all of it. If she softened now and let him off the hook with an, 'aw shucks, it's okay,' this would happen again.

That much she'd learned in life.

If she and Brodie were going to make sense of whatever was between them, this could never happen again. And she knew herself well enough to know it would take *at least* a day of solid toil in the kitchen before her anger dissipated. Maybe then, she could bring herself to listen objectively.

She held up her hand, cutting him off. "Don't you *dare* sweetheart me."

She shot a glance over to Travis. "You need to walk us out?"

"Nah. I've got paperwork I need to process. See you tonight at seven?"

Brodie stood up a little taller, looking back and forth between the two of them, understanding dawning on his face. "Wait." He glowered at her. "You're going on a date with *him?*"

She glared right back at him. "Oh no you don't, sewer breath. Not a word."

She looked back to Travis. "Eight-thirty is better. Gives me time to clean up after dinner."

Brodie harrumphed and she glared at him again. "Not a word or you walk home."

She spun on her heel and pushed through the doors that separated the holding cell from the rest of the tiny station, struggling to keep her emotions in check.

## Chapter Twenty-Six

The tires squealed as Jamie gunned the truck into reverse and spun it back around toward the ranch.

Shit.

*Shit. Shit. Shit.*

Brodie knew he was beyond being in hot water. He was in burning lava land. Although he was still pretty woozy, he was certain he'd seen real sparks coming from her hair. All the panic he'd managed to push away after hearing her voice on the phone, came rushing back.

How was he going to make this up to her? He had to start damage control fast, or she'd kick him off the property before Blake did. A tiny voice inside him raised its head. *No. Way. This is your property, man.*

Yeah.

It was his property.

Sort-of…

Mostly…

Hell, if she went to Blake and demanded it, Blake would kick him off. What if she'd already done that? Not likely. It was four-thirty in the morning. So she hadn't gone to Blake. *Yet.* And that meant he needed to start damage control right away. Question was, how in the heck would he do that? He didn't know the first thing about damage control.

Fuck.

Only one thing to do. Man up.

He needed to take the bull by the horns and man the fuck up. Fear and shame mingled in his gut, tightening into an angry black knot and threatening again to empty what little was left in his belly.

He snuck a glance at her.

She clutched the wheel so tightly, the whites of her knuckles glowed in the dim light. Her whole body vibrated in anger.

Might as well test the waters.

He cleared his throat.

"Not a word." She kept her eyes straight ahead.

He trained his eyes out the window, shutting them when the movement became too much for his stomach.

If there was a hell, this was surely it.

She slowed the truck to make the turn into the ranch, then gunned it again, taking the bumps like a bat out of hell.

"Slow down, woman. You trying to get us killed?"

She eased up slightly on the pedal, but not enough to quell the contents of his stomach. The truck skidded to a jerky halt, and he squeezed his eyes shut, willing himself to not be sick. The last thing he needed was to get sick in front of Jamey. Letting out a shaky breath, he opened the door and stumbled out, grabbing the frame for balance while the world slowly spun into place.

She tromped around the front of the truck, tossing a glare over her shoulder as she yanked open the back door to the lodge. "We'll talk after you've cleaned up and I've fed our guests. I'm already running late."

He shut the truck door quietly and took the long way around to the front door. Best let her cool off a bit more. Surely this couldn't go on forever? The bite in the early morning air helped clear his head, and he stood out front, hands on hips, taking in big gulps of air.

Would confessing to Jamey be worse than this? Right here, right now?

He let out a slow breath. Probably not.

Would it be worse than the day he'd learned about Simon?

Definitely not.

For someone who'd spent the better part of his life avoiding pain and discomfort, he sure had more than his share of both. Hell, he'd been the cause of most of it. Was he man enough to own the consequences of his actions? The question loomed large in his mind as he opened the door and quietly entered.

Thirty minutes, four Advil, and a hot shower later, he was ready to find out. He paused in the doorway to the kitchen.

Jamey's back was to him. She chopped furiously at something, then lifted the cutting board and scraped the contents into the pan on the stove. She responded to the sizzle with a little smile of satisfaction, then moved back to the counter. He watched another pass before clearing his throat and entering her domain.

Without waiting for her to speak, he moved around the island, grabbed a clean dishtowel from the drawer, and stepped up next to her as he tied it at his back.

She side-eyed him, and returned to her chopping. After a long moment, she spoke. "First, take the coffee carafes and set up the coffee. Next, bring out the half 'n half from the fridge and put it next to the sugars. While you're waiting for the eggs, you can set out the glasses, then the silverware. The plates are in the dining room, inside the sideboard."

Damn.

He'd never remember it all.

He'd always sucked with lists.

He exhaled slowly. *Man up. Man up.* "Uh, Jamey?"

She glanced at him, arching her brow. Her face remained inscrutable.

"I'm sorry. I don't do well with lists… hard to keep straight. Can I get those one at a time when I'm done with each?"

Her eyes registered surprise, but she nodded curtly and returned to chopping.

He grabbed a coffee carafe in each hand, then headed for the dining room. He knew she ran through several pots a morning, so before interrupting her, he refilled the pots and set them going again. Half 'n half was next, so he brought that out to the sideboard and placed it next to the sugars. For the life of him, he couldn't remember what was next.

She was at the stove now, stirring. The lines on her face seemed less severe.

"Jamey?" The word 'Sweetheart' almost rolled off his tongue. He sucked in a breath. The last thing he wanted was to set her off.

"Set the table. You'll find what you need under the sideboard."

By the time he'd finished setting the table, the eggs were in a chafing dish on the island, and she was bent over the oven, bringing out a tray of scones.

"No Dottie biscuits this morning?" He grinned.

She glared.

He lifted his hands, stepping back. "No offense meant. Your scones are fantastic."

Her face softened. "Yeah?"

"Yeah. I like them better than the biscuits." Hell, he'd eat a whole tray, making the appropriate lusty noises if it helped win her back.

"Take the eggs. I'll have the scones ready when you return."

She laid the final scone in the basket as he reentered the kitchen. "Take these, then bring out the juice from the fridge." She held out the basket, and his hands covered her fingers as he took it. A slow tingle stirred in his chest as he held the basket between them. Her eyes widened and she sucked in a tiny breath.

"Don't go out with him. With Travis." Great. Now he'd done it. Why couldn't he keep his mouth shut?

"Don't." She shook her head. "Not now." She slipped her hands from his and ducked away, putting dishes in the sink.

There was nothing left to do but take the scones out and try not to wallow in embarrassment. At least she hadn't shut him down.

A small victory, but he'd take it.

He finished adding the scones to the sideboard just as Mason walked into the great room. Mason stopped short, eyeing him warily. He stood stiffly, meeting Mason's gaze. Aw, fuck. He'd made a mess of everything last night. "Morning."

Mason crossed his arms, his mouth flattened into a thin line, waiting.

Brodie blew out a breath. "I was out of line last night."

Mason grunted, still eyeing him suspiciously.

"Way out of line. I didn't handle myself or my liquor."

"Touch me again, and I'll kick your ass to high heaven."

Brodie acknowledged the threat with a noise in the back of his throat, nodding. "Message received. Shake?" He extended his hand as he walked around the table toward Mason.

Mason gripped his hand. Hard. Eyes boring right through him to the point he squirmed. "I'm sorry, man. I don't know what came over me last night."

Mason leveled him with a flinty gaze. "I do. Never a good idea to mix booze and brooding. Especially when a woman's involved."

"I'll remember that."

Mason cocked his chin toward the kitchen. "You done eating crow yet?"

The comment brought a smile to his lips. "Nope. Not by a long shot."

"Better get to it then. She's worth it."

She was. If only repairing this was as easy as fixing a fence. He marched back into the kitchen where Jamey stood washing dishes. He didn't want to think of what it would be like if he couldn't repair this.

## Chapter Twenty-Seven

*B*rodie grabbed a towel and stepped up next to her, reaching for the wet items as she pulled them out of the industrial washer.

"You know where everything goes?" She wouldn't look at him.

"Yep."

Once the last of the breakfast dishes were put away, she reached for a cutting board and two knives. Finally she looked at him with stormy eyes. "How's your head?"

"Hurts."

She pressed her lips together, and nodded. "I do lunch prep while everyone eats breakfast, then one more round of dishes." She pointed to one of the knives. "You know how to use one?"

He covered a smile. "That a trick question?"

Her eyes flashed. Exasperation? Humor?

Maybe he was getting somewhere. "Probably not to your standards."

"Grab two onions."

"Yes ma'am."

Her eyes narrowed. "That's yes, *chef*."

He saluted her, grabbed the onions, and came around the island to stand next to her.

She took the onions, still not looking at him. Her knife flashed out, and cut both spheres in half, then she rapidly peeled back the skin, and deposited it in a bowl. He watched her hands floating back and forth, mesmerized. There was such ease and confidence in her movements. She placed half an onion, cut side down in front of him. She grabbed her knife, and opened her palm.

"Let the handle rest over your fingers like this." The blade balanced on her index finger. "Now close your hand and pinch here." She handed him her knife. "You try."

He'd never given so much as a spare thought as to how to hold a knife. It felt awkward, the way she presented it. Her hand encased his, helping him close around the handle. Her touch was gentle. More like a caress than brusque instruction. He shifted his weight, leaning into her touch. She glanced at him sharply, eyes widening as they held his.

She might not be ready to talk, but he'd be damned if he'd keep his feelings a secret any longer.

"Take your left hand and make a claw like this." A quaver crept into her voice, and a little spark of hope thrilled in his chest.

"Use your fingertips to hold the onion in place, and keep your knuckles bent. Then slice." She shifted away and demonstrated with another onion half, her knife silently flying.

"Wow. That was fast."

The corner of her mouth pulled up, and she shrugged. "Have to be. Now you try. But go slowly. You don't want to cut yourself."

"You think I'd do that?"

Her eyes glinted in challenge. "I've seen bigger men cry like babies because they weren't careful with their tools."

"I bet you kicked all their asses in culinary school."

"Flattery will get you nowhere, fancy pants. Chop your onion."

He grabbed the onion, spreading his fingers out.

"No. No. You'll chop your fingers off if you do it that way." Her hand whipped over his, adjusting his fingers back. "Feel the difference?"

Definitely.

Her hands stayed on his.

His mouth dried as he caught her eye. The energy shifted between them. Her eyes were so close to his, he could see her pupils widen. He'd never appreciated tall women before, but he certainly did now. She couldn't hide her emotions by dipping her head. In fact, if he thought to steal a kiss, she'd have no warning. Her lips were just too close.

He shifted, bracing his arms on the island, trapping her.

Electricity cracked between them.

"Will you give me a chance?" He spoke low, unable to keep the urgency from his voice. "Give us a chance?"

She pressed a hand over his heart. "Brodie."

Everything inside him went still.

Her eyes were green pools of emotion. Desire, suspicion, tenderness. All swirling in her depths like clips of a movie. But she held back, her body taut in his loose embrace. If it was anyone but her, he'd give up right now.

But he couldn't.

Not yet, at least.

He stepped back to rest his hips on the counter behind him. "Can I tell you something?"

Eyes still wide, she nodded.

He scrubbed a hand over his face. It was now or never.

"I can't read."

There.

It was out.

Someone knew.

The words hung between them like little bombs, then exploded as she gasped quietly.

"Not very well, at least." He kept his eyes focused on the delicate hollow at her throat. "Barely, really."

He took a ragged breath and braced himself for what he'd see in her eyes. This was the reason he was such a fuck-up. Why the whole town thought he was stupid and worthless. "I tried to learn. I still try, but the letters get squirrelly."

"Are you dyslexic?"

"I don't even know what that is." He risked a glance in her direction.

The look in her eyes made his heart thump harder in his chest. No judgment. No derision. No laughter. Only compassion.

"One of my brothers is dyslexic. It's where your brain processes language differently, so it's harder to read and write. It's not that big of a deal if you get help."

He didn't know whether to argue with her or kiss her. "Of course it's a big deal. *I can't read.*"

Her eyes grew fierce. "No. What's a big deal is that no one caught it and no one helped you."

"My mom tried. But it's… complicated." His mom had read to him until his father had told her only babies got read to. That had been in sixth grade. After that, he'd had to rely on his smarts and clowning around to get through school.

"She didn't try hard enough then."

Pain seared through him as memories flashed before

his eyes. "I hid it," he muttered, his voice thick with shame. He pushed on. "Eventually, it got too hard. I didn't finish."

Her eyes widened. "Finish what?"

He cleared his throat. "High School. I got close, but with the demands of the ranch, and... Jake on regular benders, there were more important things to do. No one asked, and I didn't tell."

She uttered a quiet curse as she stepped forward, reaching to cup his cheek. "Brodie." Her voice soothed him. Like cool water over a burn.

He brought his hand to hers pressing it into his cheek. "I get the hands mixed up on clocks. Or the numbers turn upside down and I read them backwards. Like I did last night when I was late to our date. I know it's no excuse. I never meant to hurt you." God, he wanted to gather her in his arms and lose himself in her. Bury his face in her neck and just breathe her in.

She made a clucking noise in her throat. "You know there are tutors. You can get help. Get your GED."

His head snapped back. "People would know."

She rolled her eyes, pulling her hand from his. "Don't you think they already know? At least to some degree? Why not do something about it?"

He blew out a breath in frustration. "You don't get it. There's something wrong with me."

"Puh-leeze. Wallowing is unbecoming in a cowboy. Jason, my brother with dyslexia, told me one in five people is dyslexic. He should know. Count up all the people in this town. You're not the only person struggling. You might be the only person dumb enough to hide it though."

"Hey."

"I'm sure someone at the high school can put you in touch with a tutor."

"Oh hell no," he growled. "I'll figure it out on my own."

She crossed her arms, iron returning to her eyes. "How's that worked for you so far?"

She might have a little point, but no way. He stepped back and crossed his arms over his chest, shaking his head. "I'm not hiring some teenager to teach me to read."

"So lemme get this straight. You'd rather suck your thumb than change your life?" Her lips thinned as she shook her head. "I expected more from you."

That got his hackles up. He straightened up, keeping his eyes on her. "What the hell is that supposed to mean?"

"Just that. I expected more from you."

God*damn* she frustrated him. "Just *what* do you expect from me?"

She spun and grabbed the second onion, peeling it and chopping it with lightning speed. "I want a partner. Someone who's thoughtful."

"I am thoughtful."

She shook her head and kept chopping, finishing his uncut half next. "That's not the point. I want someone I can trust. Someone I can rely on. I've been with unreliable business partners, I've—"

"Wait. Are you saying what's between us is only business?"

His heart and his stomach traded places. Had he completely misread her?

She stopped chopping and braced her arms at the edge of the island, shooting him a glare. "I don't know *what* we are, Brodie. I'd like to know. Maybe I could sleep better. You want to know what I want, what I expect? Someone I can count on. Someone I can trust. Someone I can rely on to always be there. To be solid."

She couldn't sleep at night?

Because of him?

Maybe there was hope for him after all.

She swept the onion pieces into a bowl. The tension from gripping the cutting board rippled up her arm. "I don't want fly-by-night. I'm not interested in business colleagues with benefits."

She leveled a gaze at him, her face twisted with emotion. "And you know what scares me? You don't know how to run this place, and you refuse my expertise. Now you're telling me you don't care enough about your future to learn to read. How can I rely on you?"

Her voice grew thick.

Shit.

His insides churned like he'd been sucker punched.

She grabbed the cutting boards and knives and stepped past him to the sink, rinsing them and placing them in the dishwasher. The silence expanded between them as she scrubbed the sink, then turned on the hot water, reaching underneath to grab an orange box of powder. She measured some out and dumped it into the drain, reducing the water to a trickle.

He ran his hand through his hair. "I do care about my future."

"Then do something about it, Brodie. Don't just go along to get along."

Panic fluttered again at the edge of his conscious. She was pulling away, and it was all his fault. "Please. Give me a chance. Give us a chance? Don't go on that date tonight." The last plea came out in a whisper.

She spun around, her eyes tortured. "I won't break my commitment."

His heart sank to his knees.

Jealousy surged, lighting a fire in his belly. "He's not enough man for you, Jamey."

Her eyes sparked, then shuttered. "I don't think you even know what that means."

"Yeah? Why don't you stick around and find out." The fire roared to an inferno of dragon-like proportions.

She put up her hands in surrender. "Stop. Just. Stop. God knows you're more than enough man, physically. That's not what I'm talking about. Have you ever given serious thought about your future? Do you even know what you want?"

He opened his mouth, and promptly snapped it shut.

He'd conditioned himself to never look forward. Blake and Ben had always taken lead on the ranch. He just went along. And now, he'd hit the end of the line.

"I've got work to do." He spun on his heel.

Only backbreaking labor would get rid of the ache that had settled in his chest.

## Chapter Twenty-Eight

*J*amey swept on a bit of lip-gloss as she gave her appearance one last check in the mirror. She should have canceled, but that would make her as fickle as Brodie. Wouldn't it? Although she was the one going to dinner with someone else. Not that it felt like a date. Nevertheless, a twinge of guilt tugged at her.

The conversation she'd had with Brodie rattled over and over inside her throughout the day. Unsettling her. Blowing her concentration. She'd nearly burned the onion soup, a rookie mistake that in any restaurant would have cost her a job.

Brodie couldn't read.

That explained a helluva lot.

She'd been little when her family had learned her brother, Jason, was dyslexic. As far as she could tell, it hadn't been that big of a deal. Jason had gone to special classes for a few months, and that had been that. Periodically, they'd share a laugh when he stumbled over a word. His texts and emails sometimes had creative spelling, but there'd been no shame.

She'd have to call her brother later and ask about it. There must be some way to get Brodie the help he needed. Even at his age.

She glanced at the clock on her dresser. Travis would be here any second. She spritzed on a bit of her favorite perfume. It was a luxury she rarely indulged in. Perfume in the kitchen interfered with her sense of smell and taste. But since she was out of the kitchen for once, why not?

She shut the door behind her and made her way to the great room. Brodie was settled in one of the wide leather chairs, feet stretched in front of him, head back, eyes closed.

Of course he'd be here.

She'd bet her favorite kitchen knife he wasn't taking a nap either.

He had tenacity in spades. If only he'd apply that to learning to read.

She paused, perusing him.

The hard knot she'd been carrying since the previous evening began to soften. With his eyes shut, his normally chiseled features were somehow softer. Sweeter. His nose was slightly crooked, with a slight thickening toward the bridge. Likely from one too many breaks.

His frequently furrowed brows were relaxed, forming thick, full arches over a dark sweep of lashes. His mouth, typically hard, was soft, showing a plump lower lip, perfect for nipping and sucking. The thought of sucking on his lip made her pussy involuntarily clench. She squirmed, remembering the feel of his thick cock pushing between her legs.

Shit.

Why was she going to dinner with Travis again?

Oh yeah.

Because she was a hothead. Not the first time her temper had made her regret something.

Brodie had changed from his work clothes into a pressed white shirt. It stretched perfectly across his sculpted torso, displaying his muscles and drawing her eyes down to his brass buckle and soft denim that perfectly hugged his rock solid thighs. Thighs that had held her upright in the throes of passion.

She had no business thinking about fucking Brodie while she was waiting for Travis to pick her up. None whatsoever.

But she couldn't help herself.

And when he was stretched out and vulnerable like this, she couldn't help but think of what a future would be like with him. Of what they could do and be together.

But she couldn't carry the load.

Not alone.

She'd never do that again.

She wanted a life partner. Wanted what her parents had, what Maddie had. But with the life she'd chosen as a chef, maybe that wasn't for her. The divorce rate among top chefs was astronomical. Long hours, coupled with high stress and competition for celebrity status, tended to discourage normal people from getting near. And dating within the industry? Never again.

"You done staring?"

Her eyes shot back to his face. His eyes remained shut, but a smile played at the corner of his mouth.

Devil.

He opened his eyes, boring right to her heart. How was his hearing so good he knew exactly where she was?

"You don't have to go."

Her throat began to ache. "I do."

"Stay."

Her stomach jumped into her sternum. What was she doing? Was she being stupidly stubborn to prove something to him? Or to herself? If the latter, what was she trying to prove?

The door chimed.

Her heart wrenched as his beautiful blue eyes became ice. "Go. I'll be here when you get back." His mouth twisted into a bitter smile. "You can tell me all about your date."

"Brodie, don't–"

"Don't what?" His mouth flattened to a hard line.

"Don't make this harder than it already is," she breathed out.

He pushed up from the chair and crossed to her in two steps, his eyes piercing straight through her. He slid the back of his finger down her cheek. "I aim to do just that."

The rough edge of his voice sent a thrill through her, soaking her panties.

He stepped closer, so that only a whisper stood between his mouth and hers. "You know your mind, Jamey. It's fear's holding you back."

His voice slid over her, setting every nerve quivering.

The door chimed again.

"I'll not ask you again. You have to decide what future you want, too." He stepped away. But not before he lowered his nose to her ear and inhaled. A low chuckle rumbled in his chest. "Mmmm. Delicious."

Her nipples stood at attention.

Cool air replaced the heat where his body had been, leaving her frustrated and wanting more. The door chimed a third time. Brodie seated himself again and stretched his hands behind his head.

His eyes raked over her a final time. "Better not keep your date waiting."

Indignation quickly snuffed out the desire still pulsing through her. Damn him. He wasn't going to make it easy. In spite of her irritation, her respect for him upped a notch. He might piss her off, but he was no dummy. Not by a long shot.

She sniffed loftily, smoothing her jeans and strutted – yes, strutted – to the door. Let him drink in what he was missing. She opened the door to a bouquet of flowers. Her heart sank the smallest fraction. She wasn't a flowers kind of gal. The last time she'd received flowers had been an awkward date her brothers had set up for her in Catholic school. She much preferred a bottle of Redbreast, or maybe a fancy chocolate.

"How sweet of you, Travis. Come in while I put these in water?"

Travis tipped back his Stetson and peered past her to where Brodie sat. "I think I'll wait here."

"Come in Kincaid," he called. "Don't mind me."

She hurried to the kitchen with the flowers. As soon as she'd placed them in water, she hurried back.

Brodie remained stretched out in the chair, hands behind his head. Travis stood tense in the doorway, hands in his pockets. Ten kinds of awkward.

She grabbed the door to shut it behind her when Brodie called out. "Don't stay out too late, kids. And don't do anything I wouldn't do."

She rolled her eyes and suppressed a giggle. "You ready?"

Travis placed a hand at the small of her back and guided her to his truck. Fifteen minutes later, he pulled into Gino's Trattoria. A small building just off Main, Gino's appeared straight out of the fifties, complete with a scripted neon sign, and big white lights surrounding the picture window. He opened her door and extended his hand.

"Wow. Am I gonna see Frank Sinatra inside?"

"I don't know about that, but it's as fancy as Prairie gets." He guided her inside, holding open the door, and allowing her to pass through first.

What greeted her was a crowded room that could have been any restaurant on Boston's north side. Red checked tablecloths topped with red candleholders. Italian music playing in the background, a jukebox in the corner. Wrought iron sconces along the walls lent a golden glow to the room.

And she couldn't eat the pasta. And she bet it was good, too.

Dammit.

A wave of panic lodged in her throat. God. What if she couldn't eat anything on the menu? What then?

A dark haired teenaged girl walked up with two menus. "Hope you like a booth. That's all we have open."

Travis nodded, and the girl wove through the tables, maybe twenty in all.

Jamey slid into the booth and grinned. "So you bring all your dates here?"

"Only the special ones."

"Aren't they all special?"

He smiled enigmatically. "The ravioli's fantastic."

Her heart sank. "I'm avoiding carbs." Lame. Lame. Lame. But she wasn't ready to admit she had celiac. It felt too… vulnerable.

Travis stared at her, confused. "Really? I thought chefs ate everything."

"Only if you want to end up like Tubby McFattypants."

He leaned his head back, laughing. His laugh was

warm and musical. And didn't do a thing to her insides. Brodie's laugh was rich and low and slid over her like melted butter. What would he be like on a date?

"Earth to Jamey. You in there?"

"I'm sorry. I drifted for a sec."

His brows knit together. "So soon? I'm not that boring am I?"

She shook her head. "No, not at all." She smiled wide and arched her brows. "Tell me, Travis, what's a good looking man like you doing—"

"Playing cop in a town like Prairie?" he finished.

"Well I wasn't going to put it that way exactly. But, yes."

His eyes clouded briefly. "It's quiet. No action."

She scanned the menu searching for something, anything, safe to eat. "Hmm. There's a story there, considering every other male in this town is an adrenaline junkie."

He let out a little laugh. "I've had enough adrenaline to last me a lifetime."

"Ooh, the plot thickens."

He shrugged. "Yeah. Maybe."

She quickly scanned the menu. Polenta. Praise the gods, they had polenta. And risotto. Except she'd already mentioned no carbs. Damn her for opening her big mouth.

The girl came around to take their order. Travis grimaced as she ordered a Caesar salad with no croutons.

"Sorry." She offered him a guilty smile. "Gotta keep my girlish figure."

He rolled his eyes. "I'm so disappointed. You of all people should appreciate good food like this."

Yeah. She should. Damn her pathetic life. She waved her hand, dismissing him. "I'm sure this will be the best Caesar I've ever had. What I want to know, Travis

Kincaid, man of mystery, is how you became Prairie's cop."

"That's a two bottle of wine story, and we're only having one. I'm willing to give you the short version so long as I get to ask you any questions I want."

"My life is an open book." Mostly.

An older gentleman stopped by the table with a carafe of Chianti, and filled their glasses. She plopped her chin onto her hand. "Spill. I'm all ears."

Travis shifted uncomfortably in his seat. "Not much to tell. I grew up here. My family has been here since the forties. After high school, I joined the military, eventually attended OCS and then got into the Special Forces."

"What branch?"

He eyed her. "Navy. I was a SEAL."

That was a surprise. "But you're from Kansas."

He laughed again. "We may be landlocked, but there's water. Besides, when I left home I wanted to do something... unpredictable. So I joined the Navy."

"So why'd you stop?"

His face shuttered and he studied his hands before taking another sip of wine.

"Oh... wait. You can't talk about it."

"Something like that."

"Might have to kill me if you told me?"

"Sure."

Damn. She'd opened a can of worms. "So you came back home."

"Yeah. My parents are divorced. And my dad, who used to work for the police force, died of a heart attack. My little brother, Colton, didn't want to change high schools, so I moved home. End of story."

"As if."

The girl brought their plates. Jamey's heart sank a little as she contemplated the big plate of lettuce.

This sucked.

Travis held out a fork laden with ravioli and cream sauce. Her mouth watered enviously. "Bite?"

She shook her head, bitterness lodging in the back of her throat.

"Come on," he urged. "A little bite won't hurt."

"A moment on the lips, a lifetime on the hips."

He scowled and shrugged. "Suit yourself."

God, she hated playing coy like this. But it was better than the pitying look she'd get if she tried to explain. She could handle irritation. Pity was another story.

After a few minutes of companionable silence, Travis leaned forward, eyes narrowing. "My turn. Why'd you decide to have dinner with me when you can cut the chemistry between you and Brodie with a knife?"

So. Busted.

She pushed the remaining lettuce leaves around her plate, avoiding his stare. "That obvious, huh?" She glanced up sheepishly.

"I see things other people don't. Part of why I'm good at my job."

"Why'd you ask me to dinner then, if you could tell?"

"Because you looked like you needed a friend." He paused, shoving the ravioli around his plate. Then shot her a sly grin. "And Brodie's the kind of guy that sometimes needs a kick in the ass before he makes a move."

"So you thought you'd help things along? I never took you for a matchmaker. You seem more... normal."

"Normal?" His mouth curved bitterly. "Nothing normal about me. I'm just not your brand of crazy."

Right.

That would be all Brodie. Her brand of crazy.

Travis leaned in. "You never answered my question. Why'd you come to dinner?"

A flush crept up her neck. God. She was an ass. "I was pissed as hell. I was using dinner with you to make a point," she whispered. "I'm sorry. Sometimes I'm a thoughtless hothead."

He smiled again, his features congenial again. "I'm not sorry. So long as Brodie gets the message."

"Thanks. I hope somebody, someday, realizes what a catch *you* are."

A hard edge flickered in his eyes, and his mouth hardened. "I'm not dating material. I have… baggage."

"We all do, Travis." She reached for his hand and gave a squeeze. "You'll find someone whose brand of crazy matches yours. You look too good in that uniform to be a bachelor forever." She winked at him and released his fingers.

He glanced at the dessert tray. "Share a tiramisu?"

A stab of craving shot through her. Another delicious item in a long list she'd never get to enjoy again. What she wouldn't give for even a bite of that creamy, light as air concoction.

With regret she shook her head. "Spumoni?"

"Deal."

## Chapter Twenty-Nine

*T*ravis's taillights disappeared down the dirt drive before Jamey pushed open the door, unsure of what she'd find waiting on the other side.

The great room was in near darkness. Only the dying coals in the fireplace and a lone lamp underneath the balcony offered light. She paused just inside the door, letting her eyes adjust to the dim.

She scanned the room.

No Brodie.

The small ember of hope that had briefly flickered inside her chest deflated as she let out a sigh. So… she'd bet wrong. Pushed him too hard. It was time to accept whatever lurked between the two of them wasn't enough.

Her heart twisted, and the pain stole her breath.

The office door opened, the light casting Brodie's form into relief. He'd removed his boots. Rolled up his sleeves and unbuttoned his shirt. All the way. The ridges of his abs peeked out where the material separated, demanding her full attention.

Her mouth went dry. At the same time, warmth rushed straight to her pussy, soaking her panties.

Oh, Yeah.

He was her crazy.

And was that a scotch in his hand? Knowing him, yes.

She couldn't read the expression on his face with the light so bright behind him, but she didn't miss the tension snaking through his body.

An invisible thread of electricity connected them. She stood rooted to the floor. Her pulse quickened, throbbing at her neck and buzzing through her ears. Expectation thrummed through her. Should she say something?

Suddenly, she felt shy.

Unsure.

Exposed.

Not taking his eyes off her, he downed the rest of his glass and placed it on the credenza. He closed the distance between them, stopping so close she could smell the trace of scotch on his breath, mingling with his spicy cologne.

Since when did he wear cologne? Whatever it was, it only added to the intoxicating swirl fuzzing her brain.

It would be so easy to break the silence. To push his shirt aside, run her fingers over his taut skin and kiss all the angst away. But she was tired of the angst, the not knowing. So she waited, biting her lip between her teeth.

He inhaled sharply and broke eye contact, scraping a hand across his jaw. "You kiss him?" he grated out.

The knot in her chest unraveled. She shook her head, not trusting herself to speak.

"Did you want to?"

Everything hard inside her began to melt. She shook her head slowly. His face softened, and he ran the back of his finger down her cheek, bringing it to rest under her chin.

His spoke low and urgent. "I have to know, Jamey. Was it because you wanted this?" His lips brushed hers with the barest of touches. Back and forth, their breath mingling until she couldn't stand it anymore and she leaned in for more.

"Say it," he whispered, his tongue flicking across her lower lip. "Tell me you want this."

"Yes," she breathed, slipping her hand underneath his shirt and placing it over his heart. "Oh God, yes."

She'd never been clearer about anything in her life. This man. This wild man, whose uncontainable spirit matched her own, was her home. Whatever else life threw at her, about this she was certain. Brodie Sinclaire belonged to her.

She snaked her hand up to the back of his neck where his hair curled around her fingers, and leaned into his mouth. "All of you. I want all of you."

The breathless groan that emanated from his throat sent a shiver of delight straight down the back of her neck, settling in her clit, and setting the bundle of nerves alight.

She flicked her tongue across his lip, teasing his mouth until he thrust a hand into her curls and deepened the kiss. Tongues thrust and twirled together until they were both breathless.

Growling low, he swept her up into his arms as if she weighed nothing and stalked down the hall, passing her door. When they entered his room, he kicked the door shut behind him and stopped at the foot of the bed. Want and determination filled his expression. She squirmed in his arms, but he didn't release her.

He leaned in close, brushing his lips slowly across the sensitive spot below her ear. Every brush of his lips registered in her nipples, and they hardened to tight peaks, pushing through the thin fabric of her shirt.

She skittered her fingers across his chest, biting back a small smile as his flesh pebbled under her.

He released her, and pushed her gently back to the bed, dropping to his knees between her legs as she sat. He smoothed his hands over her hips, sighing as he grazed a kiss across her collarbone. Tracing a finger inside the vee of her shirt, he paused at the top button. He flicked it open with his thumb and forefinger, and traced his tongue across the exposed skin, before raising his eyes to hers.

So many unspoken words.

Desire. Longing. Awe.

His look said she was cherished... appreciated. And dammit if that wasn't the biggest turn on ever. Every cell in her body vibrated with need. She fisted her hands in the comforter to keep from tumbling him onto the bed.

Slowly, he released the remaining buttons, slipping the silky material off her shoulders, leaving her exposed to his perusal. He took his time studying her, finally bringing his eyes back to hers. "You're beautiful, Jamey," he said, his voice rough with emotion. "So beautiful."

Her breath stuck in her throat. No one, not even her parents, called her beautiful. And yet how many times had he called her that? Her limbs grew heavy under his heated stare. The protective shell around her heart thinned a bit more. "You don't need to say that."

Something hot and possessive flashed across his features. "Like hell I don't," he growled.

He slid a finger underneath the strap of her bra and tugged. The strap slipped down her arm, pulling the lace cup forward and revealing the modest swell of her breast.

She'd always been self-conscious about the size of her breasts. Jean Luc had even hinted she could get a boob job. But the way Brodie's face lit as he took her in, the hungry glint in his eye as he ran a finger over the swell, the little noise of appreciation he made in the back of his throat… no one had ever made her feel sensual and desirable the way he did.

Reaching behind, she unhooked her bra, letting it fall to her lap.

He inhaled sharply as he took her in.

"Like what you see?" She couldn't keep the breathless anticipation from her voice. Every look he gave her, every raw stare, ratcheted her desire.

"Your tits are fucking perfect." He ran his palm over the swell, flicking his thumb across her hardened bud.

She let her head fall back as the sensation ran straight to her clit, making it throb violently.

When his lips replaced his thumb, she gasped at the sharp sensation, her skin erupting in gooseflesh. Slowly, with extreme care, he flicked his tongue across the peak, then swirled it in his mouth while he sucked gently. She clutched the comforter, writhing in the sweetest kind of agony, as he covered every inch of her breasts with his tongue.

She couldn't stand it any longer. Threading her fingers through his hair, she arched her back, thrusting her tits deeper into his mouth. The fever he was stoking inside her made her dizzy with want.

She ran her hands down his neck, bringing them to rest just below his shoulders. God, she could get off just stroking his arms. Her palms molded around his rock hard muscles, and she gave an appreciative sigh, but it wasn't enough. She wanted – needed, his bare skin under her hand.

"Brodie."

"Mmm-hmm." The sound vibrated across her chest.

"Lose yer shirt." She gave the material a little pull, and

he shrugged out of it, the cloth silently dropping behind him in a whisper.

He chuckled into her, his breath skittering across her already heated skin. "Quit your bossin'. I'm in charge here."

She grinned slowly. "Yeah?"

"Oh yeah," he mumbled as he trailed his tongue between her breasts down to her navel.

Sitting back on his feet, he pushed her bra aside and released the button of her jeans.

"Lift your hips," he commanded softly.

The denim slid down her hips in one pull. She kicked them off then leaned back on her elbows, nerves tingling with anticipation.

He gave an appreciative grumble as he pressed on the inside of her knee. "Open for me. I want to see you."

His frank perusal reduced her limbs to liquid, and another rush of heat filled her pussy. She let her knees fall open, exposing her barely-there white lace panties to his hungry gaze. "Jesus, Jamey," he groaned, brushing his fingers up her thigh, his thumb stopping at the juncture of leg and hip. He swept his thumbs back and forth across the crease until she whimpered.

Tendrils of need raced through her, firing the nerve endings. How had she convinced herself that being with him was bad when he made her feel so damned good?

This.

This connection.

She'd missed it her entire life.

He moved with deliberation. Bringing his head forward to nuzzle her thighs, and inhaling deeply. His hot breath spread over her sex like hot caramel over ice cream, finding every dip and crevice. And then his mouth was on her pussy. A scrap of whisper-thin material the only thing keeping her from inevitable bliss.

"God, you're so wet." The movement of his mouth sent exquisite vibrations across her pussy lips. It took everything she had not to grind her mound into his face.

"You're killing me here," she moaned, writhing under him.

He chuckled low, setting off another round of delicious vibrations in her pussy. "You want more?"

She was panting now. "God, yes."

With one quick snap, he broke the elastic and brushed away the fabric. "Look at me, Jamey."

She lifted her head to meet his gaze. The vision of him kneeling before her, wonder and awe softening his features as he prepared to feast on her, stole her breath.

A possessive light glinted in his eyes. "I want all of you. No holding back."

She nodded in agreement, heart in her throat. "No holding back."

He reached his hand out to cover hers. She unclenched her fist from the bedspread and opened it palm up, lacing her fingers with his.

She shut her eyes as the first sensation of his tongue splitting her pussy hit her brain. Roared through her brain like a freight train, leaving her breathless. He went slow, tasting every crevice, sliding his tongue through her wetness, swirling her clit, then down, ending with a penetrating thrust into her channel.

God, she was going to come apart.

"I'm going to make you come so many times tonight you won't know which way is up."

A little thrill went through her. "I think I'm already there," she gasped.

"Not if you're still talking." He swept his tongue up

again, this time capturing her clit with his whole mouth and sucking while he flicked the nub over and over again with the tip of his tongue.

Her hips thrust up violently as she shook with the orgasm that hit her. But he didn't stop. Blood rushed through her ears, deafening her as she collapsed back on the bed.

He moved his mouth away and nipped at her hip. "You taste so damned sweet." He untangled his hand from hers, and she heard the rustle of clothes through the fog of the orgasm that still gripped her.

"Ready for round two?"

Giving him her best come hither look, she scooted backwards.

He captured her ankle, lifting it and planting a kiss in the hollow there. Electricity surged straight toward her over-sensitized clit.

He stood naked before her, his cock jutting proudly forward. She wanted to lick him up. To taste him and give back to him what he'd just given her. She sat up reaching for him, but he shook his head.

"Not yet. You still know which way is up."

He put a knee on the bed and gently pushed her backwards, his hand skimming over her breast and coming to rest on her hip.

"But–"

"Nope." He shook his head and settled himself between her legs, his cock teasing her opening and his hips pressing her to the mattress. She bit down on her lower lip, breath catching in her ribs from the weight of anticipation.

He made a noise in the back of his throat. "God, you're so hot when you do that." He shifted forward a fraction and she gasped, rolling her hips, trying to capture more of him. "And when you do that." He pushed all the way in, filling her completely.

She groaned and ground into him savoring the friction. He slipped an arm under her and rolled them over, settling her above him. His slow, wicked grin was all the encouragement she needed to start moving slowly.

"I'll never get tired of this view." He reached up to caress her, capturing her nipples between each thumb and forefinger and giving them a little squeeze. She arched and leaned into his hands, letting instinct drive her movements.

She was still buzzing from the first orgasm he'd given her. How could she already be getting close again? His caresses and strokes were rapidly building the tightness where their bodies joined. Wrapping his hands around her lower back, he pulled her down, thrusting deeply. She could feel the tip of him touch her womb with each stroke, stoking the fire winding up her spine.

Her lips sought his, and with each thrust of his cock, she answered with a thrust of her tongue. His hands slid over her backside, squeezing hard into her ass with each upward stroke.

In this moment, it seemed her clit was somehow attached to her whole body. Every movement she felt at her tight bud, swirled outward in a spiral of intense tingling need.

He pulled away from her, eyes wild, and brought his head to her breast, alternately licking and sucking each peak. With a growl, he scraped his teeth against the sensitive point as he rolled his tongue over it.

The sensation was too much for her, and stars exploded behind her eyes. She cried out as fire consumed her body, frying nerve endings down to her fingers and toes. And still he thrust powerfully, chasing his own release while continuing to graze her nipple with his teeth. She ground into him, barely able to feel her limbs, and shuddering as wave after wave still surged through her.

He stiffened beneath her, digging his fingers into her ass. Throwing his head back, he shouted out, then buried his face – and the sound, in her neck.

A giggle spilled out as she grinned down at him. Giggling again, she gave a little twist of her hips. He groaned in answer and tucked a curl behind her ear. His other hand lightly stroked up and down her back. "You okay?"

This time she let out a full-throated laugh. She rolled her hips again, relishing the lingering sensations still zinging along her nerves. "I can't feel my body."

His eyes furrowed slightly. "But you're laughing."

"Jesus, yes." She couldn't stop the giggles or the feeling of… delight.

Uncertainty lurked in the depths of his sex-satisfied hazy expression.

"God, Brodie. I've never…"

"Yes?"

Her cheeks flamed as she confessed. "I've never come so hard I couldn't feel my body."

His face lit up with a triumphant grin. "Yeah?" He continued caressing her backside in long even strokes.

She could get used to this. Very used to this. "Yeah."

He wrapped his arms around her, pulling her down, then shifted, rolling them over so she lay pinned beneath him, his weight a comforting blanket. "Good. Now that I've got you where I want you, I need to tell you some things."

## Chapter Thirty

*J*amey's brows were so cute when they arched in question like that. Especially when her face still glowed from the intensity of her orgasm. Everything about her had softened. Brodie leaned in for another taste of her. He couldn't help himself. She tasted better than any candy from the five and dime.

Sliding onto his side, he gathered her in a loose embrace, his chest tightening anxiously as he settled them. "I've never been good at emotional stuff."

Her eyes widened slightly and she cocked her head to study him, a small smile twitching at the corner of her mouth. "Nobody's getting married here. We can keep things light."

"That's just it..." He stopped. His mouth turned to dust, and the words stuck somewhere between his tonsils and his belly. Running his thumb over the protrusion of her hipbone helped steady him, like fingering his lucky belt buckle while waiting in the box for a calf to tear out of the chute.

Her eyes shuttered, and her muscles tensed under his hand.

Shit.

He was losing his window.

He swallowed hard, trying to quell the empty roiling of his belly. Another awkward moment passed. Giving up, he shook his head. "Aw hell, Jamey, I don't know how to do emotional stuff."

Her fingers covered his mouth, and before he could stop himself, he captured the tips between his teeth, giving them a gentle nip before sucking gently.

"No pressure," she answered, her voice slightly brittle. "We don't need to name this. It's just sex."

But it wasn't.

Not for him at least.

Was it for her?

The words were right on his tongue, but his tongue wouldn't move. He'd never been good with expressing his feelings. At least the nice ones. He had no trouble beating idiots into next Tuesday.

But this…

He'd rather face down a two-ton charging bull in bare feet. Since that wasn't an option, the next best thing was diversion. He kissed her. For courage, of course. Not because he couldn't resist the way her lip curved. He lost himself in the sweet velvet of her mouth, his tongue exploring little crevices and pockets until she made that sexy noise in the back of her throat, and clutched at his shoulder.

God, he loved kissing her. He could do this. He could tell her. "It's not just sex," he rasped into her lips.

She pulled away, eyes puzzled. "What'd you say?"

"It's not just sex."

Her eyes narrowed suspiciously.

Oh, God.

He was going to puke.

"What is it then?" She spoke slowly. As if she didn't quite believe what he was saying.

That wouldn't do.

He wrestled steers with his bare hands. Surely he could confess a few things to a lovely naked woman in his bed? A woman he had *feelings* for? Big feelings. The realization ran through him like a hot poker. How in the hell was he supposed to handle that?

His chest began to burn, a flush creeping up his neck and down his limbs. He'd die of combustion if he didn't open his mouth. "I was thinking..." he swallowed, his tongue thick.

He cleared his throat and started again. "I was thinking about what you said. About what I wanted. I... I... never wanted anything. I... never let myself." His breath snagged as buried anguish from his youth burst inside, leaking all over everything. "I was an asshole. A sad asshole. It was easier to be a dick than to let anyone see that I hated I was stupid."

She made a clucking noise and brought her hand to his face. "You're not stupid. You never were."

He shook his head. "That's not the point. I've spent most of my life being an ass to people I love because I don't know how not to."

"That's not true. I see you with Simon. You're patient and gentle with him. I see how you do things. Build things people need."

His chest tightened, a lump pushing out on his ribs. "I've never... I've never been with anyone I called a girlfriend."

"Even Kylee?"

"Especially Kylee. I was a stupid, horny sixteen year-old who didn't have a clue about girls. She took advantage of that." He shut his eyes, then forced them open.

Her eyes were right there, waiting. Wide and sorrowful. The tang of bitterness scratched the back of his throat. He could handle a lot, but not her pity. "Don't feel sorry for me."

He took a deep, slow breath, then met her eyes again. "I've made a pretty good mess of my life… But I want to make it different. And I want… this… between us… to have a name."

Her eyes crinkled, and she bit her lip, a smile tilting one corner.

"Don't laugh."

"That's about the sweetest thing anyone has ever said to me." Her mouth morphed into a full on grin, and she waggled her eyebrows. "So what kind of a name? Girl-friend? Lover? Partner?" She giggled. "Ooh, how about *paramour?*"

He rolled his eyes, a small, embarrassed laugh escaping. "I don't know how to spell that."

He'd never admit it to anyone else. But with her, it felt… natural.

Normal.

Like he wasn't stupid.

She threaded her fingers through his hair, tugging him closer, so her lips were a breath from his own. "I don't care about your spelling."

"What do you care about?" He held his breath, not sure what she'd say.

"Who, Brodie." Her voice washed over him like a caress, seeping in and smoothing out all the rough, scarred edges. She kissed the corner of his mouth. Then the other corner, each touch softening the hard lump still stuck between his ribs. "It's who I care about, not what. And I care for you, you great lump." Her mouth smiled against his.

Surprise and delight rippled through him. She cared for him. *Him. Brodie Sinclaire.* He twirled a flyaway curl around his finger, studying the different shades of copper, gold, and orange, intently. Warmth settled in his chest, relaxing his limbs.

Was this… contentment?

"Brodie?" There was an edge of anxiety in her voice.

He leaned back to study her. Had he done something? Had she changed her mind already?

His voice sharpened in concern. "What's wrong?"

"I have to tell you something."

His gut twisted in sick anticipation.

She rolled away, staring at the ceiling. "No one knows this."

"Not even Maddie?"

She shook her head. "No… no. This was something… is something," her voice hitched, "I needed to deal with by myself."

Wonder that she would share a secret with him smacked him in the chest. At the same time, a lump of dread formed in his gut. Whatever it was, he would help her. By God, he'd slay dragons for her. At the very least, he'd make mincemeat of anyone who'd hurt her.

He gathered her close, protective instincts kicking into high gear. "I swear, Jamey. What do you need me to do? Did someone hurt you?"

She let out a breathy little laugh. "No, no. Nothing like that." Her fingers skated nervously back and forth across his collarbone, and she kept taking little half breaths, like she was screwing up the courage to let whatever it was out.

He shifted, bringing his fingers under her chin and

gently lifting so she couldn't look away. Her eyes were stormy pools.

"Jamey, sweetheart." He peppered her forehead with tender kisses. "Whatever it is. We can manage it together."

She let out a little sigh, a tremble shaking her body. "I have a condition called celiac disease."

Oh, God.

His chest turned to stone. He was going to lose her right after he'd found her? Yet another 'fuck you' from the Universe. Bracing himself, he asked. "Will it kill you?"

She let out a little half-laugh again. "No, no. The only thing it killed was my career."

He slowly let out the breath he'd been holding. Oh, thank God. "That's a relief."

She glanced at him sharply. "It's a relief my career went down the toilet?"

"Darlin' if you're saying that what you're doing here is your career down the toilet, then yes. And besides," He planted a kiss on her nose. "You're not dying."

She rolled her eyes and pulled back. "You don't understand."

He would not let her prickles get the best of him.

Not this time.

He tamped down on his growing frustration. "Woman, you test the patience of a saint. Help me understand."

She blew out a breath. "Celiac is an autoimmune disease. There's no cure."

"But you're not going to die?"

"No."

"So what's the big deal?"

She pushed away from him and sat up. Completely unaware that from this angle she looked like a wild spirit, sinewy and strong. His cock stirred. He couldn't help it. She captivated him.

Completely.

But whatever this celiac thing was, it was hurting her, and he wanted to help. So his needy cock would have to wait.

"The big deal is that I'm a damned good chef. And I'm brilliant at pastry. Or at least I was."

"Still not following."

She leveled a glare at him.

He ran a hand down her magnificent thigh. "Calm down. Before you get your Irish on, you need to remember I'm not a cook."

She made the cutest little grumble in the back of her throat. "Flour. My body can't digest flour. Gluten really, which is in flour. And beer... and other things. I can't touch it, breathe it, or eat it." Her lips flattened into a thin line. "Do you see where this might be a problem for a chef?"

"But you cook good food. I don't see the problem."

She raised her eyes to the ceiling. "Cockwaffles," she gritted out. "Douchenozzle motherfucking cockwaffles."

His cock stiffened to half-mast, and he stroked down her thigh again, letting his thumb caress the softer inner part. "Better speak fast, darlin'. Your temper's always been a turn-on."

She glanced down at his rapidly thickening cock, eyes widening. She covered a little laugh. "You dirty man. I'm baring my soul and you're thinking about sex?"

He grinned at her, unashamed, and lifted a shoulder. "Can't help it. You turn me on. Inside and out." He reached for her hand, interlacing their fingers. "Now, where were you?"

She sighed, dipping her head. "Do you have any idea how hard it is to be serious with... *that*... bobbing in my vision?"

He rose to an elbow, conviction thrumming through him. "If I could kiss your problems away, I would." He punctuated his words by kissing each of her fingers. "I don't mean to make light of this... flour issue... but you're overcomplicating this. You're not dying, and you cook great food."

Her eyes held a faint glimmer of suspicion, and she made a scoffing sound in the back of her throat.

He tugged on her hand. "Hey. You think I'm making this up to get laid?"

That earned him an immediate laugh.

"Has anyone here complained about your food?"

She shook her head. "But I can't work in a regular restaurant ever again."

"So stay here."

It popped out before he'd realized the implications. Technically, she was only contracted for a few more weeks. But... would she consider it?

She leveled a piercing gaze at him. The kind of look that peeled back his carefully constructed defense layers and left him bare.

He swallowed down the ache that suddenly formed in his throat. "Think about it, at least. You have options." Now he was backpedaling, but dammit if he didn't want her to stay. "We can talk about it later."

"Okay." She'd untwined their fingers, and her thumb now pressed lazy circles below his hipbone, springing his hungry cock to a new level of arousal.

"Uh... Jamey?" A wave of desire tightened his balls.

"Conversation over." She pushed him onto his back and settled on her side, her hand stroking up the inside of his thigh and only stopping when she'd cupped his balls. She licked her lips, a wicked light gleaming in her eye. "My turn to rock your world."

"You already do."

She didn't know the half of it. Once the admission had slipped out, the bigger emotions quickly filled in the holes. There was nothing left to do but to hang on for dear life and hope he survived the ride.

## Chapter Thirty-One

*J*amey stopped her mad rushing in order to pop the cork on a bottle of champagne. It had been a hectic week between guests and preparations for Maddie's baby shower. But today was going to be great. And not just for the mom-to-be. She grabbed a flute and filled it, surveying her handiwork spread across the counter.

She'd outdone herself.

But she didn't just have herself to thank. What Brodie had said to her about overcomplicating things a few weeks back had unstuck whatever hang-ups she'd had about attempting gluten-free pastry. Of course, the copious amount of sex they indulged in probably didn't hurt her creativity either.

The island was filled with plates of macarons, mini scones, and flaky, savory cheese crackers. Smoked salmon, grilled asparagus, mushroom bacon and leek mini quiches. Bison summer sausage, compliments of Blake, and flaked parmesan. Mixed olives. Strawberries dipped in dark chocolate, and almond orange teacakes. Champagne and sparkling cider.

"You look like the cat that ate the canary," Maddie called from the doorway, a questioning twinkle in her eye.

Jamey saluted her with the flute. "A feast fit for a queen. Prepare to be pampered."

Maddie's laughter trilled through the kitchen. "Don't you remember me telling you about my wedding shower? Prepare for grannies gone wild."

Her eyebrows shot up. "Are you sayin' I've met my match?"

"You know you have. That's why you and Dottie butt heads."

The observation stung.

A look of sympathy crossed Maddie's face. "I know you had to fight to be heard at home and in Chicago, too. But here, it's different. People respect you. Dottie respects you."

"Ha."

"It's true. I overheard her in the diner the other day telling someone Brodie's lucky to have you running the ship. That's high praise."

Was Dottie making room for her? Dottie as an ally would be so much better than Dottie as an adversary.

Maddie slipped around the island and wrapped her in a hug. "You're the sister I never had. You and Hope. Aunt Martha and Dottie have been the moms I never had. I love you all so much."

Jamey squeezed back hard. "Aww, Mads. You'll always be part of my family. And little wiggle worm, too, whoever she or he is." She rubbed Maddie's belly, still amazed that in only a few months, Maddie would become a mother.

Maddie tilted her head up, a sly look in her eye. "Now why don't you tell me why you *really* look like the cat that ate the canary?" She stepped back and spotted the new pair of boots on her feet. Her eyes widened and she covered her mouth. "Jameyson O'Neill, are those *hearts on your boots?*"

The flush started in Jamey's chest and rapidly moved up, setting her face on fire.

Maddie skewered her with a hard look. "Those are Tony Lamas. Do you have any idea how much those cost?" She crossed her arms over her protruding belly. "Spill."

Jamey shrugged. "Honestly, there's not much to tell."

Maddie made a disbelieving noise in the back of her throat. "Except that my brother-in-law is buying you gifts. *That you're wearing.*" She raised her eyebrow archly. "I've never seen you out of your purple Doc Martens except at my wedding."

She shifted uncomfortably, wiping her suddenly sweaty hands on her short skirt. "He's... we're... it's complicated, Maddie."

Maddie's eyes flashed concern. "Are you sure you know what you're doing, Jamey? I don't want you to get hurt. He stood you up. I know you tried to hide it, and–"

"And he's dyslexic, Mads."

Maddie's eyes widened as her disclosure sunk in.

"Severely dyslexic."

Maddie opened her mouth to speak, then snapped it shut, shock on her face.

She hated disclosing that. It wasn't her secret to share, but Maddie needed to know there was a good man underneath his blustery exterior. And a great lover. "Please, please don't say anything to Blake. I don't think anyone knows but me right now, and it's up to Brodie who knows."

"He's sharing secrets with you?" Maddie squealed, her voice incredulous.

No denying it any longer. Not with the boots on her feet. They'd agreed to be discreet, but it didn't feel right keeping *everything* from Maddie. Guilt prodded at her. If the party went well, she could tell Maddie about the gluten, after.

Maddie clapped her hands. "Brodie and Jamey sitting in a tree…"

Jamey held up a hand, trying not to laugh. "Stop."

"K-I-S-S–"

"I mean it Maddie. It's new. And we're still feeling our way."

Maddie blew out a breath, lifting her bangs off her forehead. "Well it's no surprise, really. You two have chemistry for days. He couldn't keep his eyes off you at the wedding."

The reminder of the searing kiss they'd shared down at the barn sent a rush of warmth straight to her pussy. Maddie was right. They did have chemistry for days. And it seemed like there was much more underneath.

She'd been shocked when Brodie had come into the kitchen with the boots the other morning. And the pink embroidered hearts were a sweet touch. There was a thoughtful, romantic side to Brodie she was quickly falling for. He might not say the right words, but his actions, his encouragement… the way he paid attention to little things, impressed her.

"Tell me this means you'll stick around past the end of the month." Maddie's eyes filled with pleading. "Blake would be thrilled. He said Mason Carter was really impressed with you and Brodie. He's decided to model his ranch in Montana after the lodge. You can't ask for a better endorsement than that." She rubbed her belly and grinned hopefully. "Plus, baby needs a crazy auntie."

Jamey's heart warmed. The thought of being a crazy auntie to a little Maddie or Blake was certainly enticing. Almost as enticing as exploring something deeper with

Brodie. She'd been secretly mulling it over since he'd blurted out she should stay.

"I've thought about it."

"Really?" Maddie gushed, unable contain her enthusiasm.

She nodded. Her own brothers were nowhere near having children. If she was honest with herself, she couldn't imagine life in a place with no brothers or no Maddie. The months that she'd been alone in Chicago, once Maddie had moved back to Prairie, had been lonely and cold. She didn't like the thought of pulling up stakes solely because her gig at the lodge was over.

The blast of horns honking and the squeal of tires brought her attention back to the kitchen.

"Oh Lordy, the grannie brigade is here." Maddie grinned over at her. "I'm going to need a glass of that cider." She grabbed a flute from the counter and held it out for Jamey to fill.

## Chapter Thirty-Two

*A* knock sounded at the kitchen door. "Yoo-hoo." Dottie stuck her head in. Her eyes widened at the spread on the island. "My you've been busy."

Jamey pushed down the snappy comeback and put on a smile. "Why, yes, I have. Would you like a glass of bubbles?" She'd put on a good face for Maddie today, even if it meant she had to bite clean through her tongue to do it.

"I'll pour, Jamey." Maddie reached for the bottle. "She gets a little tiddly after a few glasses." She spoke low enough only Jamey could hear.

Jamey'd make sure the champagne flowed, then. Even if she had to drive some of the women home herself.

Maddie handed Dottie a glass, and led her into the great room. Jamey followed with the champagne and a tray of flutes. The rest of the women, Aunt Martha, Millie Prescott, Gloria McPherson – the organist at which church Jamey couldn't remember, and Emmaline Andersson, the local dressmaker, were in the process of rearranging the furniture in the great room. Millie held an enormous bouquet she'd brought with her from her grocery store.

"Put that down wherever you like, Millie. I'll start bringing out the food. Champagne anyone? Once the food's out, help yourselves."

The ladies eagerly took glasses. Maddie's sister-in-law, Emma, who'd driven over from Kansas City, began to pile boxes and bags of gifts in front of the hearth. Pretty soon it would look like a pink and blue explosion had taken place.

"I hope you drove down in Blake's truck, Mads," Jamey said dryly. "You may need a trailer hitch to haul all this loot back to the Big House."

Maddie settled herself in one of the big leather chairs, beaming. Jamey kept bringing out the food while the women dug into the boxes. Periodically, she'd hear an "ooh" or a squeal of "That's SO adorable."

Once the table was laid, Jamey refilled her own glass and perched on the arm of the chair Millie occupied.

Maddie looked over at her, eyes shining, and pointed to a large wooden cradle at her feet. "Look at this, Jamey. This was my cradle. Dad and Uncle Eddie refinished it."

Jamey lifted her glass in a salute to Martha. "You must be so excited, Martha."

"Oh, we're all excited," Gloria interjected. "We never thought any of the Sinclaire boys would settle down. This is the future of Prairie."

"No pressure though, sweetie pie," Dottie patted Maddie's knee. "Little Blake can grow up to be whatever he wants."

"Are you having a boy, Maddie?" Emmaline asked from the table, the plate in her hands piled high.

Just how Jamey liked it. There was nothing quite so satisfying as seeing happy people eat her food.

"We're waiting to be surprised."

Dottie narrowed her eyes, studying Maddie's belly. "What does Ben say?"

"He won't."

"What do you mean, he won't?" Dottie crossed her arms. "You tell that boy I said to spill the beans."

Maddie shook her head. "You know how he is, Dottie. He'll say something if and when he's ready."

Emma nodded in agreement. "There's no making Ben do anything until he's ready." She pointed to the box resting on Maddie's knees. "Open that?"

Maddie pulled the lid off the box and gasped, pulling out a long and obviously very old lace baby dress.

"This is the Sinclaire family christening gown," Emma explained. "If you look inside the hem of the underdress, the year and name of every child who's worn it have been embroidered. The oldest date goes back to nineteen hundred, but I think the gown may be older than that."

Jamey's eyelids prickled.

In all the years she'd known Maddie, she'd carried an air of loneliness. Seeing Maddie glowing and basking in the love of so many people unleashed something deep inside her. Her own family was loud and boisterous. They'd as soon fight you as take care of you. They loved loud and hard.

This – what she was experiencing in Prairie – was love of community. Deep ties to place and to the people they worked alongside. Maybe it was the nature of her Irish roots to feel a bit melancholy that her family had experienced the world so differently. They'd fought and clawed to eek out a living, both in the old country and the new.

Another group squeal pulled Jamey from her reverie. Maddie held a sheer black babydoll negligee with feathers at the hem in one hand, and a hanger with a pair of crotchless panties and a see through bra with the centers cut out in the other.

"Well that ought to float Blake's boat."

The women giggled uncontrollably.

"Exactly," Gloria clapped. "If I've learned one thing as a woman, is that it's important to have as much fun after the baby as you did when making the baby."

Maddie's face turned three shades of pink.

Jamey couldn't resist teasing. "Oh I'm sure she had fun making the baby."

Martha giggled and took a sip of her champagne. "It's pretty easy to have fun when someone as handsome as Blake Sinclaire wants to twiddle your diddle."

Emmaline choked on her drink. This set off another round of tittering from the older women.

Dottie shifted her gaze to Jamey, eyes narrowing shrewdly. "And what's this I hear about Brodie being dead gone on you?"

It was her turn to choke on her drink. Her face burned.

"I saw them making out behind the livestock barn at the county fair," Millie volunteered.

She did? Jamey could have sworn they were completely alone.

Gloria tittered. "Ooh, he was always my favorite. Such big, strong muscles. And that devastating smile."

His smile was definitely that.

"And those blue, blue eyes," Dottie added with an appreciative smile.

Jamey cleared her throat. "Um. Yes, well. It seems like the cat's out of the bag."

Martha raised her glass. "Congratulations. You're the first person that's kept Brodie's attention longer than a week."

Longer than a week, huh? Was she stupid for thinking

they could be anything other than a fling? Jamey's stomach dropped to her ankles.

Dottie gave her a sharp glance. "I just hope you two've used condoms. We don't need a Sinclaire baby boom around here. Maddie and Blake have given us more than enough excitement for quite some time."

Great. Maddie had warned her about the Prairie Posse, but she hadn't been prepared for this level of frankness from women she barely knew.

Millie sighed rhapsodically. "Babies are a gift from the universe. No amount of protection would have stopped this soul from choosing Maddie and Blake at this time."

Dottie rolled her eyes. "Lord help the man that falls for you and your metaphysical mumbo jumbo, Millie."

"The universe will bring us together at the perfect time."

Maddie stood and stretched her lower back. "Oh hush. I know you're all as excited as we are."

Hearing Maddie refer to herself as *we* after so many years of *me, I,* and *my,* tugged at Jamey's heart.

Would she ever be a *we*? Could she be a *we* with Brodie? Lately, it felt like she could. And surprisingly, the idea didn't scare her. But the town's gossip did. Was she fooling herself into another heartbreak?

"These scones are heavenly, Jamey," Emmaline gushed. "They're the perfect texture. What's your secret?"

She shrugged and gave her an enigmatic smile. "That magic combination of flour, sugar, protein, and fat." Gluten-free flour, but she'd never spill the beans. Especially in front of Dottie.

Maddie spooned a bit of jam on her bite and popped it in her mouth, groaning. "God, Dottie. Have you tried these?"

A pained expression crossed Dottie's face and she coughed. "Yes, yes. Very good."

Jamey couldn't help a slow grin. "Thanks." She'd take the compliment, even if it was given under duress.

Maddie shot a hopeful smile in her direction. "It's so nice to see my two favorite people appreciating each other." She surveyed the group, her eyes lighting with excitement. "Jamey's considering staying long term at the lodge."

For the second time, Jamey choked on her champagne. Let the romance cat out of the bag, and suddenly Maddie had her living happily ever after.

"So things are that serious between you and Brodie?" Gloria practically bounced in her chair with delight. "We'd love it if you stayed."

"Oh I think it's serious," Maddie blurted, pointing to her feet. "Look at the boots he gave her."

The women collectively *oohed* and *ahhed* as they admired her new boots, giving each other knowing looks.

Jamey fought the urge to retreat to the kitchen. This was why she preferred to work parties, rather than attend them. The conversation was supposed to be about Maddie, not whether or not Brodie was her boyfriend, and she was staying in Prairie. The irony of Maddie being the gossip instigator hit her. She'd better get used to living under a microscope if she decided to stay.

Millie clapped her hands excitedly. "Would you teach me how to make the little macarons then? I want to feature them in my coffee bar at the grocery. And maybe your scones, too." She shot a guilty look at Dottie. "And of course some of your apple pie, Dottie. No one can get enough of your pie."

Jamey coughed and hid a smile. "Well, I hadn't given it much thought yet." She darted an *'are you feckin' crazy'* glare at Maddie. "But I suppose I could put together some class-es." As she spoke, the idea sprung to life.

There were enough celebrations in town, she could surely pick up a little high end pastry catering. And when there were no guests, she could offer classes at the lodge. Pastry with champagne, tasting meals, romantic dinners. The income would easily put the lodge in the black and give her the creative outlet she'd need to stay anywhere long term.

She could even host pop-up fancy dinners. Pop-up restaurants were becoming the rage in Chicago, and there was no reason she couldn't bring that concept to Prairie. Even draw day-trippers down from Manhattan or Kansas City.

Her heart pounded as the vision unfolded. It would take a few days to research, but if she spun the proposal right, maybe she could be in charge in more than name only. Her brother's voice niggled at the back of her brain. *'No more ventures without a contract, Jameyson. You work too hard to let yourself get screwed over by dick.'*

Brodie wasn't that kind of person, though. Maybe he had been, but not anymore. Certainly not since they'd become official. He helped her in the kitchen with a smile on his face. She smiled at the dirty memory.

Partnering with Brodie would never be dull.

Of that, she was certain.

"Earth to Jamey." Maddie appeared at her elbow, eyes full of concern. "Are you all right? It was okay I let the cat out of the bag, wasn't it? I'm just so excited about the possibility of having you close by when the baby comes. And I think you have so much to offer a place like Prairie."

"What about Brodie? Are you excited about that, too?"

Maddie's eyes warmed. "I want you to be happy, Jamey. And if Brodie makes you happy…"

"Aww, Mads." Jamey leaned over Maddie's burgeoning belly, and caught her in a hug. "You're adorable all bloomin' and twitterpated. Even if you can't keep your big mouth shut."

Maddie slid her a sly glance. "I still can't get over you and Brodie. You're as wild as he is. Maybe that's what you both need. Someone strong to challenge the other."

"Keep me on the straight and narrow?"

"I don't think anyone could do that," Maddie laughed.

"I'll admit, it's nice having someone in my corner."

Really nice.

## Chapter Thirty-Three

*B*rodie opened the door to the kitchen and stuck in his head. "Is the coast clear?"

Jamey entered from the great room carrying a big platter of treats. Her smile conveyed mischief and promise. "It's just us."

His cock swelled as he took her in. She wore the boots he'd given her, and a short denim skirt that swayed when she moved. He liked her in her chef's outfit, but loved it when she dressed up. The woman had a rock hard ass that begged to be palmed, and legs for days. His mouth watered seeing them bare like this.

The urge to lift her onto the counter so he could spread her wide and caress the silky tops of her thighs, the juncture of leg and pussy, propelled him to action. Not taking his eyes off her, he stepped in, pulling the door shut and locking it behind him. "Good." He waggled his eyebrows at her questioning glance. "This way no one can surprise us."

She laughed breathlessly and darted around the island. "Oh no you don't, hotcakes. I'm still on clean up duty."

"I'll help." He stalked around the other side of the island, and she sidestepped back, trying to keep the island between them.

Like that was going to divert him.

They circled the island, and when she was between the island and the sink, he stopped.

She bit her lip, eyes twinkling.

He bit back a groan, loving the way her teeth reddened her lower lip. A lip made for sucking and nipping.

"Brodie?" She spoke suspiciously, her voice going up at the end.

"Jamey?" He mimicked her perfectly.

Another nervous giggle escaped her. "What do you want?"

"You don't know?"

She gave him a hot look while her tongue darted out to wet her lips. His cock jumped, pressing hard against his zipper. The looks she gave him could bring him to his knees.

Her gaze drifted down and she cracked a slow, knowing smile. She lifted a shoulder and rolled her lips together.

"If you're a good girl," he rasped. "I'll give you two orgasms."

Her eyes darkened rapidly. She wouldn't hold out much longer.

"And if I'm naughty?" Her voice held a husky note of want.

He braced his hands on the island and leaned in. "If you're naughty, then I'll give you three orgasms and a spanking."

Her eyes grew wide and her mouth opened slightly. She swallowed, her cheeks flushing pink. "Promise?" The quaver in her voice told him she was halfway to her first orgasm and he hadn't even touched her.

"I guaran-damn-tee it."

Keeping her eyes on him, she swiped a metal canister and sauntered slowly around the island. Holding up a finger, she tipped the canister upside-down and sprayed, forming a mound of whipped cream on her finger. Slowly, she brought her finger to her mouth, her tongue darting out to lick the tip.

Holy. Hell.

His mouth went dry at the sight of her licking her finger like a goddamned lollipop. She dipped it fully into her mouth and, turning a scorching gaze on him, slowly pulled out her finger, finishing the gesture by licking the remaining cream off her lips.

All the blood in his body rushed to his cock. He fisted his hand on the counter to keep his knees from giving out. "Jesus, Jamey."

"This kind of naughty?" She squeezed another dollop of cream onto her finger, repeating the motion.

Only one outcome would be hotter than her teasing him like this. He reached for her, but she stepped just out of distance, smirking and raising her chin. "Pants."

Slowly, he brought his hand to his belt buckle, unhooking it. There was no mistaking the pure lust and anticipation written on her features. Heady stuff. In one smooth movement, he pulled down the zipper and thrust his jeans over his hips, springing his cock free.

Her gasp cut the heady silence.

God, her reactions fluffed his ego.

He raised an eyebrow, standing a little prouder. "Like what you see?"

She brought her attention to his jutting cock and slowly nodded, eyes gleaming with pure hunger. Her tongue darted out, wetting her lower lips in anticipation.

Brodie's pulse quickened, throbbing in his temple.

She sank to her knees, glancing up at him through her lashes with a naughty smirk. Sticking out her tongue, she squirted a tiny amount of whipped cream onto the tip. He groaned and his cock twitched, desire settling like a hot stone in his balls. Still keeping her gaze riveted on him, she leaned forward and licked him, spreading the cream from root to tip.

His breath locked in his throat, the myriad of heady sensations practically blinding him. "Oh God, Jamey," he hissed out when he could breathe again.

He wouldn't last long at this rate. It felt too damned good. Better than when he'd imagined it. Somewhere in the back of his mind it registered she'd dropped the canister. One hand squeezed his ass while the other gently tugged the skin behind his balls. Meanwhile, her tongue kept lapping and swirling over his cock. He threaded a hand through her bright curls.

He groaned loudly when she finally took him fully into her hot, wet mouth. "Christ you're good at this." He clenched his ass, trying not to thrust like a wild man into her mouth.

So fucking beautiful.

The back of her throat against his tip, her velvety tongue rolling over his shaft. His balls hardened to rocks as tension built up the back of his legs. "I'm gonna come, sweetheart," he panted, his eyes rolling backwards. The ripples of sensation melted his insides, rendering him senseless.

She hummed a sigh of satisfaction, setting his cock vibrating. And then sucked a little harder. The sight of her mouth around his cock, curls gently bouncing while he slowly fucked in and out, permanently branded into his memory, and sent him over the edge into oblivion.

With a cry, he released, spurting hot waves of come

against the back of her throat, and still she sucked and hummed like she was making a birthday cake instead of giving him the blowjob of his life.

He clutched at the counter, chest heaving, and waited for the spots to leave his vision. He brushed her curls, gently tugging her head up. She released him, looking like a self-satisfied kitten.

When he'd found his voice again, he started. "I've never…"

She leaned back on her heels, a little flash of pride crossing her face. "Was that naughty enough for you?"

He leaned over and helped her up. "Very." In a swift movement, he'd seated her on the counter and stepped between her legs. "Let's see what we have under here." He ran his hands the length of her thighs, fully intending to stop when his fingers hit lace. Only they hit… nothing.

He let out a hiss. "Jesus, you're full of surprises."

She smirked triumphantly, running her fingers through his hair and sending shivers down his spine. "I'm waiting for that spanking, cowboy."

In spite of the explosive orgasm she'd just given him, hunger for her, desire to bury himself deep inside her, had him thickening again. "In time, in time."

He grabbed a chocolate covered strawberry from the plate next to her on the counter. Slowly he drew the tip toward her sex, then ran it gently up and down her slit. Her thighs tensed and her eyes widened.

"Like that?" he murmured. "Tell me what it feels like."

She released a shaky breath. "H-h-h-hot… and cool."

He kept stroking. "Hmm… both?"

He withdrew the berry and brought it to his mouth. She let out a needy whimper. He took a small bite, tasting the mix of chocolate, strawberry, and her. The flavor acted like a fuse, sending a hot spike of lust straight through him.

He brought it to her lips, teasing her full, lower lip until she bit. A drop of pink juice dribbled down her chin.

Groaning, he leaned in, capturing the drop with his tongue before claiming her mouth. Her hand pulled at the back of his neck, inviting him deeper, and he thrust his tongue into the silky cavern of her mouth, tasting a heady mix of sweet and salt, hot and cool.

Driving his hand through her hair, he plundered her mouth, over and over, unable to get enough of her taste. Unable to get enough of her. He slipped his other hand back under her skirt, reaching for and finding her wet slit. She adjusted, opening for him, and he stroked up and down, brushing her clit with each movement. Her hips rolled in invitation, and he thrust one finger, then two, deep into her creamy hot channel. Her walls clenched his fingers and she groaned into his mouth.

He pulled his mouth away with a groan. Her eyes were wild and glazed, her breath coming in shallow movements. Sliding his fingers from her, he brought them, drenched in her essence, to her mouth.

"Taste yourself, Jamey. Taste how hot you are." He teased her mouth open, running his wet fingers along her lips. "Suck them. Suck them like you sucked me." He thrust his fingers into her mouth and she clamped down, sucking hard, her tongue lapping her cream like a popsicle.

The sensation brought lights to the edge of his vision. Fuck going slow, he had to be in her now. He tugged on his fingers, and she released them with a cry.

"Stand up." He pulled her hips to the edge of the counter and helped her down. Then, turning her, he rucked her skirt above her waist, baring her perfect ass. She tossed him a wanton look over her shoulder as she bent forward, tipping her ass up just enough that her glistening pussy lips peeked out.

"God help me, you're fucking perfect." He buried himself to the hilt in one hard thrust. She groaned and bucked back, the walls of her slick channel convulsing around him with the same intensity her mouth had.

The crash of a tray sounded.

"Brodie," she gasped, "What about that spanking?"

Jesus. "Are you sure?"

She nodded, her curls bouncing.

Her request hooked a place deep inside him and he nearly came undone. He brought his hand to her ass. Just hard enough to pink the soft flesh. She was gorgeous all splayed out like this, half clothed and skin flushed.

She cried out, her voice keening. "Oh God, yes. Again."

He smacked her cheek again, rubbing over the mark, then brought his hand around to capture her clit between thumb and forefinger. He gave a little squeeze, and she convulsed around him, over and over, crying loudly in her release, and triggering his own.

He thrust deep into her, his balls bumping against the wetness of her pussy with each stroke as his vision narrowed. He collapsed over her, clutching her to himself as they slowly floated back to earth.

"I think I love you," he murmured in her ear.

She hummed in the back of her throat. "You're just saying that."

"I do."

"Tell me that in the cold light of day and not after the best sex of your life."

He placed a little kiss behind her hear. "That good for you, too?"

"Mmmhmm."

"Even though it was only one orgasm, not three?"

"I'll collect later."

Warmth reignited in his chest again. He could get used to this… contentment.

The crunch of tires on gravel spurred them both to action.

"Shit."

"Oh my God, Brodie, look at this." Jamey stood, fluffing her skirt back into place, eyes wide and laughing.

He fumbled with his belt as the scene before him sunk in. Crumbled food littered the island. A ceramic tray lay broken on the floor, its remaining strawberries scattered across the kitchen.

He stepped backwards toward the door, unlocking and opening it just as Blake and Simon stepped to the threshold.

Double shit.

He scrubbed a hand across his face, his mind racing with excuses.

"What in the hell happened here?" Blake asked, scanning the room.

Jamey giggled, her face pink. She glanced at Simon, then back at him. They both spoke in unison. "Food fight."

## Chapter Thirty-Four

*B*rodie whistled as he tossed clean hay into one of the stalls. For the first time in his life, he felt like he was going someplace. Like the universe was finally on his side. The last few weeks with Jamey had been incredible. They made a great team. Not just in bed, but in how they got through a day.

The way she'd shoot him a secret smile over the head of a guest, or she'd bring him lemonade when he was working on a project, or clearing out cedar stumps. And she no longer shooed him out of the kitchen. That had to mean something, didn't it?

Content.

He kept coming back to that word. For the first time in his adult life, he had something to look forward to. He Daydreamed about the future. Hoped that if he was lucky, those daydreams might become reality.

Simon entered the barn with a bucket and shovel. Brodie watched with pride as the boy put up his tools and came to stand in front of him. "I got the coop cleaned out. Just like you showed me."

"Good job, my man." He ruffled the boy's head.

He'd come to love Simon. It hadn't been easy at first. Especially knowing that if things had gone different, Simon might have been his son, not his half-brother. Ben had straightened him out with a little counsel and perspective. Now, he couldn't imagine the ranch without Simon.

And lately, he'd found himself daydreaming of sons. Redheaded sons with green eyes... and freckles.

"When will the chickens start laying eggs?"

"Not 'till early spring."

Simon wrinkled his nose. "I hate waiting."

"You and me both, kiddo."

"Can I watch you chop wood? Jamey said that's next on our list." Simon fished in his pocket and pulled out a crumpled piece of paper with Jamey's bold scrawl, holding it out.

He waved it off. "Whatever she says. I'll get the maul."

Jamey was right. He needed to arrange for a tutor. But he wasn't ready to face the pity in people's eyes, or the mean triumph in someone like Kylee Ross's eyes, when word got out he couldn't read. And word would get out. It was Prairie.

Jamey had been bugging him about it relentlessly, and he'd finally promised to do it, but still hadn't managed to make the call.

Simon trailed him out to the woodpile. "Are we having another bonfire?"

He nodded and placed the first log on the splitting stump. "Yep. Tonight or tomorrow."

Simon stood a safe distance back and tossed bark at the tree.

Brodie swung, and the maul cracked the wood, splitting it nearly to the bottom. He heaved again and the log broke in two.

"Can I try?"

Brodie looked over his shoulder, sizing up his little brother. Simon was still on the wiry side, but determined to be a man. The protective part of him thought he was still too young. But looking back, he and his brothers had started chopping wood at a much younger age. "All right. Time you learned something new anyhow. Grab a log."

Simon grabbed a log and set it on the stump.

Brodie squatted down with the maul. "Safety first. See this?" He ran his thumb across the edge. "Feel it. Just like I did."

Simon gently rubbed his finger over the edge, fear and excitement in his eyes. "It's not very sharp."

"It doesn't have to be. It's still as dangerous as any of Jamey's knives. What do you think would happen if it came in contact with a body part?"

Simon's eyes widened. Brodie nodded. "I've seen careless people crush and even lose fingers. Treat it with respect."

He stood, and placed a log on the stump. "Safety first. Do you have your protective glasses?"

Simon sprinted to the barn and jogged back, safety glasses in place.

"Come over to the wood. See all these cracks?" He pointed out the places on the wood.

"Aim for one of those, but by the edge. They'll split better."

He stepped back, leaving the maul touching the wood. "Next, make sure you're standing in the right place to aim. Always mark your shot."

"Kind of like we do for target shooting."

"Yeah. Kinda."

Brodie brought the maul back across his body. "See how I'm holding this?"

Simon nodded solemnly.

"This is where you start. Then as you lift, slide your hand down, and swing."

The maul came down hard and split the wood on the first try.

"You'll build muscles doing this." He grinned at his little brother. "Girls will be chasing you all over the playground."

"Just like they chased you?"

"I think I chased them, too. But yeah." He stacked another piece, and prepared to swing.

"Are you going to marry Jamey?"

The question, asked so innocently, startled him. He missed his swing and the maul glanced off the wood. "Here. You try. Remember to hike up on the handle if it's too heavy." He handed the maul to Simon, hand shaking slightly.

In his mind he'd imagined them spending the future together, but he'd never named it. She was just there with him. And a few redheaded sons.

But marriage?

Getting down on one knee and proposing?

He wasn't a love and fluff kinda guy.

And the one time he'd blurted out that he loved Jamey, she'd scoffed. So he hadn't mentioned it again.

But she'd loved the boots he'd given her. Enough to wear them frequently. He hadn't convinced her to ditch the hideous shiny purple clodhoppers she favored, but he hadn't seen them on her feet as often since he'd given her the boots.

"So are you?" Simon stood staring at him, holding the maul just like he'd been shown.

"Am I what?"

"Going to marry Jamey?"

He scrubbed his hand over his face, unsure of how to answer. "You think I should marry her?"

Simon shot him a smile, then furrowed his brow in concentration as he raised the maul over his head and brought it down. It glanced off the wood. Not bad for a first try.

"I'd marry her." Simon delivered his statement with conviction.

Brodie narrowed his eyes, studying Simon. The boy was growing up quickly. And obviously trying to imitate his big brothers. "Why's that?"

Simon readied the maul again. "'Cause she's pretty."

He'd call her beautiful. Wild and strong. And beautiful. Like a mustang filly who'd never be all the way tame. "Well, don'tcha want more than pretty?"

Simon swung again, this time splitting the wood halfway down. He rolled his eyes at Brodie. "Well, duh… she cooks good, too. Everybody knows you should marry a good cook."

He snorted.

Blake had missed that message. Maddie couldn't even make decent coffee, but they seemed happy enough. Disgustingly happy.

This time, Simon's swing split the log. Brodie hid a smile as Simon puffed out his chest and tossed the log on the woodpile. Then Simon swung back around and scowled, folding his arms across his body. "You *do* like her cooking, don't you?"

"Of course I like her cooking."

"Better than Dottie's?"

God, the kid was brutal. "Yes. Better than Dottie's. But don't you tell Dottie that." He nodded at the woodpile. "You want to do another?"

Simon shook his head, a sheepish smile covering his face.

"Don't worry. Do a little every day and pretty soon you'll be chopping the whole pile." Brodie took the maul from Simon, its weight long a comfort in his hands.

He vividly remembered the first time Blake had shown him how to chop wood. He could barely lift the maul over his head, and Blake and Ben had rolled on the ground laughing. But he'd shown them. He'd gone out every day after school and made himself chop one more log than the day before. Pretty soon, he'd chopped circles around them, even though they'd been in high school.

Brodie placed another log on the stump and swung the maul high. Simon leaned against the tree, staring at him intently. "You know what the best thing about Jamey is though?"

The way she sighed in the back of her throat just before she came? Or the way she seemed to float through the kitchen like a ballerina when she was in her cooking zone. Maybe it was the look on her face at the moment he pushed into her slick heat. The look that told him he was everything she wanted.

Thinking of her hot and ready like that, heated his blood. If he wasn't careful, he'd have a lot more explaining to do for Simon than just wood chopping. "What?" he grunted, pulling the maul from the wood.

"She's good. Like Maddie. She doesn't let you do dumb stuff."

"Yep. She definitely doesn't let you do dumb stuff."

"I think that's how you know they love you."

Brodie looked sharply at Simon. How'd the kid get so perceptive? He was starting to sound like Ben. "They don't let you do dumb stuff because they love you? Yeah, that makes sense."

Did that mean Jamey loved him?

All her fussing and nagging about learning to read?

"And she taught me how to cuss. Real cussing."

Brodie covered a smile. If the look of delight on Simon's face was any indication, the boy had developed a serious crush. He chuckled. "Yeah. She's a master at cussing."

He liked the dirty side of her. Very much indeed. Especially when it involved cussing. Hell, sometimes he'd poke her just to hear her spout off.

Simon crossed his arms again. "So I think you should marry her."

"'Cause you will if I don't?" Something hot and possessive bloomed inside him. It didn't matter Simon was just a kid. Anyone looking at Jamey romantically bothered him.

Simon shot him a scowl. "Because you're just dumb if you don't." A small smile curved his mouth. "But I hope I marry someone like her."

Marriage.

How would he even ask her? She'd roll her eyes at flowers. She'd laugh outright if he got down on one knee. Not that fairy tale romance was his style. Simon had certainly given him lots to think about. "Well come on, Romeo. Let's get some lemonade. Chopping wood always makes me thirsty."

And horny.

Hopefully, once Simon was on his way home, he could find Jamey and sneak in some naughty time. They had a small window of time this afternoon before the mad flurry of activity that occurred prior to guests arriving. He meant to make use of it.

He draped an arm across his little brother's shoulders, surprised at how Simon had begun to fill out. He'd be a man before any of them were ready. They crossed the yard and entered the kitchen.

Brodie grabbed two glasses and opened the fridge searching for Jamey's famous basil lemonade. It sounded frou-frou, but it was delicious. Especially after he'd worked up a sweat. He offered a glass to Simon, who was studying Jamey's list again.

"We're supposed to clean the drains. How do we do that?"

"First we run the dishwasher." Brodie drained his glass, then flipped it upside down on a rack that held other miscellaneous dishes and pushed it into the washer. He pulled down the lever and showed Simon the start button. "Pretty easy, huh?"

Simon nodded, pouring a second helping of the lemonade.

"Then we just pour some powder down the drains. It helps keep them clean and free of food."

"That's not too hard."

"Nope. Piece of cake. There's a box on the shelf under the sink."

Simon ducked down and stood with two boxes. "Which one?"

Shit.

How the fuck was he supposed to know? Jamey'd never taught him this. Sure, he'd seen her do it a thousand times, but for the life of him he couldn't remember what color box she used.

Yellow or orange?

He pulled his fingers through his hair and squeezed his eyes shut, trying to remember the last time he'd seen Jamey cleaning the drains. He blew out a long breath. "What do the boxes say?"

"Baking soda and washing soda."

"Go with the washing soda."

Simon dumped the contents of the yellow box down the drain. He replaced the boxes under the sink, then rose to offer Brodie a high five. "Guess we're done, huh?"

"Anything else on your list?"

Simon pulled out the crumpled paper and studied it again, shaking his head. "Nope. She said I could take some kitchen sink cookies back to the Big House with me."

Brodie saw two brown paper bags tucked away in the corner. "Those them? She bribing you with cookies?"

Simon tossed him a gleeful grin as he grabbed the bags, opened one and stuffed a cookie into his mouth on his way out the door.

"See you, kiddo." Now to hunt down Jamey and investigate what color lingerie she was wearing today.

## Chapter Thirty-Five

*N*ervous anticipation thrummed through Jamey as she sat in the office, double-checking her numbers. Pulling the numbers and fully fleshing out her proposal had taken the better part of the last few days. But if Brodie went for this – and there was no reason why he shouldn't – they would be sole owners of the lodge in five years. Or less. She'd been conservative with her projections.

Restaurants failed over half the time, but their advantage here was diversifying. Between catering special events, classes, lodge guests, and her pop-up restaurant idea, they could ride out the slow months and the slow start to building repeat lodge guests. And, if she could convince Brodie to build a smoke house, they could get certified to sell smoked meats, locally and online. They could put Prairie on the map as a local food mecca.

She glanced at the notebook to her side. Being with Brodie had once again opened the floodgates to her creativity. She had more ideas than she could execute in a year, and more would come.

She knew it.

Every time she sat down to plan, the ideas kept coming.

Taking a deep breath, she hit the print button. Excitement flooded down to her fingertips. She hadn't felt this way since she'd been accepted to Le Cordon Bleu. Of course the fallout with her family once she'd told them of her plans had been epic. But she'd weathered the storm.

Her brothers remained unconvinced, especially in light of the Frenchie O'Neill's debacle. But she'd learned her lesson. She'd ask Jarrod to draw up a contract with a fair escape clause should things go wonky. But they wouldn't. Not with Brodie. And this was in Brodie's best interests. The plan capitalized on his natural talent.

"Whatcha doing' there, chef?" Brodie's voice slid over her like whiskey-infused caramel sauce and dripped with innuendo.

She turned to catch Brodie lounging in the doorway giving her body a blatant once over. She caught the faint aroma of fresh cedar. He must have been out chopping wood again. Chopping wood seemed to give him wood.

Every. Damned. Time.

Not that she was complaining.

She was half convinced her frequency of orgasm had something to do with her current flood of creativity. She leaned a hip on the desk, giving him her own perusal. His muscles perfectly filled out the blue tee he wore. The same color blue as his eyes.

Mmm, yes.

She'd take him over dessert any day.

But today, she'd postpone their afternoon tryst. She couldn't wait any longer to show him her plan. Once he'd seen it, they could take it to Blake and then go celebrate. "I have something to show you." She made the innuendo clear.

His eyes lit. "That lacy pair of panties I ordered you?"

Her pussy clenched at his words. An unmarked package had arrived for her yesterday, containing a black lace pair of cutout panties with a matching garter and see-through bra. He'd definitely appreciate what he found underneath her bulky chef's clothes today. She raised her eyebrows. "Mmm… perhaps."

He leaned forward, eyes hopeful.

"But first, I have something exciting to show you."

He stepped into the room, crowding her against the desk. "Can't possibly be more exciting than you naked in my arms."

She tilted her head and leaned in for a kiss, brushing her lips across his, then leaned back, teasing, when he opened for more. She placed a finger over his mouth. "More kisses in a minute. I want to show you something. You're going to love it."

"I'm going to love kissing you more." He growled low, dodging her fingers and laying a kiss on her neck in the spot that always made her squeal.

"Brodie, please." She giggled, then allowed herself one more delicious kiss, enjoying the swipe of his tongue as it curled against hers. Pushing him back, she grabbed the papers and his hand, and led him out to the great room.

He settled in one of the oversized leather chairs, and she climbed into his lap. The first time he'd pulled her onto his lap, she'd been surprised. Nervous even. But cuddling against him felt… right. And they'd ended up spending many evenings like that after the guests had retired. Cuddled up, talking and teasing. Enjoying a fire in the fireplace and a nightcap. Sometimes even a little teenage-style making out. This was the best place for a heart to heart about the future of the lodge. Even in the middle of the afternoon.

Brodie stroked a finger down her cheek, eyes dancing. "So… what do you have to show me that's so important sexy time has to wait?"

Her heart thudded in her chest, full of eager anticipation. "Remember a few days ago at the baby shower?"

"You mean the day we had the food fight?" He winked at her and nuzzled her neck.

Her body warmed at the memory. "Do you ever stop thinking about sex?"

"With you? No."

She giggled. There was something so sweet about that. So… reassuring. And yes, so damned sexy.

"Ok, forget about sex for a moment."

"Can't do that."

"Brodie."

"What?" He perfectly mimicked the way she said his name.

"Be serious."

"Only if you give me another kiss." He rubbed his hand along her thigh, bringing it back to rest on her hip and squeezing.

She rolled her eyes, unable to contain a smile. "Fine. But only one. This is important."

"So is this," he answered, slanting his head to hers.

She lost herself in the sensation of his mouth. His tongue slowly stroking hers, the way his cock would later. God, she would never tire of kissing this man. Never. A little sigh escaped and she tucked her head under his chin, reveling in the pure contentment that came over her. "Can we please talk about this now?"

He pulled her closer, one of his hands stroking her back. "I suppose."

"Should I move to the other chair? Out of temptation's way?"

He growled low and shook his head.

"Fine. But if you get handsy, I'm scooting over." She grabbed the papers from the side table and handed them to him.

"What's this?"

"Our plan."

"For the lodge?"

She nodded. "A five year plan for solvency."

A shadow crossed Brodie's face and his eyes became guarded. "I'm sorry, can you read it? That's… a lot."

She let out a long breath. "Have you called the school yet?" She could tell by the set of his jaw that he hadn't. His reluctance to take action was becoming a bone of contention between them. She didn't want to nag, but if she didn't, she was afraid he'd never do it. She brought her hand to his cheek. "What if I come with you next week?"

His mouth compressed. "Can we talk about it next week?"

She bit back a frustrated retort. Now wasn't the time for this argument. She nodded. "Sure. Okay." She blew out another breath, some of the excitement leaching out of her.

"So at the baby shower Millie Prescott asked if I would give her lessons on how to make macarons."

"Those are the pink oreos?"

She quirked a smile. Never let a Frenchman hear them called that. "More or less… Anyway, a few of the other women said they'd like lessons, too."

"Sounds good."

"Well, after the party, my brain went crazy. The food was a hit, and I realized that in Prairie and the surrounding areas, there are lots of celebrations where people want nice food. Nicer than Dottie's homemade pies. And that we… I… could offer high-end catering services."

He was paying attention now. "Go on."

"And then, I thought about the pop-up restaurant phenomenon that's taking place in big cities all over, even in Kansas City."

His brow furrowed. "Pop-up restaurant?"

"Restaurant overhead is notoriously costly. The biggest expense of running a stand-alone. A pop-up drastically reduces overhead. It could be someone's home, or a party space, or in our case, the lodge. We'd have to purchase some additional tables, but once a quarter, once a month, basically whenever we decide, we could advertise a pop-up dining experience."

She knew she was spinning it out too fast, but she was too excited to stop. "We could do themed nights, take reservations, even do tasting classes. Advertise in Manhattan, Wichita, even Kansas City. People will drive for a fancy food event. Especially if we brand it as high-end locally sourced, exclusive food."

"But we'd still have the hunting lodge?" His muscles tensed under her. Was he not excited about this?

"Of course. But there will be slow times. Ask any bed and breakfast owner. Even if we brand the lodge as hunting and wrangling, which we should, we'll need additional income."

He made a noncommittal noise in the back of his throat.

"What's wrong?" If he shot this down, she wasn't sure what to do. The lodge needed to diversify to stay solvent.

"What about me?"

She leaned back, surprised. "What do you mean?"

"I mean, what about me?" A tense edge crept into his voice.

"I don't follow. We're partners."

His eyes grew suspicious. "Are we? I hear a lot about cooking and classes. What about me?" The energy crackled off him.

"You'll still be doing what you do best. Wrangling, taking out guests, building."

"So I'm just the work hand."

"No, you're going to keep doing what you're doing."

He picked her up and moved her as he stood, leaving her in the chair, to pace in front of the fireplace. "Which is be the help." He practically spit out the words.

"Brodie, I don't look at you that way at all. I can barely tell a horse's nose from its ass. I don't feel comfortable mixing with guests. You're the entertainer, the host. I work best behind the scenes."

He stopped pacing to stare at her. Hard. "You mentioned a plan…"

This was *not* how she'd envisioned this conversation. "Yes. I have a plan to buy out Blake."

## Chapter Thirty-Six

*J*amey held out the papers. "I know it will take you a long time to read through it, but I've detailed a plan to buy out Blake in five years. We'd have to draw up a contract, and in the end, it would give me fifty-two percent equity, and you forty-eight percent."

His eyes flashed and his pulse throbbed wildly at his temple.

"It's not what you think," she rushed ahead. She needed to explain before he blew a gasket. "The four percent allows for the fact that I will also take over full operations so you don't have to."

"What if I want to?" he ground out, every muscle tensed.

"Brodie, you know I love you, but you don't have a handle on the numbers. It's not your strength. I'm better at it."

Anger flared in his eyes. "Wait just a second. You pick *now* to say you love me? Is that supposed to butter me up? Make this pill easier to swallow?"

TESSA LAYNE

"No... I... it just popped out. I *do* love you. But this is business. This is for both of us."

He folded his arms across his chest. "If you love me, then why do we need a contract?"

Jamey pinched the bridge of her nose. This was coming out all wrong. "Look. I've been down this road before and lost everything because I trusted the wrong person. I'm not going to risk it again."

"You can trust me."

Her heart started to pound wildly. "I know I can. I *do*. But this is still business, and it protects both of us."

"And you're making it so that I work for you." His voice was flat. Hard.

This was not at all the reaction she'd expected. Hoped for. "No. We're partn–"

"Partners means fifty-fifty split."

She folded her hands across her chest, warding off the rising panic. "I'm not going to do fifty-fifty."

He glared at her. "Why the fuck not? We're either in this all the way together, or we're not."

"That's not the point. Of *course* we're in this all the way together. The point is–"

"The point is *I'm* the boss. This is *my* family's property. This is *my* lodge to run."

"But you can't even read. How in the hell do you expect to run a big operation if you can't read?" She hated flinging that at him. Hated using his weakness to make a point. But she knew in her heart of hearts he would run the business into the ground. He'd practically done it already.

He stalked to the fireplace, then spun to face her, arms across his chest. Anger and pain radiated from his eyes. "You're just like the rest of them aren't you? You make a big act of saying it's okay I can't read–"

"I never—"

He held up his hand and continued. "But you think I'm stupid. Just like everyone else."

She crossed to him, reaching out to caress his arm. "I don't. Yes, you need to learn to read, but this isn't about your dyslexia." Her heart twisted when he flinched at her touch. "Dammit, Brodie. Don't make this into something it's not. This is about building a smart business."

His eyes glittered like ice. "Is it now?" Sarcasm dripped from his voice.

That set off the fire brewing in her belly. "Yes," she ground out. "Yes, it is. And if you would stop behaving like a spoiled, self-centered, thumb-sucking, ham-fisted baby, you could see the big picture."

"Tell me what you really think, darlin.'" His voice came out cold and clipped.

Anger rushed through her. Of all the stubborn, short-sighted, muttonheaded responses. Her proposal was brilliant. "Fine, McSnarkypants. If you're such an *idiot* that you can't recognize something great when it's right in front of your face, that's on you. I. Quit."

The words hung between them.

Only the sound of their elevated breathing cut the silence.

For the tiniest of instants, a look like anguish flashed across Brodie's face. Then his eyes hardened. "Fine. But next time you accuse someone of not recognizing what's right in front of their face, take a look in the Goddamned mirror." He stalked past her and through the kitchen, where she heard the back door slam.

What in the saints had just happened?

Had she really just quit her job?

Quit them?

Had he really just shut her down without even considering she was right? Two tears pricked behind her eye. Oh no. She would not cry. She *would not* cry. No man was worth any more of her tears. Not even Brodie. And she'd let it slip that she loved him. How stupid was *that*?

Pain stabbed through her so intensely, she couldn't breathe. She sat down hard as the room began to tilt. She squeezed her eyes shut and pinched the bridge of her nose, unable to prevent a little sob from escaping. She picked up the papers she'd placed on the side table and crumpled them one by one, tossing them at the fireplace. A solitary tear leaked out. She furiously brushed it away.

*Get a grip, Jamey. Get a grip.*

The pressure in her chest increased and pushed up into her throat. If she continued to sit here, she'd melt. She'd disintegrate into a weak, blubbering puddle. Giving herself a shake, she rubbed her hands along her thighs and stood. She stared down at the space in front of the fireplace, her dreams as crumpled as the papers at her feet. Nausea roiled in the pit of her stomach. Let Brodie pick them up. Let him throw their future away.

She whipped around and made for the kitchen. She had a job to do and guests to prepare for. She could hike up to the Big House later and give her resignation to Blake. Maybe her brothers were right. Maybe she needed to come home to Boston and set her sights a little lower. Another tear oozed out, and she brushed it away.

Damn Brodie for sweet-talking her. For lulling her into believing she could build something successful… something *meaningful* with him.

A little sob escaped her throat and she sniffed hard.

Oh no.

She was having none of that.

Opening the cupboard, she reached for the twelve year Redbreast and a tumbler. Who cared that it was the middle of the afternoon? If there was ever a time for the crisis bottle, it was now. She filled the tumbler, and took a hefty gulp, letting the smooth liquid burn her throat.

She could always go work for Mason Carter.

Another half-sob slipped out. She didn't *want* to work for Mason. She wanted to build something here with Brodie. And now she'd ruined it all by letting her temper get the best of her.

Oh God.

What had she done?

The finality of it all slammed into her with the force of a cast-iron skillet to the head. Taking another gulp of whiskey, she struggled to bring order to her thoughts. At the moment, prepping food demanded her attention. Guests would be here in a few hours. At least chopping things with her sharpest knife would calm her down. Then later, she could cry into the crisis bottle with Maddie.

Slamming the tumbler down, she stomped around the island to wash her hands. She flung on the hot water, shoving her hands under the faucet like it was a lifeline. An odd gurgle rose from the drain.

Blinding pain exploded in her eyes and across her face, doubling her over. Sound roared in her ears, and she dimly recognized her own screams.

# Chapter Thirty-Seven

*B*rodie made a beeline for the tool closet in the barn. Damn that woman. She churned him up so bad he couldn't tell which way was up.

Snatching the maul, he strode back out to the splitting stump and grabbed a fresh piece of wood. With a grunt, he raised the maul and brought it crashing down with such force the pieces went flying.

She'd fucking quit.

Just like that.

With a hard glint in her eye that brooked no argument.

Not that she'd get any from him. Not anymore. He was through begging for her affection. If she was going to throw away what they had because he wanted an equal share, then *she* couldn't see what was right in front of her eyes.

He grabbed another log, placed it on the stump, and slammed the maul down again. If he had to stay here the rest of the day to work her out of his system once and for all, then by God, he'd do it.

Anguish stabbed at his ribs.

How *dare* she?

How dare she quit them with the same nonchalance she quit a job?

The wood splintered with a crack.

His heart tore along with the wood.

He'd been a fool.

A fool to think he could woo her. A fool to think she thought of him as anything other than a dumbass fix-it guy. Maybe that was all he was good for.

Sweat began to build across his back.

Good.

He heaved at another log, sending it flying, then paused to catch his breath. Who was he kidding? He'd never once been able to work Jamey out of his system. Not with booze or labor. What made him think he could do it now, when she'd just stomped on his heart?

A blood-curdling scream pierced the air.

He dropped the maul, instantly alert. "Jamey?"

The high-pitched scream came again. From the window in the kitchen.

He broke into a run. "Jamey?"

He burst through the back door to see her bent over the sink. Inside, her screams were deafening. His heart jumped to his throat. He rushed around the island, reaching for her. "What is it? What happened?"

"My eyes. *Ohmygod* I can't see." She groped blindly for the faucet.

Her wails pierced him to the core.

"Spray my eyes. Oh God. Something got in my eyes." Her face contorted into a grimace.

He could see red welts raising on her face and arms. What the hell had happened? He reached for the faucet, turning the water to cold and pulling out the sprayer. He aimed it at her face, not caring he was soaking both of them. She screamed and shut her eyes as the water hit her face.

"Open your eyes, hon. You've gotta open your eyes."

She opened her eyes and his heart stopped. The whites were brilliant red. Worse on the left eye than the right. She took a shuddering breath, her eyes glazed with panic.

"Where's your phone? I need to call 911."

Her arm flailed toward the far counter. "By the fridge." Her voice was more howl than speech. Every cry stabbed at his heart like a hot poker.

He fought down his own rising panic, and lowered his voice, like he was talking to a spooked animal. "Sweetheart. Put your hand on mine. I need you to hold the sprayer."

She clutched at his hand, still keening. The red welts on her arm were quickly blistering.

"Keep your eyes open."

She nodded. He slipped his hand from hers and lunged for the phone. It seemed like hours before the dispatcher picked up. He quickly identified himself and their location.

"Brodie. I need you to stay calm and explain what happened." The dispatcher's voice conveyed a calm he grasped at.

"I don't know. Her eyes are red. Blisters appearing on her arms. She's spraying her eyes."

"Can she explain what happened."

"She said she can't see, that something got in her eyes."

"Sounds like a chemical burn. The ambulance will have saline wash on hand to flush her eyes. Stay with her and keep running cold water through her eyes. The medics have been dispatched. They should be on sight in less than fifteen minutes."

Brodie's hand shook as he disconnected the call.

He rushed back to Jamey, gathering her in his arms

and taking the sprayer. The skin around her eyes had turned pink and was puffing up. Whether from the ice-cold water or the injury, he didn't know.

"I'm here, now. I've got you." He slid them down the cabinets to the floor, grateful for the extra length of cord from the sprayer.

Her cries had mostly subsided. Now, she clutched at his shirt and tried to prop her eyes open with her other hand. The planes of her face twisted with pain and fear.

The minutes stretched and slowed. Could the ambulance take any damned longer? She shook in his lap, water streaming over her face. The hand he was using to help keep her eyes open ached from the cold. He couldn't imagine what her face must feel like. Finally, he heard Parker Hansen's voice calling from the great room.

"In here," Brodie shouted. "We're in the kitchen."

Three big men crowded in the door. He'd never been so grateful to see a Hansen in his life.

Parker came around the island and dropped to his knees. "Tell me what happened."

Brodie opened his mouth to explain, and nothing came out. Emotion stopped up his throat.

Jamey sniffed. "I- I-I flipped on the hot water and something gurgled, then something burned my eyes." Her voice pitched to a wail again. "My eyes. Oh God, my eyes." Her voice rose at the end, overcome with panic.

Brodie squeezed her and kept the water trained at her eyes.

Parker leaned over. "Jamey. I need to examine your eyes. We're going to turn off the water for a sec, okay?"

She whimpered her understanding.

Parker nodded at him, and he squeezed the button on the nozzle, holding the water back. Taking a small flashlight, Parker gently held open her left eye – the reddest, and examined her. He made a small noise in the back of his throat and slid a look his way. "It's definitely a chemical burn. Anything unusual go down that sink recently?"

Jamey whimpered.

"Keep flushing her eyes," Parker ordered.

Dread settled in the pit of Brodie's stomach. "Simon and I cleaned the drain this afternoon," he volunteered, drawing a shaky breath.

Parker narrowed his eyes. "What'd you use?"

He motioned to the cupboard behind him. "The yellow box. In here." He leaned forward so Parker could pull out the box of washing soda.

Parker's mouth pulled into a flat line. "You poured this down the drain?"

Brodie nodded, quelling a wave of nausea.

"You realize this can be volatile?"

He shook his head, going hot and cold at the same time.

"It can. And it can cause blindness."

The glare he received from Parker dissolved his insides to jelly.

"But it looks like you acted fast. We'll have to transport her to Manhattan and keep irrigating her eyes. An eye doc will have to look at her."

Parker's mouth kept moving, but the words didn't register. He'd fixated on the word blindness.

His stupidity had made Jamey go blind.

He'd ruined her life.

*Because he couldn't read.*

He'd done this. He'd hurt the one woman he'd ever loved. She was blind. And it was all his fault.

Somehow – he wasn't sure how, he found himself in the ambulance across from Parker, with Jamey on a stretcher between them.

Parker handed him a tube. "Here. Hold this." He clipped a bag of saline to a runner above them. "We need to improvise an irrigation device and then deal with her other burns."

It took everything inside him not to lean over and vomit on his boots. He gripped the small bit of tubing as hard as he could to stop his hand from shaking. The shaking just migrated to his knee.

Parker looked at him sharply. "You okay, man? You're not gonna pass out or anything, are you?"

Brodie swallowed rapidly, tasting metal, then shook his head. "I'm fine."

He wasn't fine.

The ache in his throat was the size of an orange. His heart pummeled his ribs like a pinball machine. He could smell the sharp tang of his sweat through his soaking wet shirt. He'd never forgive himself if she went blind.

Ever.

"Hand me that tube now." Parker held out his hand.

He let go of the tube, his vision tunneling.

Parker ripped off a piece of tape. "This is called a cannula. It's normally used to deliver oxygen, but we've jimmied it to drip saline into Jamey's eyes." He taped a nose tube down to the bridge of her nose, and adjusted the tubing, securing it in place. "Okay, Jamey, I'm going to turn on the saline. Can you keep your eyes open as wide as possible?"

Anguish crossed her face and she whimpered her assent. The noise sliced through Brodie. How would he survive a ride to the hospital? Every cry she made, every groan, reminded him that this was his fault.

*He'd* done this to her.

*He'd* hurt her.

Maimed her.

Ruined her.

Despair boiled up, stealing his breath.

Parker grabbed his shoulder. "You riding with us?"

He shook his head and swallowed. "I-I'll follow."

He stumbled out of the ambulance and Parker stuck his head out. "You sure you okay? You don't look so good."

The lump in his throat tightened to the point he could only nod.

"She's in good hands. You did the right thing spraying her eyes."

Brodie nodded again, focusing on a rock in the dirt. The ambulance door slammed shut and the tires crunched up the gravel drive.

His legs finally gave way and he welcomed the sharp sting of pebbles hitting his knees. He deserved every pain and more, for what he'd done. A sob ripped from his throat and he fell forward, beating his palm on the ground until his arm went numb.

## Chapter Thirty-Eight

*D*ark settled over the kitchen. The rest of the day had been a clusterfuck. He'd had every intention of driving up to Manhattan to check on Jamey, but the four guests scheduled for the weekend had arrived early.

By the time he'd changed, settled the guests, made arrangements for sending them to Gino's for dinner and Dottie's for breakfast, it was chore time. He'd called up to the hospital but they wouldn't tell him anything because he wasn't family.

He wanted to go to the hospital. Desperately. But what would Jamey say when he showed up? She'd already quit them, quit him, once today. He wasn't sure he could take it if she told him to leave.

He poured a measure of the Redbreast into the glass that had been left on the counter. Jamey must have poured some before she'd turned on the faucet. What had she called it? The Crisis Bottle.

If there ever was a time.

He tossed the liquid back in one gulp, tracing the burn all the way to his belly. Sweeter than scotch. Less bite.

He needed bite.

He needed a thousand needles poking into him. Though not even that would take away the pain pressing on his chest right now.

The back door slammed.

"So you want to explain why you ditched your lady?" Blake strolled into the kitchen, flipping on the light.

He squeezed his eyes shut against the sudden brightness, but not before he'd taken in the tight set of his brother's mouth. He raised a hand. "If you're here to lecture me, I already feel like a piece of shit."

"I'm not. And I see you've dug into Jamey's crisis bottle."

"Maybe because it's a Goddamned crisis."

Blake sighed heavily. "Do you know she's asked for you nonstop?"

Fuck.

He clenched the glass so hard he hoped it would break. His breath stuck in his throat. "Just tell me," he croaked. "Did I blind her?" All the worry and guilt he'd been holding at bay overwhelmed him. "Oh God." His voice came out thick and high. "Just tell me she'll be able to see again." He scrubbed his hand over his face and pinched the bridge of his nose, his breath coming out in deep gasps. Breaking down in front of Blake only reinforced the shitty theme of the day.

"I don't know." Blake opened cupboards until he found a glass and thunked it down on the island, shoving it across to him. Brodie poured them both a measure.

Blake took a sip, his gaze boring into him. "What happened?"

Confessing his shortcomings, *again* to his brother, made his stomach roil. He'd never be good enough. He shrugged. "I'm not sure. Simon and I had been working off a list she'd given him. Last one was to put some stuff down the drain."

Blake pressed his lips together and nodded. "And what stuff did you put down the drain?"

Brodie could see the gears turning in Blake's mind. He knocked his chin toward the sink. "Yellow Box."

Blake moved around the island and reached under the sink.

Brodie braced himself for the onslaught. "There was a lot of stuff under there."

He spun, holding the offending box. "And you didn't think to ask a clarifying question?"

No.

He hadn't.

He'd been thoughtless and proud, and hadn't wanted Simon to know he couldn't read. He opened his mouth to defend himself and promptly shut it, bitterness rising in the back of his throat.

He exhaled a big shuddering breath, pressing the heel of his hand into his brow bone. When he finally spoke, he mumbled, unable to meet Blake's eyes. "I can't read. It's my fault... because I can't read. I... I-I didn't want Simon to know." The last admission came out a whisper.

Silence stretched between them.

"How?" Blake finally croaked.

"Apparently, I'm dyslexic. I think mom knew something was wrong and tried to help." He risked a glance at his older brother. Shock and horror covered Blake's face.

"That explains why–"

"Why I'm such a fuck-up," Brodie interrupted.

"That's not what I was going to say," Blake's voice grew sharp.

The silence between them grew strained.

Blake scrubbed his face. "I was going to say, that's why Jake was so hard on you." He laughed bitterly and shook his head. "Jake had trouble reading too. It's how he ran the ranch into the ground. He hid it well, but I started digging into the books after he lost our land to Warren. Well, after Warren and mom made their secret deal."

"Great. I'm just like Jake. Thanks bro." He saluted his brother.

"Shut up. You don't have to be, and you know it. Why do you think Ben suggested I put you in charge of the lodge?"

"That was his idea?"

"It sure as fuck wasn't mine."

"Thanks for the vote of confidence."

"You don't exactly have the best track record. But you've done well here. You and Jamey make a great team."

"Then why'd she quit us today? Huh? Tell me that." His heart squeezed in his chest as he took another gulp and slammed the glass on the counter.

Blake's eyes grew wide. "I don't understand."

"That makes two of us."

Blake drummed his fingers on the island, as if he was coming to a decision. "Look. I don't know what happened this afternoon, but you have to remember, Maddie says Jamey's a bit of a hothead."

He snorted. "Tell me something I don't know." He poured them both more whiskey. "Jamey told me this afternoon she quit."

"Why?"

Brodie blew out a breath and stared at the ceiling. Losing his temper over four percent just seemed stupid now. "She showed me a proposal she'd created for the two of us to buy you out in five years. I got pissed because she gave herself a majority stake."

"How much of a majority?"

"Fifty-two, forty-eight."

"And you got mad over that?" Blake's voice sounded incredulous.

He nodded. "Yeah."

"Because·she created a proposal tying the two of you together?"

Well shit.

He'd never looked at it that way. What an idiot. He'd blown everything over a measly four percent. He shook his head again. "Because it wasn't even."

He rolled his eyes. "And so you went all Sinclaire on her ass."

Anger at the injustice flashed again. "It wasn't–"

Blake raised a hand, cutting him off. "Come on, be honest. We Sinclaires have a nasty habit of mouthing off or thinking with our fists before we stop and listen."

"I don't need a lecture."

"Well, you're gonna get one now, little brother. First, you and Jamey make a great team. Mason told me repeatedly how impressed he was with the way you handled the guests while he was visiting. And that was after you nearly took him out at the Trading Post. Second, given the sparks that fly between the two of you when you're together, you probably make a great team elsewhere. Why give up on that?"

"Because I always fuck it up."

"You don't have to. Come on. You wanna be different than Jake? Cowboy up. Learn to read. Ask for help. You're not alone, man. There are tutors at the high school, and I'll talk to Maddie. I'm sure there are services at K-State.

You're smart. Sometimes you stick your head up your ass. But you're not an idiot."

Brodie snorted. "Thanks for that."

"Do you love her?" Blake's voice softened.

He looked up, meeting his brother's eyes, surprised by the compassion there. "Jamey?" He nodded slowly. "More than anything. And God, Blake. I ruined her. I ruined everything." Despair sliced through him like one of Jamey's sharp knives. He couldn't breathe. All the emotion in his body seemed to be crammed tight in his throat. "What if she goes blind?"

"Then be there for her. And for God's sake, learn to read so nothing like this happens again."

Brodie nodded, stealing a glance at his brother. Blake's face looked bleak. He took a deep breath and blew it out. "For what it's worth, I'm sorry for all the times I was a dick. I saw you going down the wrong path and I didn't stop to ask why that might be. I should have noticed you couldn't read."

The hard knot that had been sitting in Brodie's stomach slowly unraveled. He shrugged. "I hid it. I didn't know how to ask for help."

Blake gave him a wry smile. "We Sinclaires have that problem. Kills us to ask for help. Even when we should." He grew serious. "I should have noticed you couldn't read. I'm sorry I didn't. Maybe I… maybe things would be different if I had." Blake drained the contents of his glass. "Thanks for the drink. I'll see myself out." He stepped out the door, letting the screen slam behind him before Brodie could answer. The sound echoed in the silence.

Brodie remained seated, contemplating his whiskey. Swirling it, then adding more when it got low. So Jake couldn't read either. What a shock. How long he sat lost in whiskey contemplation, he didn't know.

The door burst open again, jarring him back to the present. "What?" He growled. "What now?"

"Heheheh, on the wrong end of a verbal dress down?" Warren Hansen strolled in carrying half a pie.

What in the actual fuck?

"What in the hell are you doing here?"

Warren's brilliant blue eyes glittered. They were so like Maddie's it was freaky. "No way to treat a guest. How's about you invite me in to sit a spell?"

Brodie grunted and motioned to another stool tucked under the island. "You come to tan my hide?"

Warren didn't sit down. He wandered the kitchen opening drawers and cupboards, obviously searching for plates and silver. The day was rapidly moving out of clusterfuck territory and into whatthefuck land.

"Whiskey?" Brodie held up the Redbreast.

"Coffee?"

He heaved a sigh. "I can make some." He pushed up and set about making a pot of coffee.

Warren kept rummaging through drawers, examining utensils.

"Make yourself at home, Warren." He didn't bother to keep the sarcasm from his voice.

Warren continued to putter until he'd plated up two enormous slices of the pie. "From Dottie. She says to remember pie fixes everything."

"Does it now?"

Too bad pie wouldn't fix Jamey's eyes.

Or help him read.

He poured two steaming mugs of coffee, added a dollop of Redbreast to his, then slid a cup over to where Warren had perched on a stool.

"Mighty hospitable of you, son. You'll do just fine here."

"So nice to have your vote of confidence." Sarcasm dripped from his voice, but Warren remained unfazed.

Warren tucked into the pie and gave him a sly look. "Maddie Jane don't take kindly to meddling, so I'm only gonna give you a little advice. Man to man."

"What can you possibly tell me that will make this right, old man?" He stabbed his pie and shoved in a bite. It was good. Damned good. But he liked Jamey's crust better. Not that he'd ever admit it to Dottie. Dottie'd tan his hide and ban him from the diner forever if he ever told her that. But he'd tell Jamey.

If she ever let him speak to her again.

The thought of the lodge without her cut through him, settling in his breastbone.

Warren eyed him between bites, as if weighing his next words carefully. The silence settled between them. "I can tell you that yer ma was proud as punch about all of you."

Brodie scowled, his heart starting to thump erratically. "How do you know?"

"She told me. She also said she was worried about you. That you'd had a tougher time of it than yer brothers."

Why was Warren bringing up his mother? He had enough demons to wrestle with tonight. "Hmph."

"Harrumph if you want, but yer ma knew you was sharp as a tack."

"Why you bringing this up now?"

Warren raised his hand. "Jus' listen. You young folks don't listen enough. Always yappin' and talkin'. Now I was sayin'…" He took another bite of pie. "Yer ma helped you in school."

"She used to read out loud to me."

"Why do you think she did that son?"

Brodie shrugged. "Never said."

"Use that noggin of yours. I'm not gonna say nothin'

else but this. Yer ma would be tossin' in her grave to see you give up. She didn't raise cowards."

He glared at Warren. The fuck. But Warren had saved his family's ranch. What else did he know but wasn't saying?

"You don't understand," Brodie muttered, jabbing at his pie.

Warren glared back. "Damn straight I don't understand. You jus' lie on the ground when you get bucked off a bull? That's a surefire way to get trampled. You're a Sinclaire, son. Time to start actin' like it." He stood to refill his coffee.

"You think I'm a coward?"

Warren slid him an assessing glance. "I think yer ma raised you to face things head on, and in the years she's been gone, you might have forgotten that."

"You hear I can't read?" Buzzing filled his ears. Did the whole town know and he'd been deluding himself all these years?

Warren eyed him solemnly. "People talk. You can do somethin' about that, son."

He nodded his agreement. He'd call the number Jamey had given him first thing. Not like it was a big secret anymore.

"So you love that redheaded whip of a thing that Maddie runs 'roun with?"

Redheaded whip of a thing. That summed her up perfectly. His lips tilted up slightly as he nodded. "Jamey? Yeah. I love her."

A sly look crossed his features. "You gonna marry her?"

He gave a dry laugh. "It's… complicated."

"God hates a coward, son. God hates a coward." Warren put down his fork and rubbed his belly. "Thanks for the company, son. Never thought I'd see the day where

I enjoyed the company of a Sinclaire." He smiled wide and clapped him on the back, then pushed back the stool.

When Warren reached the door, he paused, hand on the screen. His eyes filled with longing and grief. "If you love her, go after her. Don't take the coward's way. I did, and I've regretted it most days." He sighed heavily, then pushed through the door into the dark.

## Chapter Thirty-Nine

*J*amey tossed on the bed in a darkened room at the Big House. Only two days in, and the enforced rest was nearly killing her. Boredom pressed in on her from all sides, leaving her jumpy and restless. How in St. Patrick's bunghole was she going to survive seven to ten days of this? Let alone staying out of the kitchen for a month?

Anything that strained her eyes was off-limits. No TV, no computer, no reading. No bright lights. And definitely no cooking.

Not that it mattered. She was done with cooking. The celiac cat had been completely let out of the bag the day before, when Dottie brought over a huge meal for everyone, and she'd had to explain why she couldn't eat it.

Once word got out, her professional goose would be cooked. It wouldn't matter how good her food was, people would fixate on the gluten-free, make assumptions, and walk away.

Maddie had been upset. Hurt that Jamey hadn't divulged her big secret. Dottie had been a surprise. She hadn't gloated or given away that Jamey had been using her biscuits. She'd just wrapped her in a hug and told her everything would be okay.

Simon brought a joke book and had read her jokes the night before. She'd taught him a few new colorful words, and then... nothing. She'd tried to listen to a baseball game, but her beloved Boston was out of the pennant race, and she had zero interest in the local team, the Kansas City Kings.

Night was the worst.

She hadn't realized how much she loved sleeping next to Brodie until his warm hard body was no longer there. The best part was his scent. That sexy mix of cedar, hay, and musk that was uniquely him. He smelled like sunshine. And she missed him desperately.

She fought off a wave of despair. "Once again in my hour of need."

"What the hell is that supposed to mean, Jamey?"

She turned her head toward Maddie's voice. "Just that."

She'd spent the better part of the previous night examining in great detail all of her life's disastrous milestones, and came to the conclusion she wasn't fit for love or cheffing. Sure, she'd been able to prove to herself she could still be a top chef in spite of having celiac disease. But this... felt more final.

"Don't you think you're going a bit overboard with the wallowing?"

Jamey's mouth pulled into a frown. "I'm not wallowing."

The doctors and ophthalmologists were optimistic she'd keep her vision. They'd warned her to be patient. But she wasn't good at that. The successes she'd enjoyed came from drive and action. Not patience and sitting around on her ass.

Alone.

And whose fault was that? Hers. Because she'd lost her temper and let her mouth get the best of her.

Maddie's cool hand brushed her forearm, skittering around the bandages and offering a reassuring squeeze. "Maybe you and Brodie need to talk. Calmly. With the crisis bottle between you."

Jamey cracked a small smile at the memory of the crisis bottle intervention she'd orchestrated between Maddie and Blake.

She'd behaved like a baby the other day. A petulant, thumb-sucking, whiny baby. Blowing up everything they shared over four percent was… ridiculous. But she didn't care. It was over. "He ruined the roast when he didn't show up at the hospital."

"He told me you'd quit."

Huh. So they'd talked.

"He's right." Her voice caught. "I did."

"Did you mean to?"

"Yes… no… hell, I don't know… He pushed my buttons."

Maddie's dry laugh filled the room. "I've never seen anyone push your buttons the way he does."

Heat blossomed in her chest. She swallowed it down. "He hated my proposal."

"That's a bit of an exaggeration, don't you think?"

"Are you putting me on trial? Speak plainly, Mads." She might have the more colorful comebacks, but when push came to shove, Maddie could always out reason her. She simultaneously loved it and hated it.

"Fine. I will." A tinge of impatience crept into Maddie's voice. "You asked me to give him the benefit of the doubt. To give him a chance. But you turn around and issue an intractable ultimatum then burn down the house when it doesn't go your way?"

Jamey didn't have to be able to see Maddie to know her eyes would be flashing.

"And then you wonder why he didn't come to the hospital?"

The question hung between them and she could swear she heard Maddie roll her eyes. Would she have gone had the roles been reversed? If he'd pushed her away the way she'd pushed him? She let out a bitter sigh. Probably not. She was too prideful to beg.

"Do you love him, Jamey?"

The question pierced her, taking her breath away.

She did.

She loved him.

Where the hell did she go from here?

A knock sounded at the door. "Can I come in?" Brodie's rich gravelly voice slid over her, pricking hot tears behind her injured eyes. She winced at the sudden ache in her eyeballs.

Great.

Add staying emotionally calm to her list of do's and don'ts while recovering.

"Did you bring the medicine?" Maddie asked.

"Yep. All the drops plus the oral meds."

"Do you want me to stay?"

"I've got it." His voice was gruff.

Maddie squeezed her unbandaged hand. "I'll be downstairs if you need anything."

Maddie's footsteps receded, leaving only silence and the sounds of their breathing. His, low and steady. Hers, shallow and shaky.

The mattress bent under her back as Brodie sat beside

her on the bed. His fingers brushed the hair at her temple, leaving a wake of electricity zinging down the side of her face. Lips brushed her forehead in a tender kiss. "Hi."

The ache behind her eyeballs intensified, nearly stealing her breath. Why was he being so Goddamned tender?

She reached out, flailing until she hit the rock hard muscle of his thigh. He raised her fingertips to his lips, kissing each digit with the same tenderness and care, before lowering her hand onto his lap. "Maddie says it's time for your meds. Pills or drops first?"

"Pills." Her voice cracked. She wasn't sure she'd be able to swallow anything after Brodie removed the loose bandages covering her eyes.

The pill bottles rattled as he removed one lid, then the another. "The pills are in my hand." His voice took on a rough edge. Was he as emotionally wrung out as she was?

He directed her hand to his palm, and she grasped the pills with her bandaged hand, accepting a glass of water with the other. She placed the pills on her tongue, focusing on the bitter, slightly metallic aftertaste, and made herself take a big gulp. She took two more before relinquishing the glass. His fingers covered hers for a long moment before the glass thunked on the bedside table.

She swallowed again, intensely aware of the tension between them. "Brodie... I–"

"Shhh. Let's take care of your eyes."

"I'm scared." She didn't recognize the high, thin sound that voiced the confession.

Or the voice, thick with remorse, that answered. "Me, too."

He lifted the tape at her temples. His sharp intake of breath jabbed at her, sending a stab of pain to her throat and eyeballs. "Oh God, Jamey." His voice pitched low and tight. "I'm so sorry."

The pain in his voice echoed her own, and she held back an answering sob, knowing if she started, she couldn't stop.

The medicine made his face blurry. But not so blurry she couldn't see the grimace of pain he tried to hide.

"I'm fine," she ground out, clenching her jaw. "I'm going to be fine." She didn't believe it. Not yet, at least. But she had to keep telling herself, telling everyone else. She would not be the object of pity. Especially not Brodie's.

"Lean your head back. Maddie showed me how to give you the drops."

She leaned back on the pillow, bracing for the pain of having his fingers on her eyes. "Did you wash your hands?"

"Of course."

"You didn't pick your nose, did you?"

That earned her a gruff laugh. "And I didn't cough or sneeze."

"Just checking. My eyes are vulnerable, you know."

His voice grew husky. "I know. Ready?"

She swallowed and nodded, holding her breath. His arm curled around the top of her head and a shock of pain darted through her as he touched her lower eyelid. She squeezed the sheet beneath her, gathering it into her palm.

"You okay? Did I hurt you?" Concern laced every word.

"Just do it," she answered tightly.

One drop, two drops. First a sting, then modest relief. He repeated the same motions on the other eye. She blinked rapidly, distributing the medicine.

"Can the bandages stay off while we talk?"

She sighed heavily. "Brodie… I… I-I'm not sure where to start."

His breath caught, and she could tell by the slight droop of his shoulders that she'd hurt him.

"I… okay." He blew out a breath. "I can accept that. Will you listen?"

She owed him that much. Her answer fell out in a whisper. "Yeah."

He took her hand and leaned over her, bracing his other hand across her body next to her hip. "All of this is my fault."

She tightened her lips and started to shake her head.

"No. It is. It's my fault because I dragged my feet about finding a tutor. It's my fault because I didn't want Simon to know I can barely read. I hope…" He took a shuddering breath, and squeezed her fingers. "I hope that someday you can forgive me, and I want you to know that I would never intentionally hurt you. Ever."

Her throat grew tight, and pain ricocheted from her chest to behind her eyes. The worst part of this whole experience was that wanting to cry made her eyes hurt worse. Like a thousand needles poking her eye sockets.

"Brodie, I–"

He rushed ahead, cutting her off. "I called for a tutor. I start tomorrow. I don't want to jeopardize anyone I love ever again."

A whimper escaped from the back of her throat, and she ducked her head.

"Look at me, Jamey."

Even with the blurriness, there was no denying the set of his jaw. "Just tell me if I'm barking up the wrong tree."

The hope in his voice melted her. She squeezed his hand and released a shaky breath, offering a tiny smile. "I love you, Brodie." The breathy note in her voice gave away the thousand butterflies that suddenly decided to launch in her stomach.

"I shouldn't have quit. I didn't mean to. I let my temper get the best of me." She took a big gulp of air. "I was an ass."

His eyes crinkled as a smile lit his face. He reached out, drawing his thumb down her jaw, sending little tendrils of warmth down her spine. "So beautiful."

She snorted. "You're nuts."

"For you I am."

"Look at me. I'm a–"

His fingers on her lips silenced her. "You'll always be beautiful to me. Zombie eyes or not."

A breathy giggle escaped. "We still have to talk. We're not–"

"I know. When you're better. Right now, we focus on healing."

"And reading."

He nodded. "And reading." He leaned in, the tilt of his shoulders conveying uncertainty.

"Can I kiss you?"

The fact that he asked made her love him all the more. She nodded, the butterflies taking flight again.

His lips were warm against hers, and a little hesitant. She moved her unbandaged hand to his neck, encouraging him, but he remained gentle. She broke the kiss and leaned back. "My lips aren't injured."

His mouth met hers again, this time with more certainty. She flicked her tongue against his lower lip, unwilling to wait. He groaned in the back of his throat and gathered her close, his mouth opening to her invitation. When his tongue slid against hers, she sighed against him as the familiar rush of warmth flooded her.

He released her, breathing heavily.

She giggled again, giddy and nervous. "It seems my lady bits are in full working order."

His laughter thrummed through her like her favorite whiskey.

He cleared his throat. "Mine too, it seems."

Silence settled between them. His hands were restless, though. Stroking and caressing her temple, her hip, her shoulder. "Jamey," he murmured. "I was so afraid I'd ruined your life, so—"

She covered his lips with her unbandaged fingers. "Hush. We've got time." She caressed his cheek and brought him forward for another kiss. A day's worth of whiskers scraped against the sensitive part of her palm, sending delicious whorls of awareness and need spiraling through her.

Once she was out of the woods... the possibilities opened before her. She wouldn't count her chickens. The future of the lodge and the inevitable wrangling surrounding it, still hung over them. But they would get through it together. Certainty filled her heart. No matter what happened, they'd face it together.

## Chapter Forty

*B*rodie hopped up the short steps to the large front porch of the Big House and flopped down next to Jamey, stretching his arm across her shoulders. Maddie's influence on the ranch had been most noticeable here, on the porch. The beat-up bachelor furniture and leftover bailing wire spools had been replaced with large cushioned patio furniture. White bulbs were looped across the porch railing and hung in graceful arcs between the pillars. They created an air of festivity when everyone sat out at night. Even now, when it was coat weather. Maddie had replaced the beat-up old beer fridge with a newer, fancier model that also held wine bottles.

"How's my favorite zombie today?" He crooked his finger underneath the dark glasses Jamey wore, and gently removed them from her face. He still cringed internally when he looked at her. He'd never get over that his care-lessness had caused her so much pain.

She tilted her chin to receive a kiss. "Eye doctor said I'm on target."

He searched her eyes for signs of permanent damage,

not that he'd recognize it. The left one was still pink in the corner. Guilt tugged at his gut as he continued his inspection. The scabs on her face and arms were slowly fading. The longest, on her left forearm, still looked nasty. He traced his finger alongside it.

"Do you think this will scar?" He couldn't keep the worry from his voice. Didn't even bother to try. She'd been a good patient, diligently following the doctor's orders. But he still didn't want her to wear a permanent reminder of his stupidity.

She lifted a shoulder and glanced down at her arm. "Won't be the first scar I've gotten in the kitchen."

"It better be the last," he growled.

She snorted, rolling her eyes. "Comes with the territory, Captain Hoverpants. You going to quit manhandling bison just because one might trample you?"

"Hell, no. But it's—"

"Different?" She supplied, shaking her head. "Not so much, hot shot. Besides…" she grinned mischievously. Her saucy grin combined with her injuries gave her an air of wickedness and badassery that had him squirming in his seat. Hell, who was he kidding? He was dead gone on her. For life. Every glance, every laugh, every smile – hit him with a one-two punch to the gut, and left him just a bit weak in the knees.

"Besides, what?" He zeroed in on her mouth, captivated by the way her teeth pulled on her lower lip.

She laughed low and husky, the sound warming his insides and settling in his groin. "You love the fact I'm as wild as you are. Admit it." She drew her finger down his neck to the hollow of his throat then traced the vee of his shirt.

Jesus.

One touch and his balls were on fire. He forced himself

to think of shoveling manure. He swallowed hard. He swallowed back the words that were ready to burst out.

Not yet.

There were things they still had to discuss. But he couldn't resist a little taste. He leaned in, brushing his lips against hers. God, she was sweet. Like one of her kitchen sink cookies, or one of those strawberries they'd thrown on the floor a few weeks back. He slipped his tongue across hers, melting a little at her soft sigh of surrender. He wanted... forever.

Reluctantly, he pulled back. "Come home to the lodge?"

She nodded, her eyes warm.

He handed back her glasses and stood, offering his hand. He pulled her flush against him. "I've missed you." His voice took on a gruff edge. "Dottie's done a good job keeping the kitchen safe, but she's not you."

She'd been an enormous help, though. Juggling all the lodge balls on top of daily tutoring these last three weeks had been exhausting. Until Jamey had been hurt, he hadn't realized all the ways outside of the kitchen that he'd come to rely on her. Dottie had saved his ass, but no one held a candle to Jamey's skill in the kitchen *and* the office. It still rankled him that it had taken a serious incident in order to recognize it.

"I don't think Dottie will take kindly to me bossing her in the kitchen."

"I think you'll be surprised. I think she respects you."

Jamey's surprised smile lit her face. "Really?"

He nodded, tipping his Stetson back so he could kiss her freckled nose. "You ready?" Keeping his arm around her, he stepped them off the porch. A tight ache briefly settled in his throat. These first steps with her felt like a new leaf. Like everything was right... well, almost right.

Just a few more pieces to put in place and then everything really would be right in the world.

They walked the few minutes down the dirt road to the lodge, enjoying the crisp fall air. Meadowlarks and robins called from the bushes, and sulphur butterflies flitted through the last of the sunflowers. The oaks along the creek bank had begun their yearly transformation to deep red.

Contentment settled over him. Something deep inside slid into place. Like a key turning in a lock. This feeling, this peace. This was why people got married.

Blake had softened since marrying Maddie. He could still be an overbearing cuss, but the worry lines had disappeared from between his eyes. And Blake had been surprisingly supportive about the dyslexia. Blake had taken an active interest in his tutoring, and offered to help him with his daily practice.

The stunner had come when Blake had asked to see a copy of Jamey's proposal. He and Jamey had floated her plan for the lodge. Blake had listened, nodded, and then had said to draw up a contract, informing them he'd help them reach an agreement on the split. With his heart in his throat, he'd made a few phone calls.

They reached the top of the gravel drive.

"Whose truck is that?" Jamey's grip tightened. "Are you ready for early guests?" Panic tinged her voice.

He gave her a reassuring squeeze. "All under control."

Rabbits starting hopping in his stomach. Instead of heading around to the back door where they normally entered, he steered her toward the front.

"Brodie?" Suspicion entered her voice. "What's going on?"

He blew out a deep breath and pushed open the door. Do or die time. He entered the great room, heart hammering, and glanced back, catching her expression of surprise and the accompanying scowl as she recognized the five men lounging with beers.

"You brought in *my brothers?*" Her voice rose unnaturally. "Did you plan on losing your balls?"

He cleared his throat, stealing a glance at her brothers. He'd expected much harsher treatment from them than he'd received. Surprisingly, Maddie had put in a good word for him, then instructed him to contact Jamey's father first. Apparently, that had done the trick. He'd never admit it to anyone, but they intimidated him just a little.

Jamey widened her stance, removed her glasses, and crossed her arms. "What are you crew doing here? I don't need minding."

Jarrod took a pull on his beer before answering. "Nice to see you too, sis. You look like you got in a brawl with an alley cat."

She snorted. "The only brawl there'll be is if you lot of gobshites try to meddle in my affairs."

Her brother Jason raised his eyebrows. "Gobshites? I see your accident hasn't affected your mouth."

"Or my brain. Now why don't you tell me what in tarnation you think you're doing here?"

Jarrod's mouth quirked. "I had some business in the neighborhood. Thought I'd stop in."

She made a disbelieving sound in the back of her throat. Brodie covered a smile and helped himself to a beer from the bucket on the floor. Watching Jamey take on her brother was entertaining as hell.

Jason piped up. "Umm. Yeah. Me, too."

Jamey rolled her eyes. "Let me guess. Because you were studying prairie fire containment… in *October?*"

He grinned back at her. The kind of grin that said he

knew he was yanking her chain. "Yeah. Something like that."

She glared at each of them. "The shit is in the pasture. Don't insult me by bringing it inside."

Jon Paul spoke up. "A little birdie may have told us you ran into a bit of trouble. We're just making sure you're okay."

She opened her hands and shimmied in a circle. "There. You can see I'm perfectly fine."

"It's true. She doesn't look nearly as bad as that time she got into a fight with Mary Pat Alexander in the eleventh grade." Her brother Cameron was usually quiet. But when he spoke, it was always with a well-timed zinger.

Her brothers chortled at the memory. "Yeah, but you should have seen Mary Pat," Jason reminded them. "She had black eyes for weeks thanks to the broken nose."

Brodie's ears perked up. "Wait." He stared at her. "You broke a girl's nose?"

A pink flush stained her cheeks, and she shifted her shoulders defiantly. "She deserved that and more. Believe me."

Holy hell.

His sassy ass-kicker.

God, he loved her.

"Actually, sis," Joe spoke up. "Brodie here invited us out for the bison round-up."

Her eyes widened and she spun around, leveling a glare at Brodie. "You really have lost all your marbles haven't you? Do you realize *not one* of them can ride a horse?"

He grinned at her, thoroughly amused. "If they're going to be visiting, they might as well learn to ride."

She narrowed her eyes. "Why would they be visiting? They never came to Chicago."

"A mistake we won't be making again," answered

Jarrod seriously. "You're right, you don't need minding. But we're family. And if you're putting down roots here, we want to be a part of it."

"Who said anything about putting down roots?"

Brodie cleared his throat. "Let's continue this discussion later." He shot a warning glance at her brothers, then turned back to Jamey. "I want to show you some changes I made in the office. Gents…" He tipped his Stetson to her brothers. "Dinner's at the Big House tonight. You can head over in about an hour." He held out his hand to Jamey, practically dragging her toward the office when she put her hand in his.

"Why'd you tell them to come?" She hissed under her breath. "I wasn't in any kind of danger."

"Just come here." He laced his fingers through hers and pushed open the door of the office. Her surprised gasp was all the confirmation he needed.

The office was neatly rearranged, a large calendar on the wall with space for each room. On the desk there were color-coded files with big labels that were easy for him to read.

Her eyes grew wide. "You did all this?"

He shook his head. "No way. Dottie and Jarrod helped me. Jarrod explained the most important parts and how to organize them. Dottie suggested the calendar for each room."

She shot him a grin that turned his insides to lava. "You're so sexy when you do things like this."

"Yeah?" Who knew files could be sexy? "Wait until you see what we've done in the kitchen."

Her look quickly transformed to worry. "You haven't rearranged have you?"

"Nope. Just color-coded, so I don't get confused. Come

on." He tugged on her hand and led her into the kitchen. "First things first. Open the fridge."

She flung a dubious glance his way, and slowly opened the door. "What's this?" She grabbed one of four large bottles standing front and center with bows around them.

"I know you miss Guinness. Jarrod did some research and found a brewery in Denver that is making gluten-reduced dark beer. This one is a rye stout. A little heavier than a Guinness, but I think you'll like it."

Her features softened in the same way they had when he'd shown her the chicken coop, conveying emotions she rarely expressed. She studied the bottle in her hands then raised her eyes, delight sparkling in her green irises. "That's…" She grinned. "Thank you."

She placed the bottle on the island and stepped up to him, lifting her chin and sweeping her lips across his. "You… I love you."

All the words he'd been patiently holding back started to push out. "Forever?" Every cell in his body stilled.

A slow sexy grin spread her mouth as she nodded. "Yes. Always. No matter what."

"Marry me."

Her eyes widened.

Shit.

This wasn't how he'd planned it. He still had… things to show her. To offer her. He still needed to woo her. Show her the Mr. Yuk stickers on the dangerous stuff, and the color-coded labels that Dottie had made. He still had to read out loud to her. The thoughts stampeded through his brain.

No taking the words back now.

What was it Dottie always said? In for a penny, in for a pound. He jammed his hand into his pocket and brought out the gold circle that had been burning a hole in there since Jarrod and his gang had arrived, two days before.

His hand shook as he captured her fingers and placed the ring in her upturned palm.

She sucked in a breath. "Is that…"

"Yes. It's your grandmother's. Although if you want something different… something fancier…"

"No." She folded her fingers over the ring. "It's perfect."

"I… ah…"

Her free hand snaked around his neck. "Stop talking and kiss me."

He didn't need to be asked twice.

He leaned in, capturing her mouth. Gently at first, then pulling her closer, he deepened the kiss, gliding his tongue against hers and pouring all his love into her. He tasted her recesses and groaned deep as she sucked him deeper into her mouth. His cock sprang to life, wanting in on the action. They were both panting when they broke away. He touched his forehead to hers, working to bring his breathing back to normal.

"So… yes?"

"Yes." Her eyes shimmered with unshed tears.

Joy exploded in his heart, thrumming against his ribs as warmth flooded his body. Sliding his fingers through her curls, he tilted her head for another kiss, taking his time and showing her with his mouth everything he'd love to do to her later.

Heat pooled low in his back and he lifted her, settling her on the island and stepping between her legs. He removed his Stetson, placing it on the counter next to her. "Jamey," he murmured against her mouth. "I have something to show you."

She leaned back eyeing him with naked lust. "If it's not your cock, I'm not interested."

He couldn't hold back the laugh. "Patience darlin'. Not while your brothers are in the other room."

"Fuck my brothers."

"No. I only want to fuck you."

She curled a leg around his hip. "Yes, please."

He slid his hands up underneath her shirt, drawing his thumbs across her breasts.

"Don't tease," she panted. "It's been too long."

He sighed. He wanted nothing more than to drive balls-deep into her and lose himself in her softness. Her slick heat. But they could wait a little longer. His cock could wait a little longer.

"Here." He reached for a folder, pulling it from underneath his hat, and handed it to her.

"What's this?"

"Just read it."

He studied her puzzled expression, heart still hammering, as confusion, then shock, flashed across her face. After what seemed like endless minutes, she finally raised her eyes to his.

"Why?"

"One. I love you. Two. I want you to be happy. Three. I didn't realize how much I relied on you until I had to do all of it without you."

And four – when he'd called Jarrod to draw up the contract giving her fifty-*three* percent equity, Jarrod had reiterated how Jamey had lost all her savings because of trusting her previous business partner. It all made sense now. Not that they'd need a contract. He'd spend the rest of his life showing her how much he loved, respected, and valued her.

She laughed quietly. "And here I was, all set to tell you we could go even-steven."

"I beat you to it."

"I really think we should renegotiate the equity. I'm fine with fifty-fifty."

"We can discuss that later then. For now, let's celebrate."

She opened her hand containing the ring. "Before we do… will you?"

He took the ring and flipped her hand over, sliding the ring into place. "Marry me, Jamey. Take my heart. Be mother to our children. Spend the rest of your life with me?"

She broke into a wide smile. "Who knew you were such a romantic?" She drew him back between her knees, looping her arms around his neck. "I'll be your wife, Brodie, and we'll figure out this contract. I have one condition though."

"Yes?"

"I boss in the kitchen."

"You can boss anywhere you like, darlin'."

# Chapter Forty-One

## EPILOGUE

*A week later…*

Jamey adjusted her sunglasses and settled deeper into the warmth of Brodie's lap. They were all gathered on the back porch of the Big House, overlooking the grounds where Blake and Maddie had held their reception. The late afternoon sun cast everything in a golden light. But there was a definite bite in the air.

Ben and Cameron crouched over a flame in the fire pit, working to bring it to life. Jamey's brothers had shown themselves to be surprisingly adept on horseback this week. The round-up had gone off without a hitch and without injury. Of course, with four firemen on hand – three of her brothers plus Maddie's cousin, Parker, they were more than equipped to handle any mishap.

Jamey sipped her gluten-reduced beer and silently offered up a prayer of thanks. Bison were not domesticated and they made cattle look small. And tame. She'd worried all week, especially because she'd been banned from the chuck wagon.

Next year.

Next year, she'd try her hand at cooking on the go.

Not much difference between a chuckwagon and a food truck. If she liked it, maybe they could add a food truck to their growing list of income streams.

Brodie's hand draped possessively across her hip and he nuzzled her neck. "Why don't we get married tomorrow?"

She choked on her beer. "But we've only been engaged a week."

"So?"

She gave him a big side-eye. "No. Way."

Maddie came through the door with a plate piled high with chips, salsa, and guacamole. "No way what?"

"I was just telling Jamey we should get married tomorrow."

Maddie rolled her eyes. "No way."

A note of petulance entered Brodie's voice. "Why not? Why wait?"

"Take it from the married man," Blake chimed in. "Let your lady make the date and the plans. Just get yourself to the church on time."

Jarrod munched on a chip thoughtfully. "Makes no difference to us, sis." He winked at Brodie. "We've already taken Brodie out back and officially welcomed him to the family."

A wave of alarm washed over her, and she grabbed Brodie's chin, inspecting his face for any signs of bruises. "I swear Jarrod, if any of you hurt him…"

She was cut off by her brother's laughter.

"Nothing that sinister," Jon Paul interjected. "We just took him out back for a good Irish welcome."

Brodie's breath was warm on her ear, sending a little shiver of delight down her spine. "Nothing more than a few shots of Irish whiskey. They tried to get me to quit scotch."

"Did you?"

He lifted a shoulder, and grinned. "Nope. Nothing will make me give up peat. But your brothers did show me how you like a hot whiskey in winter."

"They always did know how to take care of me."

"That's my job now," he growled low and nuzzled her neck.

"So Jamey, when *do* you want to get married?" Maddie asked.

"To be honest, I haven't given it much thought. I just have two requirements. I want mom and pop to be here, and I want to look pretty. Not like I just stepped out of a war zone."

Brodie tilted her chin. "You are beautiful. Right now."

Heat ignited in her chest. "I can see in the mirror."

"Jamey." His voice grew firm. "You're beautiful. *Right now.*" He didn't bother to hide the desire in his eyes.

Maddie's cousin, Axel, reached for a beer from the ice bucket. "If you're not too tied to a date, I know Hope would love to be here. She's moving back in a few weeks."

Maddie gasped. "She is? But why? Isn't she finishing veterinary school?"

Axel's face was inscrutable. "It's her story to tell. But given that we could use her expertise, I'm not complaining."

Ben scowled and stabbed the fire with a stick, sending a shot of sparks into the air. Jamey narrowed her eyes, studying him. "What's up Ben? You look like you swallowed a ghost pepper."

Ben's scowl deepened. "Nothin'… Just…" He shook his head. "Nothin'."

Maddie brightened and rubbed her swelling belly.

"What about Christmas? Baby should be here in early January, so there will still be time."

Jarrod perked up. "And that's a slow time of year for pretty much everything."

Brodie hummed and stroked her back. "I don't think we're booked yet, so we could block off the rooms and the homestead for your family.

"You could take a honeymoon right after you meet your little niece." Maddie's eyes danced.

"Or nephew," Blake added, giving Maddie's belly a proud caress. He bent and spoke to her belly. "I already have a pair of boots for you."

Maddie elbowed him. "Girls can wear boots, too. Look at Jamey's."

She kicked up her feet, admiring for the millionth time the lovely pair of boots Brodie had given her. She leaned in and whispered in his hear. "I do love them, you know."

He answered with a squeeze. She shifted on his lap, settling herself so she could see his eyes in the dying light. "I've never been one of those types who fantasized about getting married, but I do love Christmas."

"Yeah?"

She nodded, brushing her lips across his.

"So you want to get married at Christmas?"

Excitement thrummed in her veins. Was she really going to do this? Settle down in Prairie down the dirt road from her best friend and help run a hunting lodge? "Why not? That will give us plenty of time to make arrangements. I just have one small request."

He stroked his thumb down her jaw. "Anything."

"My parents... they're... devout. They'd never presume to ask or demand... but would you mind a church wedding?" She rushed on before he could answer. "If you're not Catholic, I'm sure we could go to the–"

He stopped her talking with a light kiss. "My sister Emma would know for sure, but I think we were all baptized. Original family name being St. Claire and all. We can sort out the details tomorrow."

Maddie had mentioned at some point that the Sinclaires were descended from French fur trappers. That would make sense.

Brodie tightened his grip around her and stood them both up. "It's set. A Christmas wedding."

Their friends erupted in applause.

Warmth settled in her chest, the kind of warmth that came from sheer happiness. She understood now why Maddie had moved home to Prairie. In all her travels, all her adventures, she'd never felt the pull of community like here.

She looped her hands around Brodie's neck. "I'm the luckiest woman alive."

Uncertainty flickered in his eyes. "You really want to marry me?"

She leaned her forehead to his. "Nobody else, you great lump. You put my granny's magic ring on my finger. You're stuck with me."

Love blazed in his eyes. "Forever?"

"Forever."

"Promise?"

She leaned in for a kiss. "'Till death do us part."

## THE BEGINNING OF HAPPILY EVER AFTER

I hope you enjoyed reading Brodie & Jamey's story. You will love reading about Ben and Hope's story of love and redemption in HEART OF A WRANGLER.
Secrets... did I mention secrets?

## What's a guy to do when the girl of his dreams makes a pass at him?

Saying no to Hope Hansen was the hardest thing Ben Sinclaire has ever done. Despite their age difference and a family feud, he's loved her since grade school, but a romance between them was always forbidden. Now she's back and the girl he loved has become all woman. He's finally ready to make his move, but he'll have to get around her brothers and a field of admirers to do it.

## What's a girl to do when faced with the worst mistake from her past?

Eight years ago, Hope took a chance on Ben and got shot down. Heart broken and mortified, she left town. A fiasco at veterinary school foils her plan to avoid him forever by forcing her to come home to Prairie. When her brothers meddle in her love life by placing a Cowboy Wanted ad for her in the back of Rancher's Monthly, Ben becomes her unlikely ally. As all her feelings come crashing back, Hope isn't sure if she can trust him… or herself

Ben comes up with a daring plan to win Hope, but when ice storms, weddings, and babies interfere, will it backfire? Or will Hope realize that true love has been waiting right under her nose the whole time?

*A spicy hot second-chance romance that will have you staying up all night and cheering for Ben & Hope's HEA.*

### Download HEART OF A WRANGLER now!!

*"A compelling story of second chances, family dynamics, trust and relationships."* - Kathi

*"Tessa does an excellent job of describing the true feelings of her characters."* - Lisa

**Get your copy today.**

Do you love sneak peeks, book recommendations, and freebie notices? Sign up for my newsletter at www.tessalayne.com/newsletter!!

Find me on Facebook! Come on over to my house- join my ladies only Facebook group - Tessa's House. And hang on to your hat- we might get a little rowdy in there ;)

## Meet the Heroes of Resolution Ranch

They've laid their lives on the line before but now they'll have to wear their hearts on their sleeve for the women they love…

### Police Chief Travis Kincaid Has Rules….
· Never leave the door unlocked
· Never mix work and pleasure
· And Never, **Never** kiss the object of your affection

Years ago, the former Navy SEAL learned the hard way that breaking the rules only leads to disaster. Since then, he's followed strict rules to stay focused on his career and keep his heart locked away where it won't cloud his judgment.

### Too bad the woman he's fallen for was a born rule-breaker.
In spite of her shady past, Travis finds himself bending the rules… repeatedly, for single-mom Elaine Ryder. In the aftermath of Prairie's devastating tornado, Travis must come to a decision about his future. More importantly, he'll have to decide whether breaking the rules one last time will cost him everything he holds dear… or give him his heart's desire.

### Download A HERO'S HONOR today

## Meet the Roughstock Riders

A brand new steamy contemporary romance series filled with rodeo hotties and the women that bring them to their knees…

**He's an ex-con. She's the sweet virgin he can never have.**

When disgraced bull rider Ty Sloane agreed to take a job as foreman at Falcon Ridge Ranch, he didn't count on having to share his job or his cabin with twenty-one-year-old rising star barrel racer Maybelle Johnson. She tests his patience by day and drives him to distraction by night, but she's off limits—too young and innocent for the likes of an ex-con like him.

As far as Maybelle is concerned, Ty Sloane can go jump in a lake. The cocky bull rider is a thorn in her side, both at the ranch and on the road. But he makes her feel things no man has ever made her feel, and as she learns about his past, she can't help but develop a soft spot for him.

When trouble finds Maybelle on the rodeo circuit, Ty puts it all on the line for the sweet young woman who's captured his heart, even though it may cost him his freedom.

**Download RIDE HARD today!**

## Also by Tessa Layne

HEART OF A COWBOY

*family feud/fake engagement*

HEART OF A REBEL

*opposites attract/workplace*

HEART OF A WRANGLER

*second chance*

HEART OF A HORSEMAN

*star-crossed lovers/second chance*

HEART OF A HERO

*old flame/PTSD*

HEART OF A BACHELOR

*secret baby*

HEART OF A BAD BOY

*fake engagement*

HEART OF A BULL RIDER

*Doctor-patient/second chance*

HEART OF A RANCHER

*enemies to lovers*

A HERO'S HONOR

*single parent/workplace*

A HERO'S HEART

*frenemies to lovers*

## A HERO'S HAVEN

*secret identity*

## A HERO'S HOME

*opposites attract*

## MR. PINK

*billionaire secret romance*

## MR. WHITE

*billionaire secret identity*

## MR. RED

*billionaire secret identity second chance*

## MR. WHISKEY

*billionaire secret identity workplace*

## WILD THANG

*billionaire secret crush sports romance*

## PU$$Y MAGNET

*billionaire workplace sports romance*

## O MAGNET

*billionaire fake engagement sports romance*

## RIDE HARD

*virgin/workplace/opposites attract*

## RIDE ROUGH

*secret identity/frenemies to lovers*

RIDE FAST

# Resources

## Dyslexia

The challenges Brodie and Jamey confront in this book are near and dear to my heart. One in five people have dyslexia, and if someone in your family is dyslexic, there's a higher chance that your children will be dyslexic.

One of my daughters is dyslexic, and even though I was on the look out for it, like most parents, we didn't discover this until she was in the fourth grade. She only confessed years later that she knew she couldn't read, and that she was too embarrassed to tell us. Talk about breaking a mama's heart! Often, people with dyslexia grow up with the idea that they are dumb. Incapable of learning. That's just flat wrong, and my heart breaks every time I hear a dyslexic person refer to themselves as stupid. **Any person with dyslexia can learn to read.**

**The Orton-Gillingham method is the ONLY scientifically proven method shown to dramatically improve reading outcomes in individuals with dyslexia – even adults who've never learned to read.**

Susan Barton is one of the world's premier experts on dyslexia.

**Celiac Disease**

I was diagnosed with celiac disease nearly twenty years ago – back when people looked at you like you had three heads when you mentioned 'gluten'. I'm also a self-professed food snob. Sometimes having celiac is a real bummer. I'll never get to enjoy a croissant with my coffee ever again. Or a buttery piece of sourdough bread. But I feel so much better without gluten in my life, that I'm motivated to stay clean (and yes, cross-contamination is real, and it *hurts*)

However, gluten-free baking has come a long way since the late 90's and there are many delicious pastry options on the market today, as well as some fantastic blogs!

If you have questions about gluten intolerance, visit the following sites – these are the two most comprehensive, reliable sites regarding celiac disease.

www.csaceliacs.org

celiac.org

## Acknowledgments

I am profoundly grateful to be surrounded by a team of kind hearted, intelligent, and fearless humans. Thank you all for your continued encouragement and support. These books could not come to life without you.

Amanda at Razzle Dazzle Designs – you've captured Brodie's strength and personality so perfectly on this cover. Thank you for your beautiful artistry.

To the RDs and my Chatzy ladies – Thank you for the daily laughs and encouragement. You make writing a joy.

To my mentor Kimberley Troutte – Thank you for your fearless critiques of my manuscripts, for always encouraging me, and challenging me to make my characters sing! I am so grateful for your presence in my life!

To Genevieve Turner and Sela Carson– Thank you for taking time out of your busy writing schedules to offer your expertise and feedback. You have helped make this book shine. I admire and appreciate you both!

To Jenny and Kara – Your collective brainstorming and critiques have made Brodie and Jamey's love story epic. Thank you for the wine, the extra chapters, and always making time to read something I send you. Love you both.

To my dear Cora Seton – Thank you for everything You're an inspiration on so many levels.

To my big girl – Never doubt for one millisecond that you are brilliant. You have such grace and intelligence. You are a gift to the world, creative spelling and all.

To my little girl – My book dragon, keep filling your head and your heart with words.

To my hero, Mr. Cowboy – When I got diagnosed with celiac a month after we got married, you never blinked, never once said you wouldn't eat what I had to eat. You've enthusiastically tried every dish I've made without complaint, even the few that were pretty scary. I love how excited you get on those occasions we get to share a Rickoli beer. Thank you for making sure I'm never on this food adventure solo. I love you madly.

I'd also like to give a shout out to my FAVORITE brewery ever. Brewery Rickoli in Wheatridge, Colorado. These guys brew great beer, and put the gluten-reducing enzymes in EVERYTHING

That means this Guinness loving girl can drink dark beer again!! Thank you for being a million kinds of awesome!

CPSIA information can be obtained
at www.ICGtesting.com
Printed in the USA
BVHW081045240122
627011BV00005B/108